THE WAY OF
THE JAGUAR

Bilingual Press/Editorial Bilingüe

General Editor
Gary D. Keller

Managing Editor
Karen S. Van Hooft

Associate Editor
Barbara H. Firoozye

Assistant Editor
Linda St. George Thurston

Editorial Board
Juan Goytisolo
Francisco Jiménez
Eduardo Rivera
Mario Vargas Llosa

Address:
Bilingual Press
Hispanic Research Center
Arizona State University
P.O. Box 872702
Tempe, Arizona 85287-2702
(480) 965-3867

THE WAY OF THE JAGUAR

Francisco X. Stork

Bilingual Press/Editorial Bilingüe
TEMPE, ARIZONA

ISBN 0-927534-93-2

Library of Congress Cataloging-in-Publication Data

Stork, Francisco.
   The way of the jaguar / Francisco X. Stork
     p.   cm.
   ISBN 0-927534-93-2 (alk. paper)
    1. Death row inmates—Fiction. 2. Prisons—Fiction. 3.
   Criminals—Rehabilitation—Fiction. 4. Texas—Fiction. I. Title.

   PS3569.T6489 W39 2000
   813'.6—dc21   00-039766

PRINTED IN THE UNITED STATES OF AMERICA

Cover design, interior by John Wincek, Aerocraft Charter Art Service

For my wife, Jill

DAY 1

"The worst thing you can do is think."

That's what Mr. Gómez says.

"Thinking is not good."

Mr. Gómez is a toothless little man with hairs sticking out of his ears. He's always doing something, fussing about. He shuffles back and forth with a broom, then a mop, then he gives out books and magazines, one per person and not until you return the one you got before.

"Sloth is the father and the mother of all evil. That's what I say. And it's the truth."

You have to sign for the books too, as if there were any chance that they would not be returned. Mr. Gómez is the only one on death row, or the west wing, as folks around here call it, whose number is not coming up, not the way it is for the rest of us, anyway. He has earned the privileges of the west wing by virtue of his longevity and hard work.

"I've been here so long I don't want to get out. That's how long I've been here."

One of the privileges of west wing residency is that everyone pretty much lets you be. Another privilege is that you get your own room depending on occupancy rates, but always if your due date is approaching.

Not that the privacy is that great even in a private room. There is Botswana across the hall who brazenly watches me as I contort in pain with diarrhea cramps. There is the infernal noise from Wooly's boom box next door, from Botswana's radio and Velop's television, all garbling different languages and rhythms like a compressed Tower of Babel. Mr. Gómez told me that at one time the eleven o'clock lights out and silence curfew was enforced. It didn't work. The silence made people explode or implode. No one could take it. Too much time to think.

DAY 2

"Either you find something to do or you lose your privileges," said Mr. Gómez. "Those are the rules."

"You best do what he says," said Wooly. "The commissioner can make it worse for you."

"As if anyone gives a shit," I said.

"I've been working this place for nearly thirty-four years," said Mr. Gómez, "and I've seen youngsters grow old and die on their own."

"How long have you been a west winger?" Mr. Gómez asked Wooly.

"Going on thirteen years," answered Wooly.

"Do you see what I mean?" questioned Mr. Gómez. "I mean, you can be here for years, so the commissioner wants everyone to find something to do."

"Why?" I asked.

"Because those are the rules," said Mr. Gómez. "That's the deal we worked out with the commissioner. We pretty much get to take care of our own place, but everyone has to find something to do."

"So what do you want me to do?"

"No, sir! That's your decision," said Mr. Gómez. "I got a list you can choose from if you can't come up with something by your own self. But it's mostly better if you come up with something yourself. That way all I have to do is double-check it with the commissioner."

"You can do anything you want," said Wooly with a grin. "Almost anything is satisfactory."

"What do people do?" I asked.

"Let's see now," said Mr. Gómez, searching his shirt pockets for a list that wasn't there.

"Wooly there goes down to the carpenter shop on Mondays and when else?"

"Tuesdays and Thursdays," continued Wooly. "On Wednesdays, Fridays, and sometimes Saturdays I go painting. Seems like we're always painting somewheres or another. We're starting to paint places I painted a year ago."

"Cortina fixes TVs," interrupted Mr. Gómez. "The TVs are brought to him, though. The commissioner doesn't let him go wandering around."

"Velop makes ashtrays and whatchamacallits for the gift shop," Mr. Gómez continued. "Botswana works in the laundry room. Grosvenor teaches the Holy Bible and writes prayers for folks. And . . . that's all that's in here now."

"It's ridiculous," I said.

"What'ya say?" asked Mr. Gómez.

"I said it's stupid. What's the point?"

"You never know how long you're going to be here. You never know. Some people even get their sentence computed. Right, Wooly?"

"Right," said Wooly. "I've seen it happen. If you got a good lawyer, it can happen. It's happened to lots of folks."

"Just pick something and get them off your back," snapped Cortina from the other side of the wall.

"That's true," said Wooly. "If you do something, you get left alone."

"I don't know what to pick. I don't care. Hell! Let me be. There's no time to fuck around!"

"It's no matter," said Mr. Gómez sternly. "It don't matter how much time you got or ain't got. If you don't do something you don't get privileges."

Cortina was now standing in front of my cell. Wooly had also come around to watch the interchange from a better angle.

"What did you do before you came here?" asked Cortina.

"I was a lawyer," I whispered.

"Ay, cabrón!" said Cortina.

"Motha!" yelled Wooly.

"What he say?" asked Mr. Gómez.

"He said he was a lawyer," Cortina told him.

"Oh, my," said Mr. Gómez, "you're in trouble now."

"Why?" I asked.

"Hell, man, everybody is going to be after your ass to appeal their habeas corpuses, man. Everyone is going to be after your ass," laughed Cortina.

"That's right," echoed Wooly, "after your ass."

"I did real estate," I said.

"It doesn't matter, man," said Cortina, "all the hermanos are going to ask you to help them. Ain't that right?"

"Sure is," answered Wooly.

"Everyone in this hell hole," continued Cortina, "is here because of their lawyer, right?"

"Right on," said Wooly. "I sure am. But I got a new one now."

"So what will it be?" asked Mr. Gómez. "You want to be a lawyer here or what?"

"No, I would like to be left the fuck alone," I said.

"Hey, mano," said Cortina, "this is the UNITED ESTATES OF AMERICA. You gotta work, my man. How do you think this country got to be so great? Labor, man, labor."

"So what will it be?" asked Mr. Gómez.

I yelled: "I don't give a shit! Why don't you pick something!"

"Okey dokey," said Mr. Gómez, not flinching, "I'll check with the commissioner. I'll get back to you."

"You'll be sorry," said Wooly as Mr. Gómez was leaving. "You should have picked something. You could get stuck with cleaning the shit-holes."

DAY 3

The word came down from the commissioner via Mr. Gómez that I was to lawyer for three hours a day and work with Cortina on the weights for at least one hour a day. That's what I'm supposed to do in order to hold onto my privileges, namely, a pack of cigarettes a day and the communal Friday-night Lone Stars that Mr. Gómez parcels out three apiece and that I sip ever so slowly.

"The commissioner said you gotta lawyer and you gotta lift weights with your buddy yonder," Mr. Gómez said.

Cortina appeared briefly from around his cell. He looked at me with some kind of disgust, dropped his cigarette on the floor, stepped on it, and went back to his cell.

"Lawyer? All I know is real estate."

"It don't matter. Lawyer anything as best you can. It don't matter so long as you do it for three hours a day in the library. If you don't do it you lose your smokes and other privileges."

"My smokes?"

"Yeah. I told the commissioner that losing the TV wouldn't do it for you like it would the others. I told him I thought the smokes would do it."

"I don't know the first thing about prison law."

"It don't matter. You'll see. If you can read and write you'll do. Three hours a day, including Saturdays and Sundays, starting today."

DAY 4

So I've been lawyering and lifting weights for nearly a year now. The lawyering, if you can call it that, hasn't amounted to much. Aside from helping out with appeals and drafting motions alleging cruel and unusual punishment for just about anything you can think of, mostly my lawyering has consisted of hearing detailed confessions of guilt, detailed explanations of non-guilt, and writing letters. I write letters to attorneys pointing out where they messed up, to landlords, to the parole board, to wives and children, to future employees, to the pope, to the president, to TV personalities, to innumerable bureaus of unnamable departments in unfathomable agencies. Letters and more letters. I don't know which has been worse, my duties as a scribe or my slavery to Cortina's exercise regime.

The day after Mr. Gómez gave me my sentence, Cortina woke me up around 6:00 A.M. He woke me up by sticking a radio antenna through the bars of my cell and whacking the top of my head.

"Wake up, puto," he whispered loudly.

I shot up out of bed bewildered. It seemed as if I had fallen asleep about fifteen seconds before.

"What is it?" I said annoyed.

"Time to go to work, man. Open the fucking door."

The doors to the west wing can be locked from the outside and from the inside. I lock my door at night for the protection of my lonely ass.

I put on my pants and shoes, struggled to open the door, and then followed Cortina to his cell, located next to mine, about a foot away. On the floor were cement weights and a curled-up jump rope. The weights were homemade. Someone had poured cement into coffee cans or large Hunts Tomato Sauce cans and then stuck a broomstick in the middle before the cement dried. They were sorry-looking things.

I rubbed my eyes. "Why do we have to do it now?"

"Shhh!" gestured Cortina with his mouth and eyes. He was putting a red bandanna around his head. Then he took off his shirt and rubbed his hands together, all the time keeping his eyes closed. It seemed as if he were performing some kind of silent ritual. I tried not to snicker. The slow ceremonial gestures, the ugly weights, Cortina's deep breaths of preparation, his hairless brown chest heaving up and down as if he were getting ready to jump off a cliff, all seemed comical.

"What do you want me to do?"

"Silencio," said Cortina. "Just watch how I do it."

I went over to his chair, removed a sausagelike gray television tube from the seat and sat down.

Cortina took the two smaller weights and started curling them up and down against his chest. His eyes were open now, staring at the movement of his hands. The movement of the arms was slow at first, but then after a while the rhythm picked up faster and faster until it reached a crescendo and stopped. Then Cortina held the two weights by his sides and began to lift his arms sideways slowly like an overloaded buzzard flapping its wings, trying to take off. There must have been in total about ten different lifting movements that Cortina did with the small weights. Each movement lasted about three minutes each. After half an hour, Cortina stopped and stood standing, his arms dangling comfortably at his side, his feet apart slightly. Nothing moved except his chest. Drops of sweat popped out all over his body, one at a time it seemed, and then rolled down. He stood there unflinching until his chest heaved slowly and powerfully. Then he looked at me.

"You do it," he said.

I picked up the small weights carelessly and started curling them toward my chest as fast as I could. After about a minute, I slowed down. I was puffing, and the muscles in my arms felt heavy at first and then began to ache. I stopped to catch my breath.

"This is fucking crazy," I said. "I don't need to do this."

Cortina grinned. "You're not used to pain."

"Not this kind," I said.

"You're not used to any kind. You have to do the small weights for half an hour, so pace yourself. Otherwise you'll run out of gas. Do the weights in one position until your arms don't lift anymore. Then change positions. We'll do half an hour in the morning and half in the afternoon. In the afternoon we'll jump rope too."

I started lifting again. Slowly this time. "Shit!" I muttered.

"Hey!" said Cortina. He stepped in front of me. He was shorter than I was. His black stare, his head shaped like an acorn, his stocky, round, solid body and his acne-scarred face were menacing. "You don't talk and you don't complain. You just feel the fucking pain. Do you understand?"

"I got it," I said, staring back at him.

"Think only about the places where it hurts and how it hurts," said Cortina.

The next couple of months I was sore in places I never thought I had. My Adam's apple, about a hundred places in my back, my ankles, hell, even my nostrils hurt. Every day the same. Lift in silence, lift in silence, like those oil pumps I used to see when I drove through the Texas desert, pumping up and down without rest, forever.

In the afternoons, ten of the twenty minutes is spent jumping rope. We do it in the hall where there's more vertical room. Slowly, slowly at first. Even so, I trip over the rope every few seconds.

"Concentrate on the space beneath your feet. Don't pay attention to nothing else. Concentrate as if your life depended on it, cabrón. What do you think this is? A fucking game?"

DAY 5

By my own calculations, I have about fifty or so more days. It seems like an eternity. This place is amazing that way. Everyone goes about as if they were going to live forever. Wooly goes out to paint walls. Cortina lifts weights preparing for the Mr. Universe pageant, or so it seems. Botswana, I don't know what he does, but from the evil in his eye, I can tell you that the hereafter is not on his mind. Velop goes around borrowing smokes and trying to get me to write to Merv Griffin on his behalf. Grosvenor, the slimy bastard, is about the only one who seems to have a sense of what is going to happen to him eventually. Unfortunately, the guy turns my stomach with a force I find irrational.

This morning, for example, I found this little piece of paper folded accordionlike on the stool next to my bunk. It was a prayer by who else, Grosvenor, our resident saint. His Holiness must have snuck in and placed it there during the one miserable hour that I slept last night.

"Oh, Lord, let me understand in these days the full meaning of your resurrection. Let me understand in these days that you are the Lord of the living and not the dead. Let me place my hope in you during my everyday existence, however precarious and short it may be. Let me believe with all my heart that you have a plan for me, and let me willingly accept your plan."

Now that, I must admit, is not bad. Take it from someone who has read many a prayer in his day. It's heartfelt, makes the reader feel when he reads it as if he himself is making it up, extempore, on the spot. And it contains, like all good prayers, a tinge of hidden humor. Imagine that, a fifty-day plan for yours truly. Fifty days to either make it or not make it. You could write a jingle about that, maybe to the tune of "Old Macdonald":

13

Fifty days to find you, Lord . . . . O my Lordy Lord.
Fifty days to save yourself . . . . O my Lordy Lord.
Fifty days or your money back . . . O my Lordy Lord.

Frankly, I'm surprised that Grosvenor would think me worthy
of his proselytizing after the scene I made in his "Holy Bible
class," as Mr. Gómez calls it. I accidentally walked into it after
breakfast one morning. He holds it in the library next to my
lawyering office. The class is held every day, lasts about half an
hour, and is surprisingly well attended. I say surprisingly because
I can't figure out why other people don't dislike the big fat phony
as much as I do. Yes, shit-head, I think you are a big fat phony and
I don't care if you sneak into my room and read this while I'm
asleep, you maggot.

As I write the above, I think suddenly about the Reverend Mr.
Boles and what he said that last night just before I left Boston.
Anyway, I walked into the Holy Bible class by mistake because I
was really looking for the white typing paper that is kept behind the
librarian's desk. I sat way in the back hoping to wait out Grosvenor
inconspicuously. Unfortunately, when he saw me, he lit up like a
Christmas light. Before you know it, I was getting introduced to the
rest of the class as a west winger, and everyone was turning around
and looking at me with those looks of hidden relief, the way you
look at someone who has the clap . . . you're sorry it happened but
you're glad it wasn't you.

Then Grosvenor asked me if I ever read the Bible, and instead
of walking out like I wanted to, I said that on occasion I had. He
asked me if I would care to share with the class a favorite passage
and I answered almost automatically by saying that although I
wouldn't exactly use the word "favorite," one passage sticking in
my mind from who knows where is the one where David comes
back successful from a battle and Saul goes insanely jealous when
he sees the women making merry in the street and singing that Saul
has slain his thousands but David his ten thousands.

"So can you tell us what the passage says to your particular life
situation?

Oh, boy. Here we go. My particular life situation. Now, you
would think that in my predicament I would be free to ignore all
social mores and tell pomposity to go fuck itself wherever it
appears, especially if it's in the form of a pock-faced, flabby-assed,

miserable human being named Grosvenor. But noooo! Even here and even now I am afraid to be discourteous so I blabbed out a long harangue like an idiot.

"It seems to me that Saul got a bum rap." Everyone was now turned toward me, and I sensed from the look on his face that Grosvenor was beginning to regret he ever asked me that question.

"Here's a guy—I'm talking about Saul now—who is basically a happy guy minding his own business. He loses some donkeys one day and he goes looking for them and by the time he makes it back, he has been anointed king of Israel per God's orders by Samuel the prophet. Now Saul is not a particularly bright guy, mind you, but he has lots of balls. When the Philistines want to gouge out the eyes of the Israelites just to show who's who, Saul is the only Israelite who wants to fight back. So he chops up an ox into little pieces and sends it all over the land with the message that folks are looking at their future if they don't join his army against the eye gougers. He gets an army that doesn't look like much but fights like hell and is victorious. So everyone is happy. God is happy. Samuel is happy. Saul is happy. But then Saul gets word from Samuel that God wants Saul to go out and totally annihilate the Anakites or Stalagmatites or whatever. This time God wants everyone and everything killed, destroyed, blotted out. We're talking everyone here—soldiers, civilians, women, children, sheep, cows, chickens, every living thing. And Saul does it. He kills all of them. Except he doesn't think it makes sense to kill some of the fattest cows and sheep. Instead he gives these to his army so that they can in turn sacrifice them as burnt offerings to God."

Everyone in the room was now looking at me with this get-to-the-point kind of look. Saint Flatulence in front of the room, however, was smiling beatifically. I was trembling and shaking. It didn't matter. I babbled forth on some kind of idiot roll.

"Big mistake. Big fucking mistake. God wants everything wiped out. He wants unquestioning obedience, not burnt offerings. So from that moment on, the Spirit of God departs from Saul. Samuel doesn't want anything to do with the guy so he goes out and anoints David as the future king. Saul feels like shit. Not only does God leave him, but he is tormented by an evil spirit from, you guessed it, God himself. God places an evil spirit in Saul to torment

him. Give me a break! Look it up, it's right there. Saul does everything to get God on his side. He gets desperate, talks to witches, you
name it. But no dice. Then David comes along. Everyone can see
that God is with David. He kills a giant with a rock; he has babes
dancing with timbrels on the streets; even Saul's son Jonathan likes
David more than he does his old man. That's where Saul loses it
completely. He tries to kill David, fails, goes more and more
bananas, and then finally dies."

My mind at that point was filled with an image that I don't
want to talk about right now. I looked up from the floor after what
could have been an hour and was surprised to see a group of gray
figures in front of me and Grosvenor standing Mona Lisa-like at
the front.

I didn't know what to do or say. I was standing there paralyzed
when all of a sudden I was ripped inside by an incredible diarrhea
cramp, the kind that urgently seeks to expel, willy-nilly, without
regard for time, place, or company.

"It's bullshit." I still managed to say despite the pain and the
warmness running down my leg. "All because he wouldn't kill
everything. It was a stupid order, anyway. Shit! David later kills a
chick's husband just so he can mess around with her to his heart's
delight and God doesn't abandon him or place an evil spirit in him.
He punishes him, yeah, O.K., I can buy that. But God doesn't abandon him."

I stopped abruptly with nothing more to say. Apparently no one
had anything to say because they were all silent as stones looking
at me. I ran out of the library doubled over, gritting my teeth, headed belatedly for my brown-spotted porcelain, coverless, dripping,
gentle, whooshing friend.

DAY 6

Heavenly Jesus, my evening is arriving. My day is slowly fading. I come to you now on my knees to pray. Today is the Sunday before Easter. In the coming week, my Lord, allow me to walk with you to your cross so that I may share in the glory of your resurrection. Let me walk with you to the cross. Let me carry for you your cross, heavy with the sins of mankind, so that at the end I may be forgiven and thereafter live forever in your joy. O Jesus, help me to be like you.

O.K., it's done. Grosvenor, you perverted fruitcake, your request has been honored. Your favorite prayer is in the book. Now leave me alone! That's right, you. I'm talking to you. Don't you think I know that it is you, you sly and sneaky worm, who crawls into my cell to read this stuff? The least you can do is put the pages back in the right order when you're done.

I swear that even this place wouldn't be so bad but for the fact that there are other people around. Ever since I have been pecking at this old Olivetti typewriter, I have had nothing but a series of interruptions. There is Velop pestering me about a letter to Merv Griffin. There is Grosvenor and his unending stream of prayers. There is Wooly, who wants me to sing the praises to his Josephine. Even Cortina pokes his head in now and then and asks questions about what I'm writing. Next thing you know, Botswana himself will be raconteuring.

Speaking of Botswana, I feel that he may make my early end an even earlier one. The way that he's been eyeing my beers, I am sure that he is going to—how shall I say it?—"ask" me for my lonely Lone Star and then it's going to be, as Trudy used to say, "decision time." Should I put up some kind of pretense of a fight or meekly hand it over? What bothers me the most about this is the fact that I have to think about it. It's a real pain. So many things to think about, so many moments that I would like to rescue by remembrance, and I have to think about Botswana. And it is not necessarily that I am afraid of him. Well, O.K., I admit that the thought of having my face smashed does make me twinge just a bit, but what really bothers me is that this does not bode well for that final moment. If I can't control my thoughts now, what am I going to do the night before or the final minute or the final ten seconds? What if at that crucial moment I am filled with the Roto-Rooter jingle or, worse yet, what if I'm thinking about Botswana and the fact that he took my beer? It's very serious. I would like, if at all possible, for those final minutes to have a smidgen of beauty.

A smidgen of beauty. There are, I must say, a few possibilities. There is Kate, sitting across the table from me in that bacon-odored coffee shop we liked to go to for lunch, telling me about her dream, asking me what it meant. And I, barely paying attention, because I am overcome by a suction emanating from her blue eyes and from an airy strand of sunlit hair that has freed itself from the gentle bondage of her ear, am holding on to the edge of the table doing all I can to keep from being aspirated into her and into her dream, *per omni saecula saeculorum*, amen.

Beauty? What about the image of Trudy walking down the halls of Columbia Law School looking for a Coke machine? Or maybe Trudy walking toward me down the aisle of that small church in Connecticut and I with my heart in my throat, trying to control an uncontrollable need to weep out of sheer joy, out of sheer gratitude. Or maybe Trudy on our wedding night taking me to a depth where I was not allowed to go before nor invited to again.

Shit! Ms. Navajo, I would like to answer your question now, since I don't think I properly answered it back then when Trudy and I appeared before you for our one and only marriage counseling session. It was her radiant happiness, Ms. Navajo, it was Trudy's radiant, happy beauty that attracted me to her. When she rode up that escalator at Columbia on her way to the library with her red backpack full of heavy law books on her shoulder and her dark hair flowing like a comet's tail, I wanted to latch onto her, I wanted to be a part of the way she dealt with life, her unquestioning happiness, that incandescent orbit that was hers.

A smidgen of beauty? What about the hard beauty of my Armanda? Armanda, dancing at the Nine Tails, mesmerizing a hundred eyes, but really dancing only for me as she and I both knew. Armanda, with her brown glistening beauty, squeezing out of and demanding from ecstasy the very last drop of joy that this world can give. Armanda, even in those final days in El Paso ravaged by loss and addiction, even so, beautiful in a way that is hidden to all but those who wait for beauty patiently—stalk it even—regardless of the pain, and who for some unknown reason or maybe because of their willingness to suffer, are chosen to witness it.

DAY 7

Dear Mr. Merv Griffin:

My name is Jackeline Velop and I am on death row. I have seen your show many times and my intuition side tells me that you are someone that likes to help people. Mr. Griffin, I know that you probably get many letters from people in my type of predicament. But, Mr. Griffin, I am truly innocent. I know from the way you talk and the way you look at your guests that you are a sensitive man. That is why I am writing to you. Actually, I am dictating this letter to my good friend Ismael Díaz, who is also on death row.

You probably don't remember me, but I went to one of your shows once. I was visiting my cousin Doreen in L.A. and she took me because even way back then I was a fan of yours. Doreen asked me as soon as I got to L.A. what I would like to do and I told her without blinking an eyelash that what I wanted most was to see you. That was about a million years ago.

21

Doreen said that if we went real early to the studios that we could probably get tickets. So one Wednesday morning around 6:00 A.M. Doreen and I packed a lunch and took the Number 9 bus to the TV studios. We actually ended up taking three buses, but we still got there real early. Even so, there were people already there. Some had umbrellas and folding chairs so that they would be comfortable while they waited in the sun. Unfortunately, we brought neither so we ended up taking turns standing in line. One of us would stand in line while the other would go to a little ledge that was shaded by the side of the building and sit down.

After a couple of hours, a man came out and said that he had tickets for some game shows and was anyone interested. A few people raised their hands and I could see that Doreen was tempted because of the sun and all but I gave Doreen this please-honey-just-this-once-do-it-for-me look so we didn't raise our hands.

Doreen who was not shy believe you me asked the man if there were going to be any tickets for your show and he said that tickets for your show would be available on a first-come first-served basis at around one o'clock. It was only about eleven o'clock so Doreen and I just sighed. I ended up going across the street to buy a couple of sodas so that we could eat our lunch and it was a good thing I did because I managed to find, there by the side of the store, one of those steel milk crates that I brought and gave to Doreen so that she could sit down and then Doreen and I had our lunch while we chatted and chatted.

Sure enough, at around one o'clock, just like the man said, a lady came out and asked if anyone was interested in the Merv Griffin show. You should have seen Doreen and I jump up and down and carry on as if we were two little kids. Anyway, we got the tickets and the lady told us to be at gate three at two o'clock.

I looked at Doreen mystified wondering if I heard right.

"I thought the show was at night," I said to the lady.

"It's taped in the afternoon and shown at night," she said to me.

I was so surprised. All this time I never knew that the show I was watching had already happened. It was news to me. I was kind of shocked to tell you the truth. But Doreen, who's lived on the West Coast all her life, didn't give it a never mind.

"That's show business for you," she shrugged.

So to make a long story short, we went in and got the best seats in the house because Doreen knew exactly where to go and how to get there. Mr. Griffin, I tell you, when I was sitting there waiting for you to come on, I tell you, it was the biggest moment in my life. I just knew that no matter how long I lived, I was never going to experience anything quite like that. It was a thrill. All those people, the applaud signs blinking on and off, the guy who came out just before you did to warm us up so that we could be nice and loose and loud for you. I am telling you, it was something else. I will never forget that moment as long as I live, which may not be too much longer by the way.

When you came out my heart stopped. There you were in the goose flesh and not more than ten feet away from me and Doreen. I couldn't take my eyes off you. It was all like a little miracle, the way they powdered your nose during the commercials, how you read your notes and ignored your guests when the camera was off, how you sipped from a glass of water that someone brought on a tray. I took it all in.

I don't want to take too much of your time and I can see that my dear friend Ismael is getting tired, so I am going to move on to the main reason for my letter. The only other thing I want to mention about that night is that I think you handled Zsa Zsa real good. You made Zsa Zsa tell the story about how she had been to a party where someone had said something nasty to her and Zsa Zsa Daaarling didn't take that kind of abuse Daaarling from anyone so Zsa Zsa slapped the mischiever on the cheek with all her Hungarian soul and then all hell broke lose. A real Donnybrook, as Zsa Zsa said. I thought you interviewed her real good seeing as to how she didn't really want to talk about it.

Mr. Griffin, you may remember me, I don't know. I know that you looked at me during your monologue and smiled at me because I have treasured that look and smile all my life. I know that for a brief second, you and I connected and our souls and hearts touched. I have been around for a long time and I have learned to recognize when two hearts click.

Mr. Griffin, a great injustice will be done if I am executed. You may have read about me because my story was reported in all the national papers. I am the guy who was accused of killing his momma and then cutting her up into pieces and putting her in the refrigerator.

Mr. Griffin, I do not deny that I am guilty of cutting her up. I did that horrible repugnant deed even though I was crying my eyes out with shame while I was doing it. But I swear to you on my momma and poppa's grave, on the memory of you that I treasure, that I did not strike her dead.

My momma was a hard woman to deal with. According to every psychologist that I've talked to since they locked me up, she is responsible for me turning out the way I did. I'm not talking about the things that I've done. I'm responsible for those. I'm not like those folks that go around blaming their parents for the things they do. I'm talking about the way I am. She is responsible for that.

Ever since Poppa left her she became real attached to me and she looked at me to fill all her emotional needs. I was just a little boy when Poppa left, Mr. Griffin, how could I do that? She was smothering me with attention all the time so that I didn't really have a life.

We'd get into some terrible fights, Mr. Griffin. She would call me names and I would call her names. Poor Momma. I would call her some bad awful names. But when I really wanted to set her off, I would tell her that the reason my daddy left her was because she was frigid.

"You never enjoyed making it with Poppa, and so that's why he left you," I would tell her.

I'm telling you all this because I want to be honest with you. A lot of guys come here and tell you that they're angels. Not me. I deserve to be here. I deserve to spend ten, twenty years in here. I admit that. But no way I should die.

I'm going to tell you the way it happened. One afternoon, my friend Woolf and I were in the house just relaxing and having a good time. Woolf and I had made whoopee as soon as we came in the house so afterwards we were just kind of lounging around being lovie lovie to each other. Then Woolf asked me if I wanted to do some angel dust. I told him you weren't supposed to snort angel dust, you're supposed to sprinkle a little on some grass and smoke it. But Woolf said he wanted to snort it and you just can't argue with Woolf when he wants something. So I said to him: "Go ahead, honey, if you want. Only let's go upstairs in case my momma comes in."

I was worried that Momma would return from choir practice and see Woolf in his skivvies doing angel dust. Anyway, Woolf just wouldn't move so he started doing lines right there on the little coffee table in the living room when sure enough Momma walked in. She saw him first half-naked and then she saw me in my robe and then she started yelling and carrying on like a woman possessed. I can't begin to tell you the names she called me. I don't know if you have ever been humiliated in front of your honey, Mr. Griffin. If you have you'd know what I was going through.

Woolf in the meantime was just sitting there, leaning back against the bottom of the sofa, his legs every which way. Finally, I just couldn't take it anymore so I started yelling at her.

"Leave me alone! Leave me alone! You frigid bitch! Just leave me alone!"

Momma went real quiet all of a sudden and shuffled upstairs to her bedroom. I told Woolf, "Honey, we have to split," but he just sat there like nothing's happened. Then she returned, Mr. Griffin, carrying Daddy's Dexter shoe box. That box, Mr. Griffin, had what was most precious to me. It had all the pictures of me growing up. Baby pictures, sixth grade pictures of me in a crew cut, graduation pictures in my black robe, prom pictures in my pink tuxedo. There were pictures of my poppa holding me up in the air. The pictures were all my life, Mr. Griffin.

So she sat down on her rocking chair and put the box on the same little table where Woolf had been doing lines. Out of one pocket she took out some lighter fluid and out of the other she took a match and before I could do anything she had lit the shoe box and all my life with it, all of it was going up in flames before my very eyes. I looked at her, and Mr. Griffin, I don't know if you have ever seen the Devil face to face, but I saw the Devil then. I swear to you. She was the Devil, the way she was smiling and looking at me. It was evil. It was evil incarnate, Mr. Griffin.

Then Woolf finally realized what was happening and what I was going through, the anguish, Mr. Griffin, so he rubbed my head real gentle-like and whispered to me not to worry. He went out to the kitchen and when he returned a few seconds later he was carrying Momma's big black iron frying pan. Momma looked at him wondering what he was going to do. I looked at him knowing what he was thinking but honest to God, I was unable to even flinch. Before Momma could even let a scream out of her mouth, Woolf had real quick-like brained her with the frying pan, her tiny white head splatting like an egg, her brains all over the place.

"Oh, Woolf," I said to him, "Oh, Woolf, sweetheart. What have you done?"

I bent over the mess to hold her in my arms, but she was gone before she even hit the floor. There were still tiny breaths coming out of her mouth but she was gone, her life oozing out of her every which way.

Oh, Mr. Griffin, how I cried for my momma. I cried with shame and with guilt but also with love. She was my momma after all and even though we used to fight like crazy, we were kin, and each other was all we had.

Yes, I did help Woolf carry her into the bathtub and I did help cut her up. But Mr.

Griffin, by then I was in another world. We put her in a trash bag and then, after we removed the shelves and put the groceries on the kitchen table, we put her in the fridge. Woolf was going to go get a car and come later that night to pick us both up, and I was supposed to scrub the tub. Only he never came back, and I never scrubbed the tub. Around midnight, I called the police. I called the police myself, Mr. Griffin. Didn't even bother to lie. I told them straight that Woolf had done it because while I was sitting there waiting for Woolf with Momma getting cold, I figured out that I loved Momma more than I could ever love Woolf. And that's the truth.

So Woolf gets ten years and I am about to be put to death. Turns out that the angel dust made Woolf unable to premeditate, "unable to comprehend the enormity of his crime" as his lawyer said. But me on the other hand, I could premeditate. They said I premeditated at the time I saw Woolf walk into the kitchen after he told me not to worry. They said I premeditated enough not to stop him. They said I premeditated between the time that I saw Woolf saunter out of the kitchen and the time he brought the skillet to the back of Momma's head. I premeditated enough to not even say "hey." They said that all you need is a few seconds to premeditate. They asked me if I had thought about what Woolf might do with the frying pan when he walked out of the kitchen and I answered that I had thought he might kill her. They asked me why I didn't say or do anything, and I said that right then, right at that moment as she smirked her evil smirk, right then, I wanted her dead. So my premeditation plus the drugs they found in the house met the Texas test for a boner fide capital crime, deserving of the death sentence.

I have to stop now, Mr. Griffin. I can see that my friend Ismael is having trouble writing.

This is straight from the heart, Mr. Griffin. The truth with no excuses. This is why I am writing to you, Merv. May I call you that? You are my last and only hope. I have seen in you a kindness few other men have. I know that you care about people like me, in my predicament. I am always right about these things. Please, if you believe me, help me out. There are volunteer lawyers appealing my sentence, but between you and me they are not that good. Good hearted but second rate. I need big-time help. A man like you can work miracles. People listen to you. However, if you cannot do anything, I will still remain forever yours,

Jackeline Velop,
On Death Row, Sentenced To Die Unless You Intervene.

DAY 8

"**L**isten man, you can't let him do that. The next time he tries to take your beer, you have to kick him in the huevos. You have to stand up for your rights, man, even here."

Cortina is standing in front of me with a red bandanna tied around his head. In baggy pants and a sleeveless T-shirt he looks like some kind of samurai.

"One thing you gotta understand is that the man knows you're a Mexican. So when you let him boss you around, you hurt all of us. You understand? In this place if someone messes around with a carnal they die. I don't care if they're going to get zapped the next day. You get my meaning?"

I don't know how he does it, but every Saturday night Mr. Gómez manages to bring in three six-packs of cold Lone Stars which, when duly apportioned, come out to about three cans apiece. St. Grosvenor's abstinence fortunately allows for even distribution. It is the highlight of the week without a doubt. After Saturday dinner everyone just kind of sits in his bunk straining to hear the jiggling of Mr. Gómez's keys. When Gómez comes in we all coolly walk out and line up to get our share. Mr. Gómez always gives us three apiece and always asks Grosvenor if he wants his. Even Wooly, who not infrequently gambles his share away during the previous week, gets what is rightfully his. Mr. Gómez doesn't get into gambling disputes. It is up to the interested parties to work those things out themselves.

"It's not the beer, man," continues Cortina. "It's about self-respect. How the fuck are you going to leave this world with huevos if you let people step all over you? If you're going to go anyway, then you have to go with huevos. It's all you have. It's the only thing you have. What's the matter with you, man, are you listening to me?"

When Wooly gambles his beers away, it is a real pain for everyone because then he spends the rest of the evening begging people for a "teeny-weeny sip." I made the mistake of giving him one once. He put his big lips on the can, threw his head back, and two seconds later returned it empty.

"Aaaah," he said.

"Let me tell you something, man. Do you know why Botswana never gives me any shit? I'll tell you. He knows that I'm the only one here who's not afraid to die. He knows that for a fact. He knows that I would rather have him kill me than die on a stretcher in a room with windows all over the place and people staring at me like an animal in a zoo. Man, if Botswana ever came on to me, I would smile from ear to ear and tell him: "Come on, motherfucker, come get me. This is just what I been waiting for.""

There is a growing disagreement amongst the residents of the west wing as to whether it is better to sip your three cans real slow so as to make them last as long as possible or to gulp them down at once in order to get a little buzz. Botswana, Cortina, and on occasion, Wooly, usually end up gulping them down. Mr. Gómez, Velop, and myself prefer to take small sips. Velop even swishes the beer around his mouth a few times before swallowing it. Mr. Gómez tells me that Velop has the record for making his beers last the longest. Apparently he once kept a beer alive until Sunday morning.

"How are you going to deal with him now that he knows you're a pussy? How could you just sit there and let him snatch your beer without even saying a word? I don't understand you, man. I don't get the vibes that you're a pussy, but maybe I'm wrong."

I cannot deny that there are some disadvantages to sipping. For one thing, the last can is usually warm, or at least not as cold as the first. For another thing, the longer it takes me to drink the beers the more I risk having Botswana snatch one, as he did last night. On the other hand, one shouldn't rush through something without enjoying it out of fear of losing it or out of fear that someone else may take it. I firmly believe that.

Cortina has pulled the chair from my desk and is sitting on its edge facing me as I lie on my bunk with my arms behind my head. He lights up a smoke—one of his own, I note. He is here to stay.

"Where are you from, anyway? Are you part gabacho? How come you're so white?"

Fighting over beers never happens. Even grabbing one that doesn't belong to you by force of sheer intimidation is pushing it.

Not because of any heightened sense of morality, believe you me. It is simply that you don't mess around with Mr. Gómez, who has let everyone know in no uncertain terms that if "you abuse a privilege, you lose it." That's what Mr. Gómez says when people start getting ideas. And people behave out of fear that there won't be a next time.

"De Méjico," says Cortina, grabbing a piece of tobacco from the tip of his tongue. "My old man was an Indian from Zacatecas. My mother was raza from Riverside. That's in L.A."

Most of the time I choose not to sit in the hall but rather bring my beers back to my own cell. Sometimes, however, out of fear that Grosvenor will accost me with a prayer, I'll stay with the group, listening to Mr. Gómez's stories of west wing residents or hearing out Velop's latest legal strategies. Last night I chose to come back to my room, which was just as well. There I was, about to open my third one—still semi-cold—when Botswana walked in, snapped his finger, and pointed at it. I put the beer on the desk and gave him this cold "you want it, you take it stare." Despite what Cortina might think, I was not afraid. I just didn't give a shit. Botswana stood there waiting with his hand pointing at the beer and glaring at me to put it in his hand, but I didn't give it to him. I made him take it. It was a victory of sorts, in my mind, anyway.

"My old man picked everything from lettuce to grapes. He went to school every night until he learned English. My old lady was a maid. Man, did I let her down." He looks up at the little window and lets out a stream of smoke. "I had six brothers and sisters. I was third from the top. The only one who ever got in trouble. The only one in my family who ever set foot in jail. Do you believe that? We lived in a project, gangs everywhere, crack, dope, and there we were, eight of us in this little apartment, with pictures of the Virgen de Guadalupe and little candles and tortillas and frijoles every night, all together. It was like a different world inside that apartment. Do you know what I mean? It's like it was all safe in there while outside everyone was killing one another. And I'm the only one that fucks up. Do you know why people fuck up? You're a smart guy. You sit here writing and thinking all day. Tell me why I didn't turn out like all my brothers and sisters. Can you tell me why, Mr. Smart Guy? Only maybe you're not so smart because you're here too, aren't you, cabrón? You fucked up somewhere along the line too, didn't you?"

DAY 9

No beer until further notice. All perks are canceled. Mr. Gómez mysteriously found out about the incident yesterday afternoon and dutifully informed the commissioner. Anyone else would probably have been killed for snitching. But Mr. Gómez carried it off. No one, not even Botswana, uttered one single gripe when the word came down. It was accepted with the weight of justice.

"No violence. That's one of the rules. And a rule is a rule is a rule," said Mr. Gómez.

It happened yesterday afternoon. I had, of all things, fallen asleep sitting at my desk, my head on top of the small pile of written words. I heard Botswana yell and somehow his yell fit perfectly into a dream I was having, although I no longer remember the dream.

"You mofucker! I told you not to do that shit! Didn't I tell you not to do that shit? How many times have I told you that?"

I looked up and went out into the hall where I saw Botswana holding one of Grosvenor's prayers in one hand and Grosvenor's neck with the other. Grosvenor was turning shades of red, then violet, then blue.

"I don't want no fucking prayers. You understand?"

Grosvenor's tongue was sticking out and his eyes were bulging froglike out of his head. By this time everyone except Mr. Gómez and Wooly was out in the hall. Cortina was laughing. Velop was holding his hands to his mouth and springing up and down with little bunny jumps.

With one quick movement, Botswana switched his grip from the front of Grosvenor's neck to the back. He began to lead Grosvenor head down into Grosvenor's cell. Everyone followed, including me.

"I'm gonna fuck you with your prayers," Botswana said. When I got there, Grosvenor was already on the floor with Botswana's knee on his back. Botswana was rolling Grosvenor's prayer into what looked like a poorly rolled cigarette, the kind that Abuelito used to make for himself every evening out on the porch, only bigger. Then Botswana put the paper in his mouth while, two-handed, he yanked Grosvenor's pants down over his butt, underwear and all.

"Oh, my God, someone do something!" Velop screeched. But there was more curiosity than terror in his voice.

Cortina was almost doubling over with laughter. For one very brief and mercifully fleeting second, I thought of grabbing Grosvenor's desk chair and hitting Botswana over the head. The truth is that I was unexpectedly blinded by the brightness of Grosvenor's incandescent pinkness.

Botswana stuck the rolled-up paper thermometer-like into the unwiggling Grosvenor. Grosvenor's head, sideways on the floor, was hardly visible behind Botswana's back, but I could tell that he had his eyes forcefully shut, like someone who just saw an explosion and is waiting for the bang to come. Botswana released the hold on Grosvenor's head long enough to reach into his shirt pocket for a book of matches which he struck one-handed with a flick of his thumb. Then he lit Grosvenor's prayer.

Cortina began to sing "Happy Birthday." Velop was now openly giggling and I have to admit that it was a funny sight.

"Let your light shine to all men that they may see your good works and glorify your Father in heaven," I said softly, unconsciously, not even realizing that I was speaking out loud. Apparently Cortina and Velop heard it because Cortina started laughing even louder and Velop started hiccuping and giggling uncontrollably.

"Is that what you call turning the other cheek?" Velop asked almost hysterically.

Cortina strained for a second, trying to come up with a biblical reference but nothing came and he went back to laughing.

The paper burned only half way. Pieces of black ash peppered Grosvenor's white buttocks. Botswana released his hold and humorlessly told Grosvenor that the next time it was not going to be paper up his ass. He shot me a long and meaningful "you're next" look as he left Grosvenor's cell. Grosvenor pulled his pants up, ashes notwithstanding, and sat on the edge of his bed. Velop and Cortina went back to their cells high-fiving each other. The party was over. I stayed a little longer, looking at Grosvenor. His hands were joined together, his eyes were closed, and his lips were either moving or trembling. He was whispering something.

I couldn't hear what he was saying, but it is entirely possible that he was praying for Botswana himself. That's the kind of guy he is, our resident saint.

DAY 10

Cortina sticks his head in my room and tells me that the Jimmy Olympics are on. I stop typing and go over to see what is happening. Outside in the hall, Velop is drawing a line with chalk. Wooly, Botswana, and Cortina are putting packets of cigarettes on a chair that someone has taken out.

"Now don't anybody start now. I'm going to put my outfit on." Velop finishes drawing the line and then rushes into his cell excitedly.

I walk over to where the group is standing. "It's worth a pack to you, if you want to play," says Wooly.

Botswana looks at me with a snicker that is meant to say that I'm too chicken to play. I move back. I have seen this group play Jimmy Olympics before and it is not a game for amateurs. I go back to my cell and sit down to write.

Then, suddenly, I grab an unopened pack of cigarettes and I go out and place it on the chair along with the other packs.

"Yo, my man!" says Wooly.

"Carnal!" says Cortina.

Botswana twists his lips into a fuck-you smile.

"O.K. I'm ready," says Velop. He is wearing a white T-shirt and gray tight-fitting shorts like the ones bicycle racers use. Velop stands behind the chalk line. "O.K. Everyone drop your drawers."

"Hold on," I blurt out, "what are the rules?"

"The closest one to the line wins," says Wooly.

"It doesn't matter how long you take?" I ask.

"You can take as long as your little heart desires," says Velop.

"Cut the shit," says Botswana, who by now has dropped his pants and drawers and is beginning to fondle something which I thought was already alive but which apparently is barely starting to awaken.

"Wait a minute," I say. "What about betting one of our beers the next time we get some?" These words come out my mouth and they surprise me as they do.

"Uuuu, man. A heavy hitter," says Cortina.

"I don't know," says Wooly. We won't know when we'll get the beer back. That's a big bet."

"Why should I bet a beer when I can have yours?" asks Botswana, holding something that now looks like a weapon.

"If you win, you get three extra beers," I respond, trying not to look down.

"Come on, darlings!" Velop yells impatiently.

"Let's do the beer, " says Botswana.

"La birria," says Cortina.

"Beer it is," says Wooly.

Based on the different sounds I hear at night, I suspect that Wooly is by far the most avid practitioner of the bunch. I sense, however, that despite his impeccable form, he may lack the necessary element to win at Jimmy Olympics—propulsion. I fear that Botswana is probably the current champion, although, maybe Cortina can beat him on a Botswana bad day. And it is easy to have a bad day in this contest. One slip of the hand or one too tight a squeeze and the whole thing can end in a big glob at your feet.

I myself, despite the spontaneous bravado, am full of doubts. For one thing, it has been longer than I care to remember since the old periscope has been up. I'm not sure that the gears will click again in private, much less in this public forum. Hell, I have trouble peeing in public. I remember embarrassing moments at the law firm urinals. I'd stand there with a colleague next to me asking me questions about this and that and all I could think of was the deadly silence coming from my end. I had the same trouble when I was in the bathroom and Trudy would come in to brush her teeth or something. Her drawing attention to my trickle-less stand didn't help, either.

Even assuming that I can get the drawbridge to go up, there is still the matter of projection. There is an incredible six paces between the line where the contestants stand and the line where their object of desire wants to end up. That's a long way. Still, I am hoping to draw upon a secret weapon. I think it might work. If I can get the paso lento going, I'll at least finish the race. Of course, it will be a first, if I can do it. I've never gone on to dance the paso lento solo. Armanda, let's see how good a teacher you were.

"O.K. On your marks, get set . . ." Velop is about to drop his hand when Cortina yells.

"Cut the crap and get La Mona!"

La Mona is a *Penthouse* foldout that Velop holds. Barely, through the white creases of the wrinkled paper, you can distinguish, if you squint, the picture of La Mona, legs straight up, opening her inner sanctum with her fingers.

"Oh, fine," says Velop bitchily.

He comes out and unfolds her.

"How come we never have no black woman up there?" asks Wooly.

"Sue me, mother," says Cortina.

"White women have no soul," says Wooly.

"Who needs soul?" responds Cortina.

Botswana, who has been already in a state of heightened concentration, tells everyone to cut the shit and get it on.

Velop gets the contest started.

I have unfortunately shrunk more than usual, perhaps with the anxiety of competition. I am not sure, but through the corner of my eye I think I see Botswana smirking at me. Come on little fellow, please don't let me down. Not now.

Cortina looks like he is taking an eye test that he has a high probability of failing. His eyes are fixed on a particular spot on the paper woman in front of him. Wooly has taken out a white handkerchief and is holding it to his nose with one hand. His eyes are closed and his other hand is moving as if caressing something lovely and fragile. Botswana has a look of torture on his face. He seems to be repeatedly and painfully stabbing himself and for the first time in my life I understand the term "self-abuse."

I am lagging way behind. Come on, my friend. Don't be shy. Don't let me down now. Not after all these years. Didn't I treat you as well as I possibly could? Did I ever deny you the best? O.K., yeah, the summer intern who gave me *The Diary of Anne Frank*. But you have to admit that it wouldn't have been right. Come on, don't begrudge me that. There are not too many things that I am proud of. And Armanda? I denied you the continuous glory of Armanda, didn't I? Yes I did, my little friend. I did do that. That evening in that motel room in El Paso, you urged me with all the power of your being to stay. She was your long lost home, where you belonged, the place made just for you, the perfect fit. You have never forgiven me for leaving Armanda, have you? All those times when you were withdrawn and listless, all those times when you uttered forth nothing but tears. It was Armanda, wasn't it? You were grieving for her and I didn't even know it. I am so sorry, my friend. You don't know the extent. But I've always wanted to ask you this: You have to admit that you too felt at certain times when you were with Armanda that there was more to life than . . . happiness? Didn't you? Oh, hell, what else are you going to say? You live but for one thing. You are like a Ulysses without the detours. Penelope, Ithaca, Armanda, that's all you want. I've been plenty good to you otherwise. I have. Think of Trudy and those first years when you were able to travel to countries you had never seen before. Imagine Kate and her golden beauty shining just for you. Think of all those summers in Tampico walking by the sweet-smelling whores and think of all the loving attention they gave you, one after another, relentlessly, like dedicated teachers teaching their future prodigy to play the piano. Think of Tía Lele. Remember her? There you go. You stir. You are alive after all. You still remember Tía Lele, do you?

The apartment in Mexico City was full of people from all over the building who had come to watch Neil Armstrong step on the moon for the first time. It was only one of three TVs in the whole building, so the room was full of children in shorts and men and women cologned and perfumed and wearing their best, as if they had been invited to a solemn, privileged, and long-anticipated occasion. Tía Carmelita, the older of the two sisters who lived there, had decided to charge one peso as an entrance fee to cover the cost of "la electricidad." She had also made some tostadas spread with black beans and sprinkled with lettuce, diced tomato, and a crumbly goat cheese. These she tried to sell for veinte centavos. The lemonade was free. The picture of the moon came on the screen—beige, with potholes the depth of which could not be measured. They could be potholes or they could be craters the size of Guatemala.

All of a sudden, Tía Lele got up and announced to the world that she was going to take a shower. She went into the bathroom, which no one ever locked no matter what anybody was doing there. It was lockless, in fact. I heard her start the shower and again I found myself at one of those crossroads of life. Whom should I watch? Should I watch Neil, my human representative up there taking a small step for man, a giant leap for mankind, presumably me included, or should I watch Tía Lele, naked? Tía Lele, whose body was still radiant at forty. Tía Lele, whose buttocks often rubbed against me as we passed each other in the tiny kitchen. What was more important? Which moon was more significant, more real, all things considered?

I headed for Tía Lele. I scurried, pretending to hurry to the bathroom now, so that I could come back in time for the big moment. Tía Lele was already in the shower. The old green parrot who lived in a rusty cage in the bathroom and whom Tía Lele by some kind of mysterious perversion on her part had taught how to say the rosary whenever someone defecated, turned sideways when I came in, the better to eye me. I entered slowly and closed the door behind me. I stood there timing it just right, waiting to part the curtain and take a peek when her head was full of lather and her eyes closed. I took my tiny astronaut out of his capsule. He jumped up, liberated from the bonds of gravity. I got closer to the curtain. I parted it slowly. There it was. White in its fluorescence, incredibly big and perfect.

"Dios te salve María," said the parrot.

"¿Quién es?" asked Tía Lele without any alarm whatsoever in her voice.

"Soy yo," I said.

"Ah, Ismael. Qué bueno. ¿Por qué no estás viendo el show?"

"Quería estar contigo," I said. I thought to myself that now I've done it. I should have just told her that I needed to go to the bathroom. But somehow, I've never been able to lie in life's big moments.

"Ah. Bueno." she said. After a while she continued, "¿Me haces un favor?"

"Sí," I responded.

"¿Me pasas el champú? Está en el gabinete."

The pressure was so great, I was starting to turn the color of the parrot, who by the way, was now starting with the Our Father. I opened the curtain more than I needed to and handed over the shampoo. O God, hallowed be thy name. The contrasts of whites and browns and pinks, all wet, all over. Thy kingdom come, thy will be done. Only let it come now on this very earth at this very second. The little droplets of water hung like morning dew from her fluffy blackness.

"Ismael," she said as I handed her the shampoo, "¿Lo quieres tocar?"

I touched softly and slowly as if it were a live and open socket that could kill. The parrot reverted to his God-given speech and was squawking and ruffling his feathers, all disturbed. Someone from the living room yelled at me to hurry back or I was going to miss the landing. Neil was stepping down the ladder. Tía Lele took my hand, put a bar of soap in it and began to groan and ask for God's forgiveness at the same time. Ay, perdóname Dios mío. Ay. Aha. Ahhh. And all the time she was turning around like a porcelain doll on a music box while I soaped her in the curves and in the straights and in the calves and in the caves, in the gaps and in the fullness of her exuberance, and the whole universe seemed so beautiful and loving and I was shaking and vibrating with my being as I heard roars of cheering and applause. Neil had landed on the moon!

Wooow now! That almost worked too well. Slow down now. O.K., now. Time to shift into the paso lento. I open my eyes slightly and see that only Wooly the caresser is still at it, rolling his eyes sleepily, while he takes deep, soulful sniffs from the white handkerchief that he holds wadded up against his nose. I see Velop in the distance put out a cigarette butt in Cortina's marking. It is about a foot behind Botswana, who has landed almost squarely on the line.

Suddenly, Wooly starts gasping and grunting. He has gone nowhere, but done so happily, I gather, by the broad smile on his face.

It is up to me now. I can feel everyone looking even though my eyes are closed, but not tightly. Botswana is looking too, not snickering anymore. Time to go on the paso lento. Here I go.

Armanda and I had just finished making love on the floor of her apartment. There was silence except for the gasping of lungs. Nando slept on the other side of a thin wall so Armanda and I had learned to muffle the sounds of our bodies. Armanda got on her knees and reached over to turn on a small Philco fan that rested in the corner of the room. The air conditioner was off because it had been making a metallic, whirring rattle that interfered with the intense concentration of Armanda during our togetherness.

She spoke in Spanish to me as she reached for a cigarette.

"Maybe now you are ready to learn the paso lento."

"What is it?"

"It's a dance of our bodies and then our hearts and then at the end our soul. But . . ."

"But what?"

"It's a dance of love. Es amor en carne y hueso. The paso lento never works without love."

"Ahh."

"Do you think you're ready, then?"

"Don't you think that what we just did was love?"

"Yes."

"Then what's the difference?"

"The paso lento is another kind of love. Different."

"How different?" I got up from the floor and sat on the black and white terry cloth sofa. Armanda, still glistening with sweat, stood up in front of me and leaned over to kiss me. She then went to the kitchen, opened the refrigerator, and took out two beers. Her movements were unhurried, deliberate. I could see the delicate curves of strength in her calves, thighs, and buttocks and when she came to me with the beer, I could see the expansion of her tight dancer's abdomen as she breathed in and out.

"Do you really want to know?" she asked. She sat facing me across the sofa, her legs folded underneath her.

"Yes, tell me."

"It's just that it's hard to tell. You have to do it. I will tell you a little what it's about, that way you can tell me if you truly want to learn."

"O.K. When do we start?"

"Now."

"But look at me."

She giggled. "In the paso lento, your verga is eighty years old and your heart is fifteen."

"And your mind?"

"Your mind is the music. Sometimes it's a sad ballad and sometimes a mambo caliente."

"But how?"

"I'll teach you little by little, no? It takes a long time to learn. Toda una vida." She smiled broadly and took a gulp of her beer.

"So then your verga is *really* eighty years old."

"Precisamente. The paso lento is better when you're old and wrinkled." Armanda unfolded her leg and stretched it until her toe touched the topic of her conversation.

"Look, el viejito wants to dance," I said looking down.

"Come, let's start," she said.

Armanda stretched herself on the floor and opened her arms to me.

"The first thing is to make your mind quiet. Let's rock slowly. Así. Come this way. Like when your nana Renata used to swing your hammock just before you fell asleep. Despacito. Let's sing a lullaby. Do you remember this one: "A la ru ru niño, duérmaseme ya, que ahí viene el cuco y te comerá.""

"I remember one that goes: "Cachito, cachito, cachito mío . . .""

"Mmm. That's a beautiful one. Así. Despacito. Swaying. Al norte y al sur. Al este y al oeste. Around and around. Let your thoughts go away. Be the music. The rhythm."

"I can hear the music now."

"Now feel what you're feeling. Pick a part of your body and feel what it feels."

"Any part?"

"Well, there are some that are easier than others, no?"

"Ay, that hurt."

"You weren't feeling your body. You were thinking about something else, true?"

"It's hard not to . . . rush."

"After you learn to be with your body, you will not want any more pleasure than what you're feeling at that instant."

"Ooof!"

"I know. It's the most difficult part. It takes very long to learn this part because you always want more, no? You want to grab more and more pleasure, or you want to give the other person more and more pleasure until you both burst."

"What's bad about wanting to give the other person more pleasure?"

"Nada. That's one of the steps in the dance but there's still more to the dance. After you learn to feel your body without wanting more, then you can start feeling the body of the other person. Look. Feel me now. Feel my flesh. Feel the littlest things, the tiny bumps on my nipples, the curve in my ear, my eyebrows, the hollow in my throat, the tip of my tongue. Pedacito por pedacito. Feel every part of my body with your fingertips like you're blind or like you're touching for the first time ever and I'm the first thing you touch. No te apures. We have all the time. Feel one part of me at a time. One tiny part at a time. Look. Can you feel how it feels at the very last point of your body where you connect inside of me? Feel this. Can you feel how I pull you even deeper from inside of me?"

"Ay, mi amor. Maybe we shouldn't talk anymore."

"Sí. Talking is bad. We are doing at one time what takes many times and much practice to do. Every time we make love we'll practice one step. That's how you learn to dance. You do one step over and over, then you do another, then you do all the dance and forget about the steps. Your body just responds to the music without thinking."

"Is there much more? I'm not sure I can stay with you too much longer."

"Do you see? Do you see the difference between this and what we did before? Before, when we got to a point, you went your separate way. Or I went my separate way and maybe we tried to keep up or tried to push the other to get there or tried to get there together, but we were still separate."

"What was wrong with that?"

"Nothing. But this is another way. This is a special way that I'll show you. You'll see. This way is more beautiful if you can imagine that. Look, tell me what you feel inside of you now."

"Tengo ganas de cocharte."

"Ves. This wanting to cocharme, to fuck me, is what needs to become love. Cochar has anger and selfishness in it. The paso lento is as powerful as anger but much different."

"Armanda, I need to stop for a second."

"It's O.K. Just go back to the lullaby."

"How do you know all this?"

"Come, amor mío, let's sit face to face for this next part. Sit up and cross your legs like this. Now hold me up with your hands as I come down. Hold me until I rest in you. There. Later this will be comfortable for you."

"It's not too bad."

"Yes, but your legs and back will feel pain in a little while. I don't know how I learned, it's just something I know. Maybe from Nando's father. I learned from him how his love for me was also cruel. I thought that true love cannot be like this. Maybe from my mamá, I learned too. She was a curandera and all the time people came to her for healing."

"You never told me."

"She would wrap a rosary in her hands and then feel the air all around the person. She said that she could feel where the envy or the anger or the hatred of the sick person was stuck in the body and that these things were usually the cause of illnesses. Sometimes she said it was the envy or hatred of another person that was stuck in them. Then she prayed over them and touched them with holy water and brushed them with sacred plants until the anger or envy disappeared and then the illness would go away."

"Did she teach you how to do this?"

"She tried to teach me but I was too interested in other things, like dancing or playing with my friends outside. But maybe I picked up some things. She told the people that came to see her that it was they who cured themselves. That when she prayed over them, the love of God and of the Virgen of Guadalupe that was in her stirred up that same love that was in them. She said that all she did was make this love wake up and flow through their bodies and wash away the illnesses. I don't know, I guess I learned from her that there is a true love deep in us, but that sometimes it is not easy to get to this love because of the things that we carry, like our anger or selfishness or that of others. Most of the time we don't want to get to true love, because this love is powerful and if we lose it once we have it, we feel how empty we are without it and we are afraid for ourselves. I thought that when I found the right person I would try to make true love. You know?"

"Yes."

"¿Estás bien?"

"You were right, after a while the back begins to hurt."

"It hurts because you are reclining without holding on to me. You have to balance yourself with me and learn to rest in our tension like a human bridge."

"But I can't move without falling back."

"You can move with your feelings. After dancing the paso lento for a while, there will come a feeling in your heart that is warm and strong. When that happens the paso lento becomes like dancing, a way of showing feeling with your body. The movements of your body don't have to be big. The rhythm is sometimes kept with tiny, tiny movements in the place where we unite. That's where you forget about yourself and even about the other person. Both of you are just love."

"That seems impossible."

"It is hard. It only happens if you don't have selfishness for yourself or violence for the other person. You can't make it come otherwise."

"And when it comes?"

"Then just feel what's happening in your heart. When you stop wanting the other person for your needs, something happens inside of you that's different and muy hermoso. The two persons become something like brothers and sisters or like best friends that like to be with each other all the time, only there is a power of passion too. Not the passion of grabbing, but the passion of giving completely, forever, of dying for each other. It's so hard to explain. ¿Me comprendes?"

"That's love?"

"Yes, true love. There's no words for it. You have to feel it. Maybe you'll see. I don't think you've felt this kind before. No hay palabras."

"Show me."

"I can show you the steps but the music of the paso lento comes from inside you. The music is always playing, but you have to go through the steps so you learn to hear it."

"Then what happens at the end?"

"Are you ready?"

"Which way should I be?"

"Anyway, it doesn't matter. Maybe like this."

"Armanda . . ."

"Shh . . . Now I'm going to tell you about the end as we do it but next time we won't talk when we do the paso lento so that you can listen to the music in your heart, no? At the end, the dancer and the music are one and their hearts beat together to the rhythm of the dance. When you have learned the steps of the dance then the end will just happen. In the paso lento everything is a preparation for the end, only the end is not important and you don't worry about it and you don't even care if you ever get there. You don't care about the end at all. Sometimes you forget about the end and you just fall asleep in each other's arms. That's how you know you're doing the paso lento, when you can go through the steps without thinking about them and without worrying about the end. All you do is listen to the music and let it take you wherever. When you're ready you'll know how to let go without wanting more. You just let yourself dance without being scared or worried, and without expecting anything at all except whatever the music brings. The tempo will take you wherever it wants, and you just let it take you without fear. Sometimes the tempo becomes very hard and very fast. Can you

feel the tempo now? It's like this, hard and deep, only . . . our heart
. . . and soul . . . are still calm and content even though our bodies
are pushing . . . and pulling . . . against each other . . . trying to
break to the other side . . . or bringing . . . the other person inside
of us to a place no one can reach. . . . Ever—"

"Armanda . . ."

". . . the other person is in us deeper and deeper . . . inside of
us . . . our bodies welded together at every surface . . . until mind
and body lose track . . . and now you are the woman . . . and you
open to me . . . and now I am the man that penetrates you and
makes you give—"

"Ahh . . ."

". . . and now we are man and woman together and you can't
tell where you end and where I begin . . . and now we are not man
. . . or woman . . . we have no sex . . . we are just the music . . . that
is always there . . . in our hearts—"

"Amor . . ."

". . . until we unite so much that we are like one person that is
made with two spirits. Así. Una . . . Dos . . . Así. Dos personas en
una con su amor, todo uno."

Armanda, I never even came close to dancing the paso lento
back there in El Paso. When it was time for me to leave for Boston
and law school and Trudy, I left. Never looked back. I never gave
myself completely to you as the paso lento required. And when I
received your last letter I put it away and did not feel the pain that
it conveyed until much later. I didn't have the courage to accept
your love for me and all its consequences. And now, even though it
is too late, I take you and give myself to you. All of me, even in this
poor form. Take this of me, all that it is. Take this all of me in memory of you. Armanda . . . Armanda . . . Armanda.

I open my eyes when I hear Cortina yell: "¡Ay! ¡Ay! ¡Ay!
Armandita. Amorcito mío. Panochito de mi alma. ¡Ajúa!"

"Fuck!" I hear Botswana swear.

"Yo, mama!" says Wooly.

In front of me in a world I barely begin to recognize stands
Velop wiping from his right eye, in essence, my love and my
remorse.

"Oh, my goodness!" I hear him say in the distance. "Oh, my
goodness!"

DAY 11

This morning, after our half-hour of afternoon weight lifting torture, Cortina followed me into my cell and asked me if the small wooden animal on my desk was a jaguar.

"Maybe it's a jaguar. I always thought of it as a mountain lion."

"No, man. See here. These are big brown spots like a jaguar." Cortina picked up the wooden figure and showed me with his fingers where he thought the big brown spots were.

"Maybe," I said. I was looking for my cigarettes, which I must say tasted particularly good after the exercise.

"Where'd you get it?"

"An old man gave it to me a while back. I kept it."

"Mean anything to you?" He nodded for one of my cigarettes. I gave him one and then lit both of ours.

"For some reason I've kept it. I don't know why. I only knew the old man for about an hour."

Cortina shook his head as if he understood. "Maybe it's not a mountain lion but a jaguar. Maybe you kept it because one day you'll want to be a jaguar."

"I don't know what you're saying," I said.

"Ahh," said Cortina, waving away the previous conversation and the smoke from his nostrils with his hand. "Why don't you ever answer your mail?"

"It's bullshit mail. From anti-death-penalty groups who want to represent me in an appeal."

"So what's wrong with that?"

"They're not interested in whether I live or die. They're just interested in a social cause."

"What's the fucking difference?" asked Cortina, knitting his eyebrows. "Maybe you don't answer the mail because you want to die."

"Maybe I'm like you. You told me that Botswana didn't mess with you because he knew that you're not afraid of dying."

"Yeah, puto. I'm not afraid of dying, but that doesn't mean I want to die. You get it? It's none of my business, but maybe you want to answer those people about the appeal."

"I had my chances. I lost."

"I don't care what the fuck you do, but whatever you do should be because you believe it's the right thing. Not just because you don't give a fuck. If someone is offering you an appeal for free, take it. The way I see it from here, if you're not guilty you owe it to life to keep on living and if you're guilty the same but for a different reason. You know what I mean?"

"Yeah. I'll think about it."

Cortina accepted that as an invitation to leave. Before he entered his cell, he turned around and came back to mine. He closed the barred door behind him as though that would prevent anyone else from hearing what he was going to say.

"Do you want to be a jaguar?" he asked solemnly. The way he said it, you could tell he thought it was a big honor, something that you just didn't ask anyone.

"I don't know what a jaguar is. If a jaguar is someone who's not afraid to die, count me out 'cause I'm scared shitless."

Cortina laughed and hit me on the back and knocked a puff of white smoke out of my mouth like when you shake an eraser on the blackboard. "Eres un gran cabrón," he said amidst a coughing fit of laughter.

"You can't be a jaguar just like that. It takes time and hard work and huevos to be a jaguar."

"What do I have to do?"

"Hey, guess what, man? You've been doing it."

"Lifting weights?"

"Not just lifting weights, man. Lifting them the way we lift them and jumping rope. You've been getting ready for battle, man. Now you have to get in there."

"Where?"

"Here, man, or here or here," he pointed at his head, then he put his hand on his heart, and then he grabbed his crotch. "Anywhere where fighting needs to be done."

"Who do you fight?"

"Whoever. When I lift weights, I am saying to myself, to whatever it is that's in my head, miedo, hatred, anything. I say to it,

'Come on, motherfucker, I'm here. Come get me if you can 'cause I'm not running away from you.' I just look at it and stare it down, whatever it is. Sometimes I stare down the love I have for my Guadalupe and the fact that I'm not ever going to see her again. Sometimes it's guilt. Sometimes it's lonesomeness. That's what the fight is all about. Every day. Every day is a fucking fight with whatever is there. What about you?"

"What do you mean?"

"What is it that you're running away from?"

"Running away?"

"Yeah, man. What are you a cobarde about?"

"Muchas cosas."

"No, come on, man. Don't bullshit like that. You got huevos about something. It takes huevos to lawyer every day for the fuckers around here and it takes huevos to write every day like you're writing, just like it takes huevos to fix fucking TVs some days. Some days I feel like nothing's worth doing. ¿Para qué? ¿De qué sirve? But I get up and do the TVs. It takes huevos to do that."

"Yeah, in a way it does."

"Now let me ask you this: Why did you start writing? It's not part of your trabajo, is it?"

"No. I don't know. I guess I started a few days ago when I heard rumors that . . ."

"Yeah, that you're going to get fried pretty soon."

"Yeah."

"Yeah. You're writing because the weight lifting is making you into a jaguar."

"Making me what?"

"I've been seeing that in the past few months you are finally looking at the pain of weight lifting and jumping rope without calling it good and bad. Right?"

"I guess."

"It happened, man. You developed the eyes of the jaguar. Now you have to use that same power to look at other things in your life. That's why you started writing. You wanted to look at things straight as if someone else had done them."

"Look at what things?"

"The things you fear. You have to figure out what those are."

"Botswana, for one," I said.

"Shit, man. He's nothing compared to what you have to face. You have La Pelona to face. That's a big one. We all have to face her."

"La Pelona. I had a dream about La Pelona yesterday."

It's the same dream that I had when I was a teenager. One of the one or two dreams that stick with you for life. Last night I had it again. The last time I talked about that dream was with Kate. I told her my dream about La Pelona and she told me her dream about the nuns. Now there I was telling it to Cortina:

"I'm in some kind of bus station standing in a very long line of people. I'm not sure why I'm standing in line. There are buses somewhere, but I'm not particularly aware that I'm waiting for any kind of bus. Then all of a sudden the line of people is filled with fear and so am I. At one end of the room this tall, handsome, but very scary woman has entered the room. It is La Pelona. La muerte. Death herself. She has entered the room. She is picking people from the line at random and everyone knows what happens to the ones she picks. The fear increases as she moves down the line. People who are picked are reacting with shrieks, some are grabbing her long dress begging her to change her mind. She is cold and direct but not mean. She is moving slowly toward me. When she is about three or four persons away from me and before she has noticed me, I jump out of the line like a jack-in-the-box and I start making clown faces at her and waving my arms and my legs. I'm trying to make her laugh and am laughing myself even though inside I am terrified. I'm jumping up and down, grabbing her hands, trying to get her to do a jig with me, hugging her and kissing her frozen cheeks. And she lets me do all these things, not angry or even surprised by what I am doing. Then all of a sudden she smiles at me, a small smile that lasts only a fraction of a second, but in that fraction of a second I recognize some kinship with her. Then she moves on. She moves down the line and I am not picked."

"There you go," said Cortina. "You got it, man. At least in your dreams."

"Yeah?"

"Yeah."

"Is that what being a jaguar is all about?"

"That's it, man. You were scared of La Pelona, but you didn't run away. You stayed there and stared her down. You even made her laugh. Yeah. It was good. That's it. See, whenever we're in a line like that, we try to hide, right? Don't pick me. Oh, shit, don't notice me. But you went ahead and got yourself noticed. That's it, man. That's the way of the jaguar."

We lit up a cigarette and puffed in silence. After a while I asked Cortina where he had picked up the stuff about the jaguar life.

"I guess I picked it up from my old man. Every Saturday my old man used to take one or two of us to the public library and we would look up books about the Aztecs and the Mayas. Sometimes he would take one out and he would read to us after dinner. I would just as soon be out playing with the vatos at the time, but I guess some of that stuff stuck, 'cause later in prison I got to thinking about it."

"You have to think about something," I said.

"Yeah, what else you gonna do? One night I woke up dreaming about a picture that I had seen in one of them books. It was a picture of an Aztec warrior wearing a jaguar skin, head and all, and for a long time I couldn't get that picture outta my head. There he was, the sonofabitch staring at me. You know what I mean?"

"I think so."

"Then I remembered those books. About how the warriors had ranks and the highest you could be was a jaguar and how you could only be a jaguar if you killed or captured many enemies. That was what a jaguar did. He lived to kill and capture enemies so he could feed the sun with their blood so that the sun would be satisfied and not destroy the Aztecs. Didn't you ever read about that?"

"A long time ago."

"Yeah. The fucking Aztecs were assholes. They could have beaten the Spanish, but they just sat back and let themselves be conquered. They thought the Spanish were gods. That's the only part I don't like about them."

"They fought back."

"Shit! If you fight back when it's too late, it's like not fighting at all."

Cortina got up and paced up and down for a few seconds. Then he continued. "Anyway, there were a lot of good things about them. The way a jaguar is trained is by getting used to pain little by little. Even as kids, the ones that are going to be warriors are introduced to pain so that when they get older they don't run away from it. Pain's natural to them. They don't think of it as bad or good. Then when they get older they start getting used to their own dying until it's not a big deal to them. If they get caught and are sacrificed, the important thing is to die like a jaguar."

"Is that what you want to do?"

"Yeah, when it's my time I want to die like one. Just like you, right?"

"Yes, if I could."

"That's what you want. The only difference is that I'm trying to live like one too. I don't know if this stuff about being a jaguar is right or if the Aztecs really thought about it. But I figure, what the hell, I can make up whatever I want. Who's to stop me? One thing I like about the Aztec jaguars is that they saw themselves as killers. They didn't feel bad or guilty about it. That's what they were. Así no más. Era un hecho nada más. ¿Me entiendes?"

"Sí."

"So that's me too, man. I've killed four people in my life and when I stopped bullshitting myself, I realized that I enjoyed killing them. I enjoyed fighting with them and killing them because if it wasn't them it was me. Some I killed for vengeance, some I killed because they were trying to get me. No importa. I liked it. That's a simple fact. So I figured I might as well go on doing what I liked best because that's what I was."

"A killer."

"And a fighter. Only now I don't kill people unless I have to, to keep on living. Now I fight whatever it is that needs to be fought. . . . Anything that makes me want to run away, I fight with it; I stare it down. Everything that comes my way is to fight or to stare down or to look at with the eyes of the jaguar, not moving back. The fight doesn't always end in killing. Sometimes you even beat your enemies with your stare alone, and then they become your slaves to serve you and help you. Sometimes I remember my Guadalupe and how she's still waiting for me, and I stare at the pain of that. Sometimes I think about my jefita or my jefito or my carnales, and I just look at that shame too without backing down."

Cortina turned around and stared out the window intently, dragging on his cigarette. After a while he squashed the cigarette butt with his thumb and index finger and put the dead cigarette in his pants pocket. Then he turned around and looked at me directly.

"What about you?" he asked.

"What about me?"

"What is your thinking about how to live?"

"I don't think I have any one truth like you have. Little pieces here and there."

"I don't know if they're truths or not. All I know is that it makes sense to me and it's about as good as anything I ever heard. I thought that's what you were doing with all the writing, coming up with something."

"I don't know if I'm coming up with anything. I'm just writing about things that are happening around me."

"That's good, man. You're beginning to show interest and curiosity like the jaguar. But you won't be able to see clear like a jaguar until you spend some time looking at what happened to you. Who are you? How did you get here? What's your truth, man?"

"My only sorry-ass truth is that I am and always have been a coward."

"¿Y qué?"

"Me da vergüenza. I don't want to die like one."

"Shit, man, being a cobarde is nothing to be ashamed of as long as you don't act like one. But that's good, man. You discovered you're a cobarde and that's good. If you do te apuesto a que you won't die like one. You just gotta look at the Pelona every day and stare her down without running away. Ojo a ojo, cabrón. Every fucking day if she's there. Then maybe she'll smile at you. ¿Me comprendes?"

"Sí."

"Ya vas en camino. All you have to do is do what you already started doing."

"What?"

"Lift weights the way you've been doing. Forgetting about yourself and just feeling what you feel. Then you'll eventually feel a calmness and a fuerza que sale de dentro. All you have to do is use that fuerza wherever. When a fear or something else comes at you, you have to meet it and fight it and make it your slave and then your friend, or else you kill it. You've been training for a jaguar, pendejo, and you didn't even know it. But now you need to want to be one. Eso es todo."

"Bueno."

"Ah, y otra cosa. From now on you're on your own. You have to make the jaguar life your own. There's no one way of being one. Do you understand? It's not going to help you any to look to me for answers. It's up to you. ¿Me entiendes?"

DAY 12

lthough I know it is not true, for some reason I want to say that things began to fall apart the day I received a phone call from Arnold Valenti. There I was, about to open a can of water-packed tuna, Trudy having called to say she would be late, when Arnold Valenti, senior deacon of the Church of Jesus our Shepherd, called to ask if I would tape a funeral.

"Virginia died," were the first words uttered by Valenti. No hello, no nothing. Just "Virginia died."

"Oh," I said, as I scrambled through my mental files for a picture of Virginia.

"She just up and died. She was gardening and just fell over. Apparently a blood clot burst in her brain."

"Gee, she seemed so healthy." I located, tentatively, an image of Virginia.

"Actually, she was ill for some time," said Valenti, correcting me. "Her husband is a wreck. And of course, her granddaughter lived with them. You knew that, didn't you?"

My image of Virginia was, in fact, accompanied by the image of a very thin man and a dimple-faced girl with braids. It was an image, I now realize, that came from the Church of Jesus Our Shepherd yearbook.

"I think I did," I said.

"Anyway. The services will be held next Saturday at 2:00 P.M. and we were wondering if you would tape them."

About a year before, Reverend Boles asked me if I would parallel record the Sunday service. The job seemed simple enough. Put in two tapes, press a few buttons on a nonintimidating Sony T-500, take out the tapes, label them, and place them in a little black suitcase in the church secretary's office. It seemed simple enough. Unfortunately, everyone in a congregation of 1,000 or so was so incapable of accomplishing this technological feat that I was anointed by default as solo recorder of every Sunday service, and on some occasions, funerals and weddings.

"Sure, I'll tape it. Be glad to do it," I remember saying.

Oh, Valenti! You dumb fuck! Do you know what wheels you set in motion?

DAY 13

I sneaked in the back door to the church around 1:55 p.m. The black hearse was parked in front and next to it was the driver and another man who, I guess, was paid to ride shotgun. They had black suits with yellow carnations. I don't know if the image of white gloves slightly tattered at the edges came from here or from some other funeral.

The organ was already playing when I entered the small room in back of the sanctuary where the tape recorder was located. It was a tiny room about the size of the one where I am now. At one point the room had been used by the choir to put on and take off their purple cassocks. This joint tenancy became a problem because, with me there fiddling with the tape, choir members could not linger afterward to leisurely gossip about each other and other church members.

So they moved across the hall and shared a room instead with the bunny ears and angel wings and Magi staff of the Christmas pageant.

Most of the time, whenever I taped a funeral, I put the tapes in and left. Later, after the funeral, I returned to label the tapes for Reverend Boles to deliver them to the grieving parties. This time, for some reason, I sat down on the upturned trash can that doubled as my command post, twisted the 40-watt bulb on the side wall until the light went off, put the headphones on, and listened. I don't know why I did this except that there was something about the organ music that was sweet and melancholy.

By then I knew who Virginia Lamars was. After Arnold Valenti hung up, I looked her up in the Jesus Our Shepherd yearbook and found her there, smiling like some kind of fairy next to her husband and the dimple-faced girl with braids, whom the yearbook identified as her granddaughter Louise. Virginia was thin and had pointy Cat Woman glasses that no one wore anymore. Her husband stood by her side with his hand resting on Louise's shoulder. He looked as if he was just about to smile when the photographer clicked the shutter.

I thought about Virginia as the organ prelude played. Not that there was much to think about. I had not said to her more than a "Hi, how are you?" on a few occasions. But something about her had stuck with me. During one of my first coffee hours, while everyone was milling around in groups of threes and fours, I was standing in front of the bulletin board trying to look absorbed in the Cherub Choir's upcoming bake sale, when all of a sudden Virginia walked by and gave my elbow a tiny squeeze. I turned around and she winked and kept on going. That's it. She had walked by, squeezed my elbow, winked elflike, and disappeared.

She was now lying cold no more than 30 feet from where I sat. We were separated, it was true, by the sanctuary wall. But, in the darkness, the tape recording room seemed like the inside of Virginia's coffin, now shared with me.

I now believe that this is where I started to come unglued: The Reverend Mr. Boles's voice coming through the earphones with a high-quality directness, as if my brain were manufacturing the words and not simply receiving them. I remember only a few words. Ordinary. Simple. Humor. Peace. Life. I remember words like that. I don't think I was listening to the words at that point. I was instead feeling the tone, the rhythm, the cadence of deep and hopeless sorrow behind the words. It was as if Reverend Boles could no longer resurrect for himself and others the promise of the Resurrection. Virginia was dead. That was the fact for which there were no words of comfort. She was as dead as we would all soon be. Dead, apparently, forever and no faith would alter that.

DAY 14

*O*r maybe it all started the day I met Kate. The day she popped her head into my office for one of my old memos. I had the good instincts to tell her that I did not have the memo readily available, although I did. Sometime after 6:00 P.M., I made my way up to the 32nd floor with the long-lost copy.

What was it about Kate, anyway? I was convinced that she did this to every man that met her. I was sure that half the men in Boston and almost all in Italy (where she hitchhiked the summer before law school) were in love with her. And it was not just because she was beautiful, although she was, but because she had some kind of unexpected something that made people want her. I have tried to define this unexpectedness over many sleepless nights in many sleepless places, including this one, but still I cannot pinpoint it.

The best I can say now is that there was something about Kate that reminded men of some kind of dream that they had lost through their own fault and which became forever unattainable. I know that to be true in my case. Kate reminded me of something in my past that I had lost and something in my future that I would never have, although I didn't know then what that was.

When I walked into her office I was struck by the fact that it was plastered with pictures. Pictures on her desk. Pictures on her bookcase. A collage of pictures on the wall. Pictures of Kate and Philip eating cake at their wedding, of Philip all in white accepting a tennis trophy from a bearded man in white shorts and a blue blazer, of Corky on tiptoes poking his head out of his crib, of Corky, Kate, and Philip, in that order, in a rowboat floating peacefully in the pond outside Philip's parents' home in New Hampshire, and my favorite one of all, of a diapered Corky at the beach bending over and looking at the camera from between his legs.

"Looking at the world ass-backwards," Kate said.

So that's how it began. One day she came into my office with her sun red suit, her white shirt buttoned to her neck, and she asked if I had a copy of my famous memorandum on the property rights of structures that extend beyond low water tides. Before she left my office, I myself felt extended, reaching beyond some primal boundary line.

Thereafter, I found in me an urge to go up to the 32nd floor with more frequency than I ever had before and pop my head in through the door and ask about work and later about Corky and later about Kate herself. Then one day out of the blue, she called me and asked why I was in a bad mood, which I was.

"How do you know I'm in a bad mood when I haven't even seen you or talked to you today?" I asked, surprised.

"I can tell," she answered.

Then she told me to look out the window. There, over the Charles River, was a sunset magnificent in purples and yellows and orange reds. When I hung up, I was drenched all over in the agonizing colors of the sunset. And that's it. From that moment on she occupied my mind—how shall I say—not like a siege that came later, but like a constant memory.

DAY 15

Or maybe the seed of my Now was planted and fertilized by my decomposing marriage. I remember that around the twelfth year of our marriage, I convinced Trudy to come with me to talk to a marriage counselor. We went once and only once because we mutually, albeit silently, realized that nothing would finish off the marriage faster than to meet face to face with unblinking truth.

We sat there in two wooden Windsor chairs in front of a soft-looking woman who seemed to have been transplanted from the Southwest somewhere. She wore a white chiffon blouse with a long red skirt that I had not seen on anyone since the sixties. She had a Navajo-looking belt, the silver and agate kind with matching bracelet and ring. Randy Nevits, our firm's divorce lawyer, recommended her.

"So what brings you here?" she asked.

Trudy looked at me and with a movement of her eyebrows indicated that the question had been directed at me. I hemmed and squirmed for a few seconds before answering.

"Something is not right," I said nervously. "We don't talk much and when we do, we fight. We don't make love. We don't seem to like each other very much."

I stopped for a second, hoping for someone else to say something, but no one did. I looked at Trudy and whispered, "You seem to be disappointed in me."

"Pardon me?" asked Ms. Navajo.

"I said that she seems to be disappointed in me."

Silence.

"Is that true?" This question was directed at Trudy.

"Look," said Trudy, "this is really not productive."

"What isn't?" asked Ms. Navajo.

"This session, this conversation. We shouldn't be here before a total stranger blabbing about our life."

Ms. Navajo ignored her reply and came back to me.

"Why do you feel that she is disappointed in you?"

"She just seems to be. The way she says things. The way she doesn't say things. Nothing I do ever seems to be right or enough."

"Do you agree with that?" Ms. Navajo asked Trudy.

"No, I do not agree with that," said Trudy with some finality. She thought about this for a second and then continued.

"I was disappointed that you didn't make partner. And I was disappointed that you're willing to settle for a lifetime associate position doing residential closings, but not for the reasons that you think."

It was beginning to get a little uncomfortable.

"Please continue," urged Ms. Navajo.

"If I am disappointed at all it is at the fact that you seem to have given up on yourself. I don't care about you not making partner. I don't care about the money, as you seem to think I do. I care about the fact that you stay in situations that you don't like."

"Like our marriage." Ooops. That one slipped out.

"If you want to go, go," said Trudy without anger.

Silence.

Continued silence.

"Why do you stay together?" asked Ms. Navajo.

This one was up for grabs. Trudy responded.

"I don't have a problem with this marriage. We've had our rough times and we seem to be going through one now. But I think we can work it out."

It was my unavoidable turn to say something. Preferably about why I couldn't or wouldn't leave Trudy if I wasn't happy. But how can you articulate a gut feeling that you just can't leave someone who basically doesn't give a damn whether you leave or not? Instead I said, "I do like what I'm doing. There's nothing wrong with doing residential closings. I was disappointed too in not making partner. But things worked out for the best. I probably would have been miserable as partner."

"You seem miserable now," said Trudy.

"Right now?" I asked.

"I mean, you seem miserable in your job, now."

"I like what I do. I feel helpful to folks."

"Well, you don't act like someone who likes what they're doing."

"What do you mean?"

"I mean that you mope around all the time. You seem to be depressed. Real depressed. You walk around the house, your shoulders hunched, you sit on the sofa and watch football games and drink, or you go down to the basement and read your religious books, lives of saints, prayer books, which lots of good they've done you, and you're also smoking again. You don't do anything around the house. You never want to do anything with me. You talk about not making love. Maybe if you were a little bit more interested in me, in life in general, we would make love."

This last statement by Trudy was totally untrue. The doing things together part, I mean. First of all, she was always working late. Second of all, on weekends she was totally dedicated to her "babies," Aladdin and Alhambra, until we sold the latter horse. Furthermore, we did go out every once in a while, for Chinese, et cetera. Why I didn't say this I don't know. I sat there semistunned.

"Do you know why I agreed to come here today?" Trudy was asking me something.

"Why?" I answered listlessly.

"Because I think you are the one who should be seeing a psychologist by yourself. You are the one who needs help to crawl out of the hole you're in. I'm surprised that you're willing to come with me to see someone, but you're reluctant to go alone as I have suggested to you many, many times. I agreed to come today because I thought this would help you. After all, it's not as if there's no history of mental illness in your family."

Silence on my part concurrent with a long, menacing, and deep where-the-hell-did-that-come-from? glare.

Was there mental illness in my family? Well, let's see. There was Uncle Pancho, who at the age of twenty-eight proposed marriage to Eulalia García, was rejected, went back to his room, and never left the perimeters of the house again until he died at the age of eighty-two. I see him on the green front porch of the wooden house that Abuelito built for him across the street from Abuelito's house, getting a haircut from the traveling barber who came once a month carrying a wooden suitcase full of scissors and a soft white brush and the deadly steel snappers that crawled up your neck, cold and pinching like a wet crab. Abuelito took care of the hermit Uncle Pancho like he took care of the other assorted loonies of the family, my mother, or Lilia as I called her, included.

Was there mental illness in my family? What about Tía Lele, she with the dark areolas and the resplendent bum. What about her? She was nuts. Who besides a lunatic would teach a parrot to pray the rosary at the site of genitalia, and who but a madwoman would let my adolescent fingertips touch that furry terror and all her electric smoothness while asking for heavenly forgiveness? Ay. Sí, sí. Perdóname Dios mío. Ay. Aha. Oh, yes.

What about Theodore? You had to be somewhat skewed to crash intentionally against that train overpass. Even if the motive was some kind of misguided love, some kind of warped but effective sacrifice. Love can be a product of mental illness too, you know. I am convinced of that. And the way he looked at me that Sunday morning before I took off for church, those eyes that knew they would never see me again. The way he let me kiss him on his stubbly cheek. How could he just sit there and let me go unless there was something upstairs that had frozen, that had already been killed?

Mental illness? There are all sorts. And not all of them keep you from functioning day in and day out, motoring from one errand to another, going to malls and catching an occasional baseball game.

Mental illness in my family? I haven't even gotten to Lilia. Lilia, who had been rotting away not so gently in a world of make-believe. Talk about a life of misfired connections, wrangled mental synapses, twisted and short-circuited aspirations. And even worse, what about her momentary lapses into icy and detached rationality?

And what about me? Up to then, except perhaps for a brief encounter back in my college days with a force so uncontrollable that its origin could very well have been the other side of sanity, and except for bursts of blind and unaccountable rage, I thought of myself as a little different but normal. Yes, I had been privy to a glimmer of universal blackness, but that's not the same thing as being insane. And to tell you the truth, total darkness had been rare. Most of the time when it was bad, it was just a constant gray, a drizzly sadness coming from who knows where and staying as long as it pleased. Even when it felt as if I were wedged deep in the devil's asshole, even then, I don't think that I was crazy. But I do believe that there is a fine line between having all your marbles in place and missing a few. A mighty fine line.

Trudy was right as always. If I only managed to look beyond myself, to dedicate myself to a job, to daily tasks that needed to be done. If only I made myself a list of things to do, accepted my ambition, manufactured a future of some sort. It is a question of drive. Man is a teleological creature. He looks forward naturally. He is purpose-oriented. He aspires as easily as he expires. Being crazy and being hopeless are not that far apart. Suicidal thoughts were, for Trudy, something that were dealt with, handled. You got a haircut or you changed your diet. You exercised. You fixed the goddamn faucet that had dripped, dripped, dripped for so long there was a stain on the porcelain sink the size and color of a rotten yolk. The thing is, Trudy was right . . . but. Have you ever met an "always right . . . but" person? I tell you, they are unbeatable.

Something was going wrong. I was pinned by Trudy. I needed Ms. Navajo to come to the rescue and gave her a look to that effect.

She responded by addressing Trudy. "If I may be allowed to take this in just a slightly different direction. It seems to me that in different ways and perhaps for different reasons, both of you are recognizing there is a problem here. That's a very valuable start which I think we can build on. I have noted some of the things that have been mentioned here. We're going to come back to those at some time, so I don't want you to think that what has been said has been lost, but now I would like to ask you a separate question. What initially attracted you to each other?"

For the first time I wondered whether Randy Nevits was right in recommending Ms. Navajo. Maybe he sent his clients over here so that he could kill the marriage for sure and move on to the hefty divorce fees. This last question was like some kind of coitus interruptus. I felt like I still wanted to answer Trudy's charges about my so-called depression. And that statement about "my" books. What the fuck did that mean? My books. She was always after me about this. To the point that I would feel guilty if I ever sat down in my very own house, the mortgage of which I was partially paying with my tiny lifetime associate salary which perhaps was not as grandiose as her partner's cut, but which helped. What was I supposed to do? Be out in the stable cleaning horse poop and brushing horses the way she did? I liked reading my books. What the hell is wrong with that? It wasn't just the books that she was referring to, either. It was the subject matter of the books. The "God" books and going to that second-class church on Sundays burned her up quicker than anything. And depression. I wasn't depressed. I was sad. Sometimes I get sad. What can I tell you? Life is such. Trudy got sad too. Depressed. What about the time when for two noble (and in many ways memorable) years we tried to have a child and nothing came of it? Nothing. And the doctors could not find anything wrong with her (or with me, I hasten to add). She was sad too. She was more than sad. I never lost hope. But she lost hope. One day, when we were about to make love, Trudy pushed me away and without explanation she went to the drawer where she kept all her nylons and she pulled out her dusty diaphragm kit. Just like that, after two years of not using anything, she goes to the bathroom, comes back to bed and lies down, legs akimbo. She said nothing. Post-coitally, she still said nothing. Finally I asked her a week later why the diaphragm. For God's sake, I am her husband. The child, were he or she conceived, would be part mine. Not having a kid is a loss for me too. I have a right to know even if her body is hers and all that crap. All she said was that now was not the time to have a kid. She wanted to go all out and make partner. Maybe after that. But "after" never came. Not even after Trudy was well ensconced in one of the oldest and most venerable legal institutions in the blue blood tradition of Boston. She could have a child, take a few months off. Her clients would still be there when she came back, well taken care of in the meantime by the army of eager-to-please brightest that her firm employed. We could have adopted a child, for God's sake! The money was not a problem. The house was big enough for a small kindergarten class. But the matter of children was dropped. Aladdin and Alhambra kept on getting a shine on their coats. The diaphragm came back. Then, when this became a nuisance, the prophylactic. And then, after the Act itself became imbued with a sense of dry obligation, the safest of all birth control methods came into use—or lack of use—and the matter of our child was sucked into a vacuum, the depth of which I could not begin to fathom then.

DAY 16

I am unable to remember how much time lapsed between the afternoon Kate asked me to look at the sunset over the Charles River and the day my own inner river became a rushing waterfall. Time seems to be doing a number on my head and memories of events are losing their before-and-after continuum. I think it was a while before Kate the meandering, deep river became Kate the rapids. Despite my attraction and what I suspected was hers, I believe there was a friendship, the likes of which people say only comes along once or twice in a lifetime. I remember feeling, when I talked to Kate, as if I were talking to myself, only Kate was a woman and I was a man. We seemed to be some kind of twins. I would pick up the phone to call her when it would ring and it would be her calling, asking what was up.

We talked whenever we could, almost daily it now seems, over lunch, lingering in doorways, sometimes after work over a beer, and the talking seemed to be enough, an end in itself, even though inside the river was stirring.

We talked about all kinds of things. I remember long conversations about dreams. Kate, my Pharaoh, would tell me her dreams which I, Joseph-like, would interpret. Then I would tell her mine, and we would discover connections between what she dreamt and what I dreamt or characters that appeared in her dreams and then jumped into mine, continuing the story that started in her dream or vice versa. Sometimes she would tell me dreams that did not fit with her life so far as we could figure, but which fit perfectly with mine. We decided that some very persistent but mute messenger was using either one or both of us indiscriminately to get some point across.

We talked about my "books," as Trudy called them. She herself had a small collection which she partially hid from Philip's harmless but annoying ridicule, and I borrowed her books just as she borrowed mine. We underlined special passages or key thoughts in each other's books, and in that subtle way we conveyed messages back and forth with other writers' words. We also wrote small notes in the margins so the reading had double significance, the text itself and what the other person thought of it, when reread by the original owner.

We talked about Corky and later about Philip and about Trudy when we had attained emotional intimacy. I never left a conversation with that vulnerable feeling of having revealed something that should have stayed inside. Although now, if truth be told, I regret having told Kate Trudy's secret.

Then one day, that fragile dam holding the river on a semi-orderly course did break, and Kate became a constant torrent.

We were at the office outing held as always at Walter Preston's country club. Walter was the managing partner, and the firm outing was when Walter graciously received the adoration of the young associates and when he reciprocated to the female half with squeezes and not-so-fatherly hugs.

Kate and I were in the pool, Philip happily destroying tennis opponents and Trudy (happily?) playing golf with lecherous Walter himself. We were chest-deep in chlorinated green-blue water, innocently holding hands and making a swing for Corky, when all of a sudden her hand accidentally, or so I think, grazed a part of me that had been of late forlorn. I didn't have time to focus on the nascent swelling because Corky was pulling my chest hairs like a maniac, but there, amidst all the giggles and hilarity, as we swung the little fellow back and forth, was that same touch again, only this time the movement of her fingers was decidedly, as we say in the business, premeditated, or was it that there was now more of me to touch? Still, one must go slow, proceed lawyerlike from facts to legal application to conclusions, avoiding assumptions at all costs, or at least recognizing them for what they are. It was entirely possible that in fashioning the swing, a finger had strayed here or there. No need to make a big deal out of it. Except that when I looked at Kate, her smile told me it was no mistake, and anyway, the "deal" had gotten big of its own accord—bigger, in fact, than it was by nature meant to be, and was now struggling out of its confinements, like a deep-sea diver without oxygen desperately headed for the surface. Now

Kate's hand could not help touching that which had become a veritable obstruction to the free flow of Corky's pendulum. Mercifully, the little fellow—I am talking about Corky now—was thrown on the count of three into the shallow end of the pool amidst a squeal of joy and terror, while I myself got, Oh Kate, an electrifying life-affirming squeeze as you dove to his, that is to say, Corky's, rescue.

That night, half buzzed by afternoon beers and evening wines, I wound myself to where Kate was sitting. Despite the entire firm's curious gaze—Trudy included—I asked her to dance with me. The four-piece combo was playing a melancholy song, the words to which I still remember. She took my hand and led me to the little square of wooden floor under the big white tent, and we danced along with a couple of old retired fogies who had been coming to Preston's outing since the days of Justice Holmes. We didn't say a word. I held Kate at a respectable distance and made sure the expressions on my face reflected nothing more than a casual conversation, but in my mind, and I am sure in hers too, we were as tight as we could be and the music was so slow we barely needed to move at all. Still we slowly swayed with so much electricity between our bodies that if a moth had flown into the improbable wedge between us it would have been instantly zapped. And all the time as we danced, her hand and her breath and my melting hardness were telling me a thousand, thousand, thousand yeses.

So that's when the siege began. For me, anyway. The next Monday I went to see Kate, propelled not only by the memory of that last dance but also by the fiasco with Trudy at home that same night. I found Kate friendly and joking but somehow subdued. Her eyes were unable to rest comfortably on mine the way they did before. There was a certain reserve, a certain way of not pursuing my opening leads that told my inner radar some topics were better off intuitively recognized, even mutually and secretly accepted, but not pursued openly and explicitly. Without ever mentioning anything, I knew Kate knew what I felt, and I knew that during the Saturday and Sunday following the outing I had fought a fierce battle with Philip and Corky and the future, and they won. Just barely, perhaps. But they did.

DAY 17

Maybe it was the sight of Kate and me dancing that rang a bell in Trudy. I don't know. But when we got home from the outing, Trudy wanted to reclaim what was legally hers.

I had seen that determined look in Trudy before. Our relationship had not yet fully settled when María, who had sat next to me in corporations class, had begun to show a fledgling interest in me.

One day after class, María and I had been making plans to study together when Trudy descended upon us from the back row and with precise ruthlessness made it clear to María (and to me) that my stock was not for sale; it was off the market.

"You have a commitment with me on Wednesday evening," was all that Trudy had said. And it was enough.

I had been flattered then as Trudy stood her ground while María scampered away. But on the way home from the outing things were different.

"Did you have fun?" asked Trudy.

I was so full of Kate when Trudy asked that question that I felt as if I were made of glass and all my thoughts and feelings could be seen.

"I did," I said after a few seconds had gone by.

"Is there anything you want to tell me?" Trudy asked.

"No, why?" I nervously answered. I glanced at her and sure enough she was reading my thoughts. Every single one of them. I turned red but somehow managed not to blurt my whole guts out.

"I don't know," said Trudy gently. "I just want you to know that you can always tell me whatever it is you want to tell."

She reached over and held my hand and I held hers, somewhat bewildered. After a little while she said, "When we get home, I want to make love, O.K.?"

Now here's the thing. I want to get right to the point, this part of the story not being one I am inclined to linger on. I don't think I ever in my life turned down this kind of offer from Trudy. If you knew her and saw her you would immediately understand why. On this night I did not turn the offer down, either. But the point I am urged to make at this moment is that Trudy and I never made love again after that. Not that this was very different frequency-wise from the state things were in before, only that this was, somehow, the final touch, the coup de grâce. That night making love with each other finally ebbed out of the repertoire of human options available to us. It did so naturally and, but for that night, painlessly, like the death of the very elderly in their sleep.

When we got home I went upstairs and got in bed while Trudy went to the bathroom to wash her face. I sat on the bed waiting for her in a state of what can best be described as paralysis. She came into the bedroom, her body reflecting the light in the hall, which she clicked off after she lit a tiny French vanilla candle on her dresser. It was summer and hot, and I remember my palms sliding on the sweat of Trudy's hips. I had not thought of Armanda for a long time, but I thought of her then and of her lessons in the paso lento as I fixed my gaze out the window on the summer stars shining behind the oak trees.

Now as I write this, I remember without shame the muted sobs and burning tears that overtook me even as Trudy was being overtaken by her pleasure. And now, I am grateful to Trudy for her respectful silence, the way she had gently dismounted, put on her robe, and gone downstairs to make herself a cup of coffee.

DAY 18

The morning after Virginia's funeral I was in a foul mood. The whole sleepless night I had felt as if I were locked inside Virginia's coffin with Virginia and the coffin kept getting smaller, packing both of us in a single and tight darkness. I looked out my bedroom window as soon as I got up and decided to go outside to have my morning coffee and cigarette (the latter was banned from the house and was a source of eternal irritation between Trudy and me). It was a sunny spring day, cold enough for only a sweater. When I opened the door, my lungs and nostrils were filled immediately with the smelly smoke of burning wood and oak leaves.

"Son of a bitch!" I yelled. "He's doing it again!"

It happened every goddamn nice spring day. Every weekend day for the past three years, every Saturday or Sunday that had any possibility of being a nice day was the perfect day for Computer Brain, my dear next-door neighbor, to burn piles of dead leaves and not-so-dead wood on his property.

Computer Brain's real name was Bartholomew Meagher II or III, I don't remember which. I never saw the guy except peripherally as he drove his baby-blue Mercedes down his driveway. He and Trudy, however, had met and struck up an acquaintance from the time that Aladdin managed to clear our fence and end up on Computer Brain's expansive property.

I talked to him only once (one time too many!) on the phone and did not know anything about him except what was conveyed by Trudy. He was unbelievably successful, the inventor of some new microchip or other, a bachelor who had been written up in *Boston Magazine* as one of the city's most eligible catches.

He was also, I am convinced, a closet pyromaniac. As soon as April rolled around and the town of Oakridge announced that licenses were available for spring wood burning, Computer Brain would rush off to get one and immediately begin to feed his arsonist instincts. Every dead branch (and some fully live ones too), every leaf that hit the ground, every twig, would be incinerated. And as if that weren't enough, Computer Brain would chain-saw anything still attached to a tree that happened to dangle the wrong way or that somehow did not make it past his standard of binary perfection.

When they asked me in one of my many mental examinations if I had ever thought of killing anyone, I had to say in all honesty, although this probably got me into deeper trouble, that yes, of course I had. Who hasn't? Killing? I would sit on my terrace, my eyes stinging, my iced tea tasting like buffalo piss, and I would fantasize about the different ways that I could fulminate the bastard.

One day Trudy and I were having some people over for the afternoon. This was around the time Trudy had decided Alhambra and Aladdin were one horse too many and had advertised to sell Alhambra. A young couple who had visited us before were bringing their ten-year-old to ride the mare. During the previous visit I learned the little girl had a bad case of asthma, so just before they arrived I had taken it upon myself to telephone Computer Brain and ask very politely if it would be at all possible to extinguish his pyre before our little asthmatic friend arrived.

There was a long pause on the other end of the line and then Computer Brain imperturbably replied that he did not think that would be feasible; he had already called the Oakridge police to see if the wind conditions allowed burning and the police had given their O.K. Because this was almost the last weekend to burn, and because one could never tell if the season would permit another good wind day, he was afraid that it would not be feasible at all.

"I'm sorry indeed," he said.

"I'm sorry indeed, too," I said.

Now here's the thing. I conveyed the contents of my conversation to Trudy shortly after I hung up and she seemed annoyed with me for making the phone call. The people that were coming were Trudy's friends, primarily. They were coming over to look at her horse, which she was trying to sell. I was trying to help out and all I got from Trudy was a one-sentence dismissal and a look of "that's what you get for doing something without checking with me."

"If you want to live in the country you have to put up with country inconveniences," she said to me summarily as she headed for the stables to get Alhambra ready.

Oakridge was a "rural suburb." That's what the real estate agent called it when we were looking at houses. By this she meant that you could have ten acres of land and still see your neighbor's house across the fence. You can work in the city, only an hour away down the Massachusetts Turnpike and still have the feel when you get home that you are on a farm somewhere. Horses and horse shit and flies and mosquitoes along with the asphyxiation of burning wood are some of the privileges of country living.

But on this particular Sunday morning, as I opened the door and choked on the smoke, I felt as if something or someone had removed the tiny lid that ordinarily kept my creeping and lately chronic irritation bottled up. For one thing, I had spent a miserable night among my books unable or unwilling to shake off the restlessness that started at Virginia's funeral and that was spreading like some kind of fast-forward cancer.

I put my cup of coffee down on the deck and walked toward Computer Brain's house, but only after I picked up a shovel from the garage. He was raking leaves into the fire when he saw me coming toward him, shovel in hand.

"What are you doing?" he asked, taking a small, hesitant step toward me.

I pointed the shovel to hold him at bay, although it wasn't necessary. Computer Brain was not going to do anything. I could tell.

"I'm going to enjoy my morning coffee if it's the last thing I do." I then began, calmly I believe, to shovel dirt into his early morning sacrificial offering to the Gods of Manicured Yards Everywhere.

He stood there, Mr. Baby-Blue Mercedes, Mr. Software Genius, Mr. Concave Antenna Dish, Mr. Self-Confidence, looking at me with white, hot anger, seething with the urge to jump me, grab the shovel from me, and brain me with the steel end. But he stood paralyzed, I assume, by a rationality that had already played out instantaneously and in color graphics all the ramifications of all possible courses of action and then had picked the one that would produce the most desired result.

Then he said it. He said those wonderful, symbolic words that have been uttered time and time again in one form or another since the Pilgrims landed down the road, felt at home, and claimed this land as their own.

"Why don't you go back to where you came from?"

Ahh, there it was. Out in the open. It was almost a relief to hear Computer Brain mouth THE words as he headed back in toward his house and, I imagined, the phone. He walked tight-assed with his spine very straight and his pride full, in total control, responding, no doubt, exactly as one should respond in situations such as these.

I continued putting out the fire as best I could because my arms were trembling something fierce. When the fire was out, I walked back home, sat on the deck, drank coffee, smoked cigarettes, and waited for the police to show up, but they never did. Maybe Computer Brain was more of a human being than I thought he was. When Trudy began to stir upstairs, I got in my car and drove out of our "country" setting as fast as I could go.

DAY 19

I was sitting in my office the Monday after Virginia's funeral watching a single-engine Cessna circle around the downtown area. The plane was nearly even with the skyscrapers, and I was wondering why in the world the FAA would let a plane fly over the city. I thought that there was some rule about planes not being able to fly over packed stadiums, et cetera, for fear of the carnage should the plane come down. Just then, Louise came in and announced there was someone in the lobby with an envelope for me.

"Can you sign for it?" I asked.

"He will only take your signature," she said in her typical haughty fashion.

Louise was about forty-five and bitter. She had started out some twenty years earlier with a bang of promise as the executive assistant to one of the firm's biggest rainmakers. When he suddenly shifted firms, Louise was unceremoniously left behind. She became the secretary of a not-so-important partner for a short time and then was shifted (or shafted as she put it) from associate to associate. She was not fast enough, pretty enough, or for that matter, nice enough to fill the bill for any one of the people that she worked for, but not bad enough as well as too dark-skinned to fire outright. It was Preston himself who, in a flash of brilliance, came upon the perfect solution to the Louise problem. She would be my secretary and help out with any typing needed by the firm's two real estate paralegals.

The day that I came down from my partnership review with Preston's offer that I could stay with the firm as a salaried attorney doing primarily residential closings, her last flicker of hope for any status or professional advancement was snuffed out. What was a once-powerful ambition to make it in the big time became instead a concentrated focus on (a) retirement, (b) her bad luck, (c) the evil and racist machinations of Preston and Matilda, the office manager, and (d) me, with a wary eye to make sure that the last stopgap in her professional descent did not fuck up.

"It looks like some kind of service of process," she said with her back to me.

In the lobby was a tall man with gray pants and a blue shirt similar, now that I think about it, to the uniform that we wear around there.

"Are you Mr. Díaz?" he asked.

"Yes."

"Would you please sign here?"

I did. When he left I was holding a white envelope with a law firm's name etched in blue on the corner. It was not the name of any of the firms that I was currently dealing with. I took the envelope back to my office, opened it, and began to read slowly at first. Then, when the meaning of the words began to register in my brain, faster and faster, I started skipping the nonessential verbiage, looking for verbs and nouns that would confirm what I was fearing.

"Whereas on the fifth of April . . . trespassing . . . tortious assault . . . threatened complainant with a shovel . . . damaged property . . . mental anguish and distress . . . emotional anguish . . . pray for relief . . . $850,000 . . ."

I put the papers down on my desk and went to close the door to my office. Louise, with an uncanny instinct for detecting when something was wrong, gave me a "I knew it was going to get worse because all the shit happens to me" look.

There was some definite humor in the phraseology. Mental anguish, brandished a shovel. Pray for relief. Whoever said legal documents were boring? This was funny. It was a joke. Computer Brain had a sense of humor after all. But then I remembered Computer Brain walking toward his house with his back very straight and his ass very tight and I knew that no, this was no joke.

I looked up the name of the lawyer who signed the complaint and dialed his number.

"Is Mr. Segall there?" I asked.

"Who shall I say is calling?" asked someone who sounded like she was ten years old.

"Ismael Díaz," I said.

"May I tell him what it's about?" she asked.

"Tell him it's about my fucking life," I said. I was in no mood to be my usual polite self.

"One second please," she said, totally unperturbed.

"Ron Segall here." I could tell immediately he was from the tough school of negotiating. Start off mean. Never give an inch. Be a son-of-a-bitch from the word go. O.K. I could play that game too.

"I just received a complaint in my place of work signed by you. It's a joke, right?"

"It's no joke."

"How can you sign something like this? Threatened with a shovel, emotional anguish. This is total bullshit."

"Listen, the complaint and my client's affidavit speak for themselves. Get yourself a lawyer."

"I am a lawyer."

"I know. That's why I'm talking to you in the first place. I think it's a mistake for you to call me, but I took the call out of professional courtesy. And out of the same courtesy, I will tell you this: I've advised my client to file criminal charges in conjunction with this action. You really should get yourself a lawyer. That's my advice, one attorney to another."

When I was a kid growing up in El Paso, Texas, long after Theodore died and I had persuaded Lilia that we should continue Theodore's dream for me to grow up as an American, my best buddy Norberto and I would get into these humongous snowball fights on the rare occasions when it snowed. Most of the time the battles were between Norberto and me, but sometimes we would pick a fight with the other vatos in the government-subsidized neighborhood where Lilia and I qualified to live. That was real war. When we fought between ourselves, we only loosely packed the snowball. But when we fought with the enemy, the balls were more like rocks. I remember getting hit in the face by one of those rocks. Once the pain had gone away and Norberto and I had time to congratulate ourselves for still being alive, all things considered, it always amazed me that even though the snow was cold, the pain of the cold hitting your face was a hot, burning hot, pain.

That's what it felt like again that morning as I talked on the phone with attorney Segall with the Cessna still circling outside like a wacky vulture.

"Fuck you and your goddamn 'one attorney to another'! What the fuck is the matter with all of you? Goddamnit, I could kill the whole bunch of you!"

I hung up so hard that the phone bounced. Louise, even though I could not see her because the door was closed, began to curse her fate . . . again.

DAY 20

It was a melodramatic gesture, to be sure, but it made me feel good to do it. In the left-hand drawer of my office desk there was an envelope addressed to Kate. The envelope was sealed and taped so that Louise would think twice about opening it. My thoughts were that if something ever happened to me, say, if I got creamed on the Massachusetts Turnpike, then whoever tearfully cleaned out my desk would come upon the envelope and give it to Kate. The envelope must have stayed in the drawer a good year, I guess. Every once in a while I would take it out and hold it against the light to see if you could read its contents. But no, the envelope held its little secret, patiently waiting for me to hang it all up. Not that I needed to see what was there. I had the poem memorized, engraved in my mind.

One night I had shot straight up in bed with all the lines there flashing in the darkness of my brain as if by teleprompter. I spent the rest of the night still as a log not to wake Trudy, but wide-eyed and restless nevertheless. I went through the poem line by line, editing an adjective here and a comma there, and when I got to the office the next morning, I wrote it on a sheet of yellow legal paper and typed it myself that afternoon after Louise had gone home.

Kate never really told me whether or not she liked the poem. I had placed it on her empty chair just before I exited, lugging my briefcase and a Xerox box kindly given to me by Ralph from the mailroom. It was a small box, and even then it seemed half empty. A few personal trinkets, old Christmas cards, mementos from departing associates, my Mexican vase, a couple of books: *Crocker's Notes on Common Forms* given to me early in my career by my appointed advisor and mentor, Kevin Niven, and a worn-out and stained copy of *The Diary of Anne Frank*, which I'd found stuck to old Lifesavers in the back of my desk drawer, given to me by a summer intern who I'd had reason to believe had a crush on me.

I wonder what would have happened if Kate had still been in her office. It had only been 6:30 P.M.—early by law firm standards—except that it had been Friday; on Fridays Kate usually left early to pick up Corky at his kindergarten.

Why is it that bad news at work is always delivered on a Friday around 4:30 P.M.? Louise had already been putting on her coat, getting ready to make her early Friday escape when the summons came from Preston.

"Preston would like to see you in his office," she said with a look of impending doom.

"Right now?" I asked.

"Right this very second," she said.

"Sounds bad to me," she said, as I walked by her.

"Don't worry, I'll take you with me wherever I go." This had not come out as humorously as I'd intended.

"Shit!" she retorted.

Preston was sitting behind his big mahogany desk. In front of him and across his desk in one of two chintz chairs sat Kevin Niven.

"Please sit down," said Preston.

Kevin Niven winked at me.

"I got a call from Ron Segall a couple of days ago," said Preston. "I'm afraid he didn't sound too happy."

"What did he say?" I asked.

"Well, he said quite a bit. He said that he was representing a neighbor of yours who is suing you for tortious assault. He said that criminal charges were a possibility. He said that you had called him names and threatened him over the phone. He said that he was considering reporting you to the Massachusetts Bar Association. He said that he was calling me out of consideration for our old friendship because he did not want to see our firm dragged through the mud. That's more or less what he said."

"And you believed him?"

"You tell us if we should believe him," said Kevin Niven softly, kindly, coaxing, like a father confessor.

I have always noticed this about myself. That at those times when it is most in my interest to defend myself, to speak up on my own behalf, I get filled instead with a kind of "fuck you" pride that makes me clam up in silence.

"Well?" asked Preston not quite so kindly.

"Well what?" I asked, losing track for a second of what we were talking about.

"Did you assault your neighbor and did you threaten Segall on the phone?"

"No," I managed to say. "I lost my temper with Segall. I was angry. The whole thing is petty and ridiculous."

"Did you tell Ron Segall that you felt like killing him?" asked Kevin Niven in a soothing whisper.

"I might have said that," I said. "I was upset. I had just been served with a bullshit lawsuit."

"Did you threaten your neighbor with a shovel?" Now it was Preston doing the interrogating.

"What? No. I did not. I jumped over a fence and put out a fire that was choking me. Every damned weekend he burns brush. It was choking me. I put it out. The fire. With a shovel. I threw dirt on it. That's all."

"Calm down, Ismael," said Kevin Niven, touching my kneecap. "We're trying to get the facts, that's all."

"When did Segall call you?" I asked, pulling myself temporarily together.

"I don't see what difference that makes," said Preston.

"So you did jump over into your neighbor's yard?" asked Niven.

"I jumped over into my neighbor's yard," I repeated.

"You trespassed," said Preston conclusively.

"I trespassed . . . with intent."

Preston did not think it was funny.

"What about Ron Segall?" asked Kevin Niven.

"I told you. I called him up to find out about the lawsuit. I was upset. I already told you." This last I said quietly, not looking at either Kevin Niven or Preston, but wondering whether Kevin was there as a mentor or as one half of a Mutt and Jeff negotiating routine.

Preston started to say something but Kevin Niven held him off with his hand, asking for a few more moments.

"What has been happening to you lately?" he asked.

"What do you mean?"

"I mean that we've all been wondering what's going on with you. You seem to be drifting. You have no umph! We've received a couple of calls from First Home Equity about mathematical errors on adjustment sheets. What's wrong?"

A big, big question, Kevin Niven. Too big for me to answer.

"How long have you been with the firm?" continued Kevin Niven. "Is it fifteen years now?"

"Fifteen years, yes." I said.

"Look," interrupted Preston, who was losing patience with Kevin's prosecutorial style, "the point is that we cannot have attorneys assaulting their neighbors or threatening to kill other attorneys. That's the point."

"What Walter is trying to say," said Kevin Niven, glaring at Preston, "is that this may not be working out for either one of us. And I want to stress that it's a two-way thing. You're not happy here, are you?"

I was tongue-tied. My brain numbed.

"Are you happy here?" repeated Kevin Niven.

"I do good work for you," was all I managed to say.

"You do work that someone with a third of your salary could do," said Preston.

I could tell by the quick and scared look he shot at Kevin Niven that Preston was wondering if he had said something that could be used against the firm. A complaint with the Massachusetts Commission Against Discrimination, for example.

What Preston said happened to be true, what with the new real estate software recently introduced into the market, which I was still trying to master. What he said was true, and I was not in the mood to refute the truth.

There was a long pause which Kevin Niven interrupted.

"We've been good to you, Ismael. You know that to be the case."

Yes. I knew that to be the case. The fact is that they could have fired me way back in the early days when I stumbled and fumbled my way through multimillion-dollar construction loans and complicated purchases. I got them done all right, but somehow the transactions were not smooth. There were wrinkles, complications, last-minute details that were forgotten. There were the reviews too. All carefully conducted by Preston and carefully documented by a follow-up letter. Failure to negotiate aggressively. Failure to work fast and accurately under intense pressure.

"Is something funny?"

Preston was reacting to the smile on my face. In fact I was smiling at the recognition of one of those little ironies of life. I remembered Preston telling me in my partnership review that I was

not a closer. I asked what a closer meant. Preston defined it for me:
"A closer. Someone who closes deals, who pushes the negotiations
or the transaction to a point where the job is done, someone who
goes for the jugular, someone with a killer instinct."

Now there I was in front of Preston, about to be canned for bran-
dishing a shovel over my neighbor and threatening to kill his lawyer
(and here I am now!). How's that for being a closer, Preston old boy?

"You've been good to me," I said. I was calm. The ambiguity
of the situation had disappeared and I gratefully regained a sense
of clarity. "But I've been good to you too. I have done a lot of closings and a lot of leases and a lot of things that needed to be done.
No client ever complained about me. I never turned down any
work, even when it had been turned down by others. Look at my
billable hours. You didn't lose any money on me."

Preston made a "so what" face and was about to say something
when Kevin Niven spoke.

"That's true too. You are a good worker."

Preston grimaced. Kevin's words were apparently going counter
to his "dismissal for cause" legal strategy.

Kevin Niven pushed on. He had that courtroom look that I
admired so much. Soft but persistent and direct. Earning the witness's trust even as he pushed him gently toward self-destruction.

"You're always willing to pitch in, and that's appreciated. But
here's the thing. I want you to answer my previous question honestly, as I know you will. Tell me that you enjoy what you do. Tell
me honestly that you like what you are doing and you can stay."

Preston was clenching his jaw. Kevin Niven had clearly devi-
ated from the charted course and was now winging it in a way that
had not been prediscussed.

But now I was faced with Kevin Niven's question and with my
own resoluteness for some modicum of truth. There were too many
contradictory things going through my mind and it was hard to
pick which one of those things was accurate. It was the whole mess
that was the truth, but how to communicate it? There was that
wrenching intestinal cramp that mischievously waited for me to
step inside the office's chrome elevator every morning and which
increased its clamp on my entrails in direct proportion to the elevator's ascent to the thirty-first floor. There was the satisfaction of
helping someone buy a home and doing it in an unstressful way.
There was the pleasure of a well-written lease, in discovering the

phrase that succinctly hit the heart of all concerns. There were the nuisances and nuances of dealing with attorneys who felt that they should win every single negotiating point, minor or otherwise. And when the work slowed down, there was the almost physical pain of not feeling useful, the shame of not truly earning the monthly paycheck and the peculiar envy of those who were busy.

There was also the sense that I was no Kevin Niven. Kevin came to work every day and methodically went through a list of tasks that he had prepared the previous day just before he went home for the evening. Kevin plowed through his work with a sense of perpetual curiosity. He went home and read the law or things related to the law. He was motivated by a desire to be the best, not just to be considered the best, but to actually be the best. To say that he liked what he did would not be fully accurate. He was what he did. Not that he did not do other things or that he did not have other loves, including the love for his wife and two teenage sons with whom he spent all of his extra time canoeing or camping or playing tennis. It was simply that despite all the many headaches of the job, including partner backstabbing and the yearly catfights about how to divide the revenue pie, Kevin Niven enjoyed what he did. He enjoyed. He delighted even.

No, I was no Kevin Niven. Every night I would take a briefcase full of work home and most of the time I would lay it in the basement unopened as I reached instead for one of my books or languished word by word over yet another love poem.

As I sat there waiting to come up with the right word, just one word that would allow me to construct some kind of sentence, I remembered Kevin Niven's words to me at the end of my very first interview with the firm. It was in the spring of my third year of law school. The firm flew me up from New York to meet with several partners and associates. Kevin said of course he would put it in writing, but he wanted to tell me that everyone who had interviewed me that day was impressed, and that the firm was inclined to make me an offer right then and there. He and his partners were sure that candidates like me did not come along that frequently. He wanted me to know that, if I so chose, they would be very happy to have me work with them. God forgive me, but when I thought of Kevin's words, it was all I could do not to cry. I managed to knot the welling feelings into a hard lump, which stuck uncomfortably somewhere in my throat.

What happened along the way? Where did I lose the drive and the ambition that Trudy was so sure I had somewhere deep inside? The urge to shine, where had it gone? The letter from Kevin Niven arrived in New York a few days later with the particulars of salary and benefits. I could take as long as I wanted to respond to them. The job was mine. I could take my time deciding. But there was no need to think about it. There was no anxiety around the decision. I called Kevin Niven back that very afternoon. With an overwhelming sense of peace that I was doing the right thing, I accepted the firm's offer. Trudy was going back to the Boston firm she had clerked for the summer before. Now we could be together. Everything was falling into place. I too had arrived. I belonged. I was going to a place where I was enthusiastically accepted, wanted even. I would be doing real estate, why not?

"Ismael, are you all right?" Kevin Niven's words came from a distance.

"Yes. I was just thinking about something. . . . I don't know if I can answer your question right now. . . . I'm not really sure that you're interested in an honest answer. You seem to have made up your mind about what you want from me."

Preston and Kevin Niven looked at each other. It was time to choose one strategy over another. I was prepared to wait for their answer in silence for as long as it took. An old negotiating trick that Preston himself taught me during our first deal together.

Preston started to speak, but Kevin Niven interrupted him and with a flick of his eyebrows indicated that he wanted to give it one last try.

"I'm not playing tricks with you here. I happen to think that leaving a job is not the end of the world. In fact, leaving a job that you don't like is sometimes the best thing that can happen to you. I'd wanted this to be a mutual decision. Something that's good for both of us. For you and for the firm. You deserve to be happy. Find something that makes you happy. Remember that time you and I went out for drinks? The day you were told that you would not be offered a partnership with the firm? Remember I asked you why you went to law school? Do you remember what you said? You told me that in college you had spent your summers with migrant farm workers in Alabama and about the mentally handicapped persons that you lived with. Do you remember that? You said that you had accepted that scholarship from Columbia because you thought that somehow law school would give you the tools to contribute, to help. Do you remember that? Ismael, it's not too late. You have a lot going for you. You just need to find your niche. Take some time off. Work off whatever it is that's bothering you and find something that you like."

Kevin Niven's words surprised me. First Trudy; now him. Did I really appear that miserable to other people? Or was it just Kevin's keen sensibility and human insight and Trudy's daily contact with me that had detected something that even I did not fully apprehend? In any event, Kevin Niven had me in a clinch. His words seemed imbued with a concern for the right thing, for the overall right thing. Whether this concern was authentic or whether Kevin had led me with elegant craftsmanship precisely to where he wanted to go, I could not tell.

"I'll leave," I said.

Kevin nodded. Preston appeared to let out a small sigh through the corner of his lips. He waited a second or two and then, pretending he was straightening some papers on his desk, said, "The firm is willing to provide two month's salary to help you in your future job search. You're free to take the money in advance as soon as you wrap up any pending matters."

"I would like to leave today," I said.

"Today?" asked Preston, surprised.

"Today. There is nothing I'm doing that someone else can't pick up Monday morning. Louise knows where everything is."

I was on my feet and turning toward the door when Kevin Niven asked, "Is there anything you want us to tell the other associates?"

"Tell them the truth," I replied softly.

I went back to my office. I looked around at the bookcase, the file cabinets, the walls, the desk. It would take quite a few boxes to pack fifteen years of existence. Real estate treatises, blue plastic notebooks filled with my favorite leases, which Louise had put together for me as a "don't ever say I never gave you anything" birthday present, closing "bibles," drawers full of memoranda of law that could be useful in the next job. I saw the Currier & Ives painting on the wall that Trudy had bought at an antique store in Maine for "practically peanuts." On top of the book case was my Mexican vase, a brown water jug really, from Oaxaca. I brought it down gently and cuddled it against my chest like a baby.

DAY 21

I was driving home from work, the half-filled Xerox box with my belongings rattling in the back seat, when a truck on elevated wheels appeared in my rearview mirror and started tailgating and downshifting and blinking its lights and communicating to me in no uncertain terms that I was driving too slowly. When you start getting close to Oakridge, the roads become country roads, narrow and winding and almost all of them marked in the middle with a no-passing yellow line.

In one of the New Testament classes that I took with Father Pearse at Spring Hill College, we were asked to try our hands at writing a modern-day parable just to get the hang of what Jesus was trying to do, stylistically anyway. For the Kingdom of Heaven, we were supposed to substitute: "America is like . . ."

So I sat there and sat there and could not come up with anything. I, the person who wrote short stories and plays for the Spring Hill literary magazine, was totally stumped. Then, with one minute left, I managed to scribble something to the effect that America is like driving on a country road on a winter Sunday morning when all is white with freshly fallen snow, the sunlight almost emanating from the very trees themselves, and you are driving aimlessly really, with no other purpose than to enjoy a Sunday drive, when suddenly there is someone behind you who wants to get someplace fast and is itching to pass you so that there is no way you can enjoy the drive anymore. You try to ignore Speedy behind you by resolving not to look in the rearview mirror, but even so you know that he is there. You can feel him and there is no way to ignore him; no matter how hard you try, you just can't.

So there I was in the midst of my very parable, only this time I was not looking at the scenery but was lost in thought, replaying in my mind the events of the day and wondering how the fuck I ended up working in a law firm in the first place. All I could think of was that it was something that happened almost despite myself.

It was not something I intended or willed, it was just something that I allowed to take place. How far back did the allowing go? I couldn't tell. Maybe it went as far back as the day that I unexpectedly received a letter from Columbia Law School saying I had been accepted, and a few days later another letter saying tuition had been waived, and then maybe the allowing was clinched when a beneficent foundation had decided to kick in room and board for three years. That was it. Those were the sacred omens that I deciphered as some kind of message, some kind of call for what I was to do with the rest of my existence.

Now there I was jobless. By most accounts, including my own, a failure. Something got twisted along the way. Some kind of trap was laid and sure enough I stepped into it, but how, how did it happen? It was I after all who undertook the motions of studying for the law admission tests and applying to Columbia. It was I who spent hours on a personal essay that must have impressed someone in the admissions department enough to let me in despite the low test scores. Somewhere in my basement it still lay, this essay that spoke unsentimentally about growing up fatherless in El Paso; about going from almost last to almost first in the class rankings of the local Jesuit high school; about discovering to my amazement that I was smart enough; about the honors scholarship that paid my way through Spring Hill College; about foregoing the pleasures of college dorm life and living instead in halfway homes for the mentally handicapped; about summers spent with the Mexican migrant farm workers that each year filled the back sheds of Alabama's farms with their brown-eyed children and their portable gas stoves and their hands cracked and scaly from uprooting potatoes; about how law school seemed the natural fulfillment of my concerns, a way to befriend the intellect and the heart, the twins that labored in my womb.

What happened along the way? I felt as though, with just a little more time, I would be able to discover those one or two junctures from the past that I had blithely stepped over, unaware of their future impact, and I could use that discovery to readjust the future. If I just had a bit more time. But I had no time. I could no longer ignore the present, which was now flashing bright lights on and off in my rearview mirror. The GMC was behind me pushing me to go faster. Not that I was going slow, mind you. I was in no hurry to get home, that's true, but still I was doing the speed limit.

Anger, bitter and deformed, was suddenly at my throat like burning vomit pushing to come out. I slowed my car to a crawl and the elevated truck started fuming. It started honking and the driver started yelling out the window. The truck tried but could not pass me because there were cars coming in the opposite direction or curves blocking the driver's vision. I slowed the car even more and then the truck began to bump the back of my car. I slammed on the brakes and the truck rammed into me, jolting my chest against the steering wheel. I looked in the mirror and saw the trunk of my car almost underneath the truck's giant silver bumper.

I got out of my car and walked toward the truck slowly, although inside I felt my blood gushing from my brain to my arms and my legs. I saw two men in the truck, although I had to strain my neck to do so. One of them was wearing a yellow cap and had a scraggly beard. The other one, the driver, had Groucho Marx eyebrows and was wearing a grimy Red Sox cap. He rolled down the window when he saw me coming.

"What the fuck's the matter with you?" he asked menacingly.

"If you have a problem with the speed that I'm driving, pass me." I said this as calmly as I could, only the words gushed out fast and were laden with an accent I hadn't heard since my growing-up days in El Paso.

I waited for a second to see if Groucho was going to come down, tire iron or worse in hand, but instead I got a "suck my dick" curse while he shifted into a screeching reverse and then proceeded to slam into my car. Pieces of red and white plastic from my Subaru's rear lights flew all over the place. I reached up to open the driver's door but the truck was moving back again so I missed the door handle. Only now my car was stuck to the truck, the top of the car's bumper to the bottom of the truck's bumper, making the two vehicles seem as if engaged in some kind of unnatural fornication. Groucho and Scraggly Beard were laughing and cursing as they tried to shake the truck loose by going forward and backwards.

Someone watching the scene from the top of a hill would have laughed. A giant silver and black truck lurching back and forth with a red Subaru stuck to its bumper and some kind of idiot in a suit dangling from the side door of the truck trying to grab the driver's throat through a slit in the truck's window.

The truck lurched backwards one more time and managed to dislodge itself from my car with a thud, its shock absorbers bouncing up and down. I didn't hear the final jeers as the truck peeled away and swerved away from an oncoming car because I was on the side of the road, shirttail hanging out and sweating, wondering where in God's name all the anger was coming from and where, oh where, was it going to take me?

DAY 22

The lights in the house were on. Trudy was home. I got out of my car, tried to pick up the box of belongings in the back seat, but my arms were unable to do it. The incident with the truck had drained all the energy from me. I looked up at the early evening sky and took a deep breath. Then I pushed myself to climb the porch stairs and open the door to the house.

I heard Trudy's voice in the distance. I could tell that she was on the cordless phone somewhere upstairs by the way the volume of her voice undulated. Trudy liked to do more than one thing at once. She opened letters and discarded them while talking on the phone. She could write a brief and watch television at the same time. It was as if doing only one thing left too much of her brain unoccupied.

I went over to the kitchen refrigerator to get ice cubes for a drink. The clinking of the ice cubes in the glass was followed by a lowering voice upstairs. The conversation was wrapping up. Then there was silence. I poured myself a Johnny Walker and waited for Trudy to come down. When nothing happened, I yelled half-heartedly.

"I'm home!"

No answer. I heard footsteps and then a door close—not slam—but close with enough force to let me know that it was being closed. I sensed trouble. Then I remembered that, among other things, I had lost my job that day and that this was something that probably should be communicated to Trudy. The thought of this filled me with apprehension.

I took a swish of scotch and went upstairs. It was the bedroom door that had been closed. I opened it and went slowly in. Trudy was in the midst of putting on her blue jeans. The ones she wore around the horses. She gave the pants a final tuck to take them over the hump and then she sucked in her stomach to button them, all without looking at me.

"Is something the matter?" I asked.

"You tell me," she said. She disappeared into the walk-in closet and came out a few seconds later with her boots. She was still not looking at me.

"You know about my job."

"Yes, I do." She said this with a smile that was not a happy smile.

"How do you know?" I asked. I was genuinely curious about this.

"You are something else, you know that?" She was sitting on the edge of the bed putting on white socks. "What has gotten into you? What the hell has gotten into you?"

This last she said with a hot, controlled intensity that I had seen her use before in the courtroom. It had the effect of rattling the witness. For a second I thought of responding with the anger that was beginning to well up again inside me. I remember consciously telling myself to not lose it, to stay in control.

"Are you crazy or something?" she continued. "Why do you persist in destroying yourself?"

"I lost a job. It's not the end of the world. It really is not that big of a deal." I said this firmly, without anger.

"Not that big of a deal? Not that big of a deal?" She was standing up now in front of me, her arms at her side. "You threaten to kill someone with a shovel, then you threaten to kill someone on the phone, then you get fired, and it's no big deal. No big deal."

"Who told you all this?" I was getting more curious.

"What difference does it make?"

"I'm curious, that's all. Maybe you should ask me if it's true."

"Who cares if it's true? It's all over town." She looked at me for a fraction of a second with a look that wondered whether she should have said that.

"Is that what's bothering you? That it's all over town?"

"Yes. You're damned right that's what's bothering me. Why shouldn't it bother me? Maybe your reputation isn't important to you, but it is to me." She wasn't screaming, but she was loud and forceful.

"My reputation is important to you, or your reputation is important to you?" I wasn't trying to be cute. I was trying to understand exactly what was bothering her.

"Your reputation, my reputation, our reputation. All of that matters. What you do affects others, you will be happy to know." She was staring at me with a frozen smile.

And now out came that rush of anger. Again. For what? The second, third, fourth time in that interminable day? The problem is that anger makes me illogical, unable to respond to the point at hand. And what's worse, anger brings back this Mexican accent that makes it hard for me to be understood.

"That's all you care about? That's the only thing that bothers you? What others think?"

"Yes! Yes! Yes, goddamn it! I care about what others think. It's part of being a responsible adult. Why do I feel that I'm talking to an adolescent? Grow up, will you!"

I was having trouble answering her. I wanted to lash out with my arms or my legs. I wanted to lash out at Trudy. I wanted to break her giant antique dresser mirror, with my fist shattering the reflection of both of us. If I didn't find a way to say what I wanted to say, I might end up doing just that, and I was doing everything I could to keep myself from being violent once again.

"I am not a kid! Quit talking to me like a kid!" I managed to say. It wasn't the best of all retorts, but it was a relief to get that out, anyway.

"You are an idiot," Trudy responded without missing a beat. "You are about to lose everything. Profession. Home. Marriage. And for what? What is the matter with you? I don't understand. You have everything." Her tone was more mystified than angry. She sat on the edge of the bed. I saw two tears streaking down her cheeks leaving black marks. I hadn't seen Trudy cry in a very long time. This was not courtroom stuff. I felt ashamed that I was causing her pain. I went over to where she was sitting and put my hand on her shoulder. She twitched her shoulder and my hand fell off.

"You better go," she said.

I wanted to say something. I wanted to apologize for the trouble that I was causing her, but that didn't seem quite right because it would not have been heartfelt, and I didn't want to say things I didn't truly mean. Not at that time.

"I'll be down in the basement," I said.

"I want you to go away," she said, looking up at me, unblinking.

I asked her with my eyes if I had heard her correctly.

"I want you out of the house by the end of the day tomorrow."

"Just like that? Out?" I asked almost with a laugh.

"Yes."

"What exactly did I do? I lost a job. I didn't kill anyone. Not yet, anyway." I was trying to put some humor into the situation. But the words, and more significantly, the tone, did not come out the way I wanted them to.

"You are a violent, repressed, fucked-up individual. You're a sneaky, lying bastard. You're as fucked up as your mother." She was standing up again, saying this directly to my face with a scathing hatred that scared me.

"My mother? What is this all about?"

Trudy went over to her dresser and opened the top drawer. It was the drawer where she kept her silk designer scarves. When she turned around, she was holding my brown leather notebook.

"Is this for me?" she asked with sarcasm.

I looked at the book for a while. I was in no hurry to answer. I could have said yes. I could have said that the poems in that book were about Trudy. After all, even though they were clearly love poems, I never used any names. The poems were all addressed to a mysterious "You." I could have even told Trudy that those were poems to a Divine You. Trudy, after all, knew about my "books." Those poems could have been another poor imitation of the Song of Songs or of St. John of the Cross. They could have been. I myself wasn't sure anymore who the You in those poems was. I wasn't even sure that the You wasn't Trudy herself.

I said almost in a whisper as if afraid to inflict pain: "They are not about you."

"I didn't think so," said Trudy. She tossed the book at me. I reached out reflexively to catch it, but she threw the book more at my body than at my hands. The book bounced off my chest and landed at my feet.

"I have never been unfaithful to you." I thought that needed to be said.

"It might have been better if you just fucked the person instead of wasting yourself in some adolescent illusion."

Trudy's words brought suddenly to mind an image totally unrelated to the current circumstances. It was Trudy walking back and forth outside Renata's house fighting off the mosquitoes that were attacking her. We had gone to Tampico the summer before we were married. When we were there, Trudy, Lilia, and I decided to go visit Renata, the nanny who took care of me from birth until I was adopted by Theodore and Lilia and who lived about an hour away from Aunt Consuelo's house. It was a hot, humid day and I and everyone else could tell that Trudy was having a miserable time. The heat and constant sweating drained her of all energy and on top of that she developed an allergy to mosquito bites. Renata lived in a little wooden house that was almost totally shaded by tall banana and guayaba trees. From a side window of her house, Renata sold bottles of soda and beer that she kept in the kitchen refrigerator. I remember that Renata's leg was bandaged to cover a blood clot that had burst. We took some chairs from inside the house and sat outside where it was cooler. Renata gave Lilia and Trudy a Coca-Cola and I took a beer. We had been sitting down for only a few minutes when Trudy excused herself. The mosquitoes were attacking her. She would feel better if she could walk a little, so she went outside on the unpaved street next to Renata's house and began walking back and forth. Renata, Lilia, and I tried to have a conversation, but we all felt uncomfortable and rushed. Later, when Trudy asked me if I had enjoyed seeing Renata again after so many years, I told her that I had been worried about her and so had not enjoyed the visit as much as I would have liked. "You could have taken as much time as you wanted," Trudy responded. What flashed through my mind as I picked up the leather book full of poems was the image of Trudy walking back and forth while Renata, Lilia,and I tried to talk. And then I remembered something that I had not thought about for a long time. I remembered how I had told Renata that I was going to marry Trudy and how Renata had replied that yes, she had heard that those were my intentions. I sensed that Renata was holding back something. I asked her if something was the matter. Her words came back to me as I stood in front of the angry Trudy:

"Creo que ella te quiere, pero que tú no la quieres a ella."

"I think she loves you, but that you do not love her."

I remember being shocked by Renata's words. I remember feeling annoyed, even, that Renata would say that, like the times when I was little and living in Abuelito's house and Renata persisted in telling Abuelito and Lilia that I wasn't sick enough to stay home from school.

Now there I was, Trudy in front of me waiting for an answer and I, gazing at her but looking way beyond her to that time in front of Renata's house, and realizing, for the first time, that maybe, after all, it was I who had not done right by Trudy.

"This is my house too," I said to Trudy absentmindedly.

"My lawyer will contact you in a few days. I would like to settle this peaceably if at all possible. I want the house. I earned it. If you try to fight me, I'll leave you penniless. I have a copy of those poems and I have your admission that they are not about me. I have a good case if you don't agree to the proposal that my lawyer will make to you."

It was almost a relief to see my old Trudy again, full of legal exactitude. Trudy, Trudy, another follower of the Preston School of Negotiation. Aim high. You just never know when you have a sucker in front of you.

"By the way," she continued, "inside that book you'll find a check for five thousand dollars. I have just transferred all the money from our joint checking and savings account to my own account."

"That was fast," I said without sarcasm.

"Yeah, well. It's something I've been thinking about for a while." When she said this she looked into my eyes with a look of pain that I had never seen before. Then she walked out of the bedroom and headed downstairs. I heard the back door open and shut. Through the bedroom window I could distinguish her shadow heading toward the stables. She was going to groom Aladdin.

DAY 23

I stood there in the bedroom not knowing where to go. I went to the closet, opened it, and then closed it. I went to my dresser and did the same with the top drawer. Then I headed down to the basement. Through the years, the house that Trudy and I shared had become more hers than mine. Like a huge boundary battle between feuding countries, Trudy's presence had slowly and imperceptibly increased her domain over every room of the house except, perhaps, the basement. The basement was mine. The few battles that I had won, I won there. First I had won the major battle over whether the floor should be carpeted, although I lost the minor battle over the color and texture of the carpet. A couple of years later I won the battle of the heat (I called the plumber on my own and unbeknownst to Trudy had the heat installed while she was away at a conference).

There was a minor skirmish when Trudy noticed the newly installed hot water baseboard pipes on one of her trips to the laundry room, but it did not amount to much. The war was won, however, when I decided to hang up Abuelito's rifle on one of the walls. As a concession to Trudy, I spent hours polishing its long thin barrel and sanding and varnishing its oak handle. I even went to an antique gun store and bought a gun rack that I was told dated back to the American Revolution. Then one Saturday morning I hung it up and waited for Trudy's reaction. But it never really came. One morning on the way to work about a week after I hung the rifle, she said, "If you're going to put the rifle on the wall, you should at least take a tape measure and make sure it's centered." After she left for work I went downstairs and found out that she was right. The rifle was closer to one end of the wall than to the other.

Abuelito's rifle, as I called it, was a single-loading twenty-two. To load it you pull the hammer with your thumb as far back as it will go. After the shot, the empty shell is discharged by cocking the "western" lever. I don't remember when Abuelito gave it to me. I believe it was on a summer trip to Tampico after Theodore had died. I remember bringing the rifle across the border by hiding it in the spare tire compartment of the white Falcon Lilia had bought with Theodore's life insurance proceeds. I had probably shot it about five times in all of my life. Norberto and I went bullfrog hunting with flashlights one evening when I came back from Tampico. I remember how the small-caliber bullet had splattered the hypnotized bullfrog and how hot the barrel of the rifle got after the shot went off.

That night I was in the basement looking but not really looking at the rifle. I was thinking about Trudy's words. "I want you to leave," she had said. The words were filling me with anger and pain at the same time. I wanted to go out to the stable and let her know how much I hurt, and it was taking all of my concentration and strength to stay put, to keep myself from letting go. It was taking all my strength to remind myself that the anger I felt at Trudy was to some extent misplaced. It had to be. How could it possibly be all Trudy's fault? She was hurting too. She must be. I had seen her tears a few minutes before. But now she wanted me to leave and part of me wanted to leave also. Only where would I go and what would I do? There was no place.

That night even my basement felt uncomfortable. I noticed in my hands the leather book of poems that Trudy had thrown at me upstairs. How did she find it? I had placed it there on that shelf, not without some humor, next to a translation of *Rilke's Selected Works*. Trudy, who never came to the basement except to look for a screwdriver or a hammer or on her way to the laundry room, had taken the time to look over my books sometime when I was not there. There is love in that, I thought. I thought of Trudy and the first time we made love. The jeans dropping to the floor, the soft smell of her hidden flesh as I knelt to finish her undressing, and I remember feeling fear, as she was slowly revealed to me, that it was all a cruel dream from which someone would awaken me at any second.

I thought that night about a line in one of the first poems I had written in the notebook which I was then caressing the way Trudy caressed the neck of her Aladdin. Something about life being like an onion of goodbyes that peeled every day until there was nothing left. Trudy, my job, the place I called my own were that day's goodbyes.

I put the book down on the sofa and reached over and grabbed Abuelito's rifle. In my red toolbox I had three 22-caliber bullets that I had found on my walks through Oakridge and which I had saved for some unknown occasion. I knew exactly where they were because I saw them every time I looked for a drill bit or a screw, and every time I saw them I wondered the same thing: "What am I saving these for?"

I placed a bullet in the rifle's one and only chamber. I cocked the hammer back until it clicked into its locked position. The rifle was not that big. If you were right-handed you would have to hold the barrel with your left hand against the temple. Or even easier inside the mouth, stretching your right hand outward as far as it would go and using the tip of your forefinger to pull the trigger. It was awkward, but it could be done.

The phone was ringing. As I heard it, I realized that it was not the first ring and that in fact the phone had been ringing persistently for the past minute or so. The ringing had no intention of stopping. I put the rifle down and went upstairs to the kitchen to answer the phone, the basement being phoneless.

"Hello," I said.

"Ismael, is that you?" It was Kate's voice.

I looked out the window and through the night I could see by the floodlights in the stable that Trudy was still out there.

"Kate?"

"You weren't asleep, were you?"

"No, no. I wasn't." Although it was the first time that Kate had called me at home, it seemed appropriate for her to call just then.

"I heard about this afternoon," she said.

"You did?"

"Yes. After my closing I went back to the office and saw your . . . poem on my chair."

"Oh," I said.

"I went down to your office and saw that some of your things were gone. So then I didn't know what to think. I went back to my office to wrap up some things, and while I was there Preston called me."

"He called you?"

"Yes. He wanted me to come in tomorrow to work on loan documents that he needs by Monday. He's an asshole. Anyway, after he finished telling me about all the stuff he needed done he asked me if I had talked to you."

"He asked you that?" I was getting tongue-tied again.

"Yes. Are you O.K.?"

"Yes."

"So I told him that I hadn't, that I hadn't talked to you and I asked him why he was asking. So then he said, 'You're friends with him, aren't you?' And I didn't know what he was getting at. So I said, 'Yes, we're friends.' So he said that you had resigned earlier in the afternoon. Is that true? Did you resign?"

"More or less," I said.

"Well, I mean, he told me the whole story about the lawsuit and all that. They're a bunch of assholes. What are you going to do?"

"There's nothing much to do," I said.

"They're such jerks. You're better off getting away from there."

"I suppose." I was silent for a few seconds. I wasn't sure why words were not coming readily. Usually I would try to get in as much communication as possible in the few minutes here and there that I could talk to Kate. But the inside of my brain seemed gummed up with a thick substance that prevented any kind of pro-longed mental connection. "What did you think of my poem?"

"What?" Kate asked. I wasn't sure whether she hadn't heard my question or whether she wondered why I would ask her about that at that particular moment.

"Did you like the poem?" I asked.

"Ismael, are you sure you're all right?" There was concern in her voice.

"It's been a hard day, that's all."

"Have you talked to Trudy?" she asked with some hesitation.

"We talked. It's not good." I said. I looked out the kitchen win-dow toward the stable, with no apprehension this time.

"Oh," I heard Kate say.

I said, "I'm going to be O.K."

"Look, Ismael," Kate said this in a slower, more serious voice, "if you need anything. If you need to talk to someone or something. Even Preston was worried. He's probably just afraid of getting sued by you, which by the way is not a bad idea, but anyway, call me if you need something from the office or something."

"Thanks," I said. Then I thought that if I didn't say something soon, Kate would hang up and that too would be another goodbye.

"I'm sorry I'm not very talkative. I would like to talk to you. I just don't know where to start. And this is hard. I mean, it's hard to talk now." I noticed through the window that the flood lights in the stable were now off. Trudy was probably walking back to the house. "If there was only some way to see you."

"You want to come in for lunch next week?"

Next week wouldn't do any good. Next week was too, too far away.

"Can I see you tonight?" I blurted out of the blue.

"Tonight? I guess, if you want . . . sure . . . I can meet you for a cup of coffee after I put Corky to sleep . . . and after I find a baby-sitter for tomorrow. Philip is taking the 10:30 A.M. shuttle to New York and I have to work . . ." There were pauses between her words as she thought of the mechanics and perhaps possible repercussions of my request.

"Can I do it?" I asked. At that moment Trudy walked into the house. She glared at me as if surprised that I was still there and then passed by me on her way upstairs without looking at me anymore.

"Ismael, are you still there?" Kate was saying on the phone. "Do what?" she asked.

"Take care of Corky tomorrow?"

"Are you sure?"

"I would really like to," I said.

"Well . . ." I could tell that she was thinking about how that would go over with Philip. She and Philip had had conversations about our friendship, Kate had told me, and Philip, I gather, had conveyed to Kate via body language that he was not warm to the idea. "Yes. You may. If you want to," she said this with some finality. She seemed to be taking some kind of stand in her mind.

"What time should I be there?" I asked.

"So . . . do you still want to go out tonight?" I could tell by the way she asked that this would be hard for her to do.

"I can see you tomorrow," I said.

"O.K.," she said. Relieved, I think. "Can you be here around eight? I want to leave early so that I can get back early and Philip

needs to get to the airport at least an hour before the plane leaves
or else he's a nervous wreck. This is really nice of you. Are you
sure you want to do this?"

"I'm very sure," I said.

"O.K. See you tomorrow then."

"O.K."

"Oh, oh, do you know where I live?"

"Yes."

"How do you know?" she asked.

"One day I looked up your home address in the firm's directo-
ry and I drove by your house." I don't think that this sounded as
weird as it could have sounded because her response was gentle
and full of quiet knowing.

"Oh, you did, did you?"

"I'll see you tomorrow," I said.

That night I thought of Trudy's secret and felt ashamed that I
had told Kate about it. That night I myself went to the stables with
Abuelito's Remington still loaded with the sticky bullet and came
within a finger twitch of blowing the brains out of the unblinking
Aladdin. That night, late that night, I heard Trudy talking urgently
to someone in her sleep, perhaps to me, as I tiptoed through the
house in the dark touching its walls like a blind man.

DAY 24

I did not need an alarm clock the next morning. I had been lying on the sofa mummylike, my hands over my chest for hours when 7:00 a.m. finally rolled along. In the workshop where I kept all those unused tools there was a small chest of drawers with extra clothes. I noticed for the first time that I had slept with my wool suit pants on and now they were all wrinkled. I changed into khakis stained with the varnish of some failed restoration project or other and found a long-sleeved flannel shirt, for it seemed cold. One of those New England mornings that cling to winter.

Upstairs everything was quiet. I used the downstairs bathroom quickly and then went out through the basement. Everything seemed fresh and new. The dogwoods that Trudy and I had planted on the edge of the long driveway were budding pink.

The grass coming up was soft like baby's hair. I stood there looking at almost every tree and remembered something about each one. There were the ten-foot pines I had transplanted from out back when they were only knee-high and had placed along the fence that separated our property from Bartholomew Meagher's to give us extra privacy. How many hours had I spent trying to save each tail-like root, digging with my fingers and uncoiling it from the ground with my hands? As I stood there taking it all in, feeling the coldness of the morning on my face, the yard seemed unusually beautiful but also precarious, even strange.

As I was driving to Kate's I thought about how some people have the knack for living and others don't. It seemed as if along the line when it was my turn somebody forgot to tell me the secret, forcing me now to float around clueless. It was a simple secret—I had a feeling about that—but still beyond my grasp. Trudy had found it, and so had Kate, I think. Kevin Niven definitely had it and so did Renata, but in a different way. Theodore had it and then lost it. Bartholomew Meagher overflowed with some form of it. These

115

people functioned. Maybe with different degrees of enjoyment, but they functioned. They motored on, more or less painlessly, and when there was pain, they trudged. They got up in the morning and had something to do. They invented errands. They had hobbies and pleasures and ambitions. They looked forward. They competed. They went into the daily fray and were not afraid of it. Some welcomed it, even. So where had I missed it? Was this something that you learn or something that you are born with—this lightness, this unstuckness?

I remembered the first time I was invited to visit Trudy's parents before we were married. My bedroom was upstairs about a thousand creaky steps from Trudy's. The first morning there I took a shower and dried myself with one of two teal-colored towels that hung over a porcelain rack at the end of the bathtub. As I was drying myself, I noticed for the first time that the towels had a seashell embroidered with silver thread. The reason I noticed was that when I looked down, my balls sparkled like tinseled Christmas ornaments. The silver embroidery was disintegrating before my very eyes. I learned later that those particular towels had been hanging over the bathtub since the beginning of the universe and were FOR DECORATION ONLY. The towels for daily use were the two white fluffy ones that hung in front of the commode. Trudy's mother went into the bathroom that afternoon to "straighten up a bit" and did not fall for the closed bathroom curtain or my careful folding trick. She walked out of the bathroom past me as I was going upstairs to get a book and went straight to Trudy with evidence in hand of what she'd been saying all along, that I was not the right man for Trudy, that Trudy was making a mistake. The towels were ruined. A few moments later as I shamefully pretended to refold my shirts, Trudy walked in, and, not as sympathetically as I would have hoped under the circumstances, told me that the towels were bought by the family during a trip to Yugoslavia when she was a little girl. They were hand embroidered and the thread was real silver. I apologized, but in my defense, I asked how I was supposed to know that those towels were not meant to be used. Trudy looked at me suddenly and incredulously, as if in a flash she had seen that maybe her mother was right, after all; maybe I was not the right one.

So where does one learn about these things? How does one know which of life's towels are FOR DECORATION ONLY and which for daily use? Who is supposed to teach you about these things and why didn't I get taught? Or maybe the lessons were there, lessons presented in various classrooms taught by different teachers, and maybe it was I who had the faulty equipment, I whose radar did not pick up the blips that life had to offer. Was I with some form of dyslexia reversing the consonants and vowels of daily living in such a way that even the simplest of all messages, the most elemental signs of how to live, could not be apprehended?

It was around 7:30 A.M. when I pulled into Kate's driveway. I was half an hour earlier than expected. Noticing which car was absent, I could tell that Kate had already left. As I stepped outside, I heard a noise I recognized a few seconds later as machine-gun fire aimed directly at me. Here was Corky skidding to a stop right in front of me on his yellow-and-red three-wheeler, the kind with a seat low to the ground and a front wheel bigger than the rest.

"You're dead, turkey," he said.

I grabbed my stomach, doubled over to my knees and fell on the front lawn, lifting my legs way up in the air for extra emphasis. Corky screeched hysterically. As I was getting up, I saw Philip coming out of the house. He was putting on his sunglasses and had a serious expression on his face. It had been almost a year since I had seen Corky and Philip. Corky seemed to have grown spades in that time. The little boy that Kate and I rocked back and forth in the pool during that historic summer outing was now a more defined human being, with a grown-up haircut and facial features all his own. He did not look like Kate, except maybe for his reddish blonde hair. But neither did he look like Philip, especially with that smile. Philip never smiled, or if he did, it was not really a smile but a sort of calculated movement of the lips meant to convey a smile. Philip's look was intense. After the pool episode, and while I was still reeling from Kate's magic touch, Kate and I took Corky to watch his father play tennis. I remember looking at Philip's face there on center court. It was a grim all-business face. When he scored a point, he would hit his racket on the side of his hand, rather hard I thought, as he whispered to himself "yes, yes." When he lost a point, he hit himself also, only harder and he "god-damned" himself through his teeth. I remember that after only a minute or so of watching Philip, Corky began to pull Kate's hand in the direction of the pool.

"Don't you want to stay here and watch Daddy play?" Kate asked.

"Daddy looks mean," Corky replied.

That's more or less how he looked as he approached me that early morning. I was shaking the dust from the back of my pants when I saw his outstretched hand.

"You're half an hour early," he said. He made that movement with his lips that people were supposed to consider as a smile.

"Sorry," I said, shaking his hand and immediately regretting having said that I was sorry, for I was not, and I did not want to yield in any way to Philip.

"Aw, that's all right. As long as you don't expect to get paid for an extra half-hour." This was supposed to be, I think, a "ha, ha" kind of statement, but with Philip one never knew for sure.

"I'll give you a discount," I said. The truth was that I was sorry that I had lost track of time in the car. I wished I had stopped somewhere to drink a cup of coffee. Spending time with Philip on this particular morning was not something I looked forward to. Perhaps I could stay outside with Corky while he finished packing or whatever. No such luck, it seemed. I was being led into the kitchen and there next to the kitchen table was a black overnight bag with *The Wall Street Journal* tucked inside its handle. Philip was packed and ready to go.

"Cup of coffee?" Philip asked pointing at a chair for me to take.

"Sure," I said.

Philip went to the coffeemaker and poured a cup of coffee into a white mug. I noticed that the pot was almost empty. Kate must have filled her Exxon traveling mug before she left for work. Philip placed the coffee in front of me.

"Milk?"

"Yes, thank you." I also take sugar but Philip did not ask if I wanted any and I was not in the mood to request it.

"So . . ." He was looking at me, waiting for me to start the small talk. I deliberately took my time pouring the milk into the cup of coffee. "What are you going to do?"

"Pardon me?" I was not sure what he was referring to.

Philip sat down gravely in front of me. "Kate told me about your job," he said, looking at me straight in the eye.

I took a sip of the coffee, which was not piping hot. Perhaps it was natural for Kate to tell Philip about my job or lack thereof, but for a moment I felt betrayed. That information had made me vulnerable to Philip, and besides, it implied an intimacy between Kate and Philip that I had fancied as my and Kate's own province.

"Oh." It was all I could do to respond.

"Are you going to look at other firms? Kate tells me that it's an employer's market right now. Everybody and his grandmother is getting a law degree."

"I don't know," I said, looking at him in such a way as to let him know I did not want to talk about it at that time. The look was much too subtle for Philip.

"You might want to try the public sector," he said. "I do some business with people in state government. If you like, I can hook you up with them."

"Thank you," I said. I couldn't tell whether Philip was being helpful or hurtful. His tone of voice was neutral and factual. It contained neither sympathy nor, for that matter, arrogance. There was a very long pause during which I think even Philip felt uncomfortable because he twitched in his chair a little not knowing whether to get up or to stay seated. He finally decided to stay seated.

"You know, Kate talks a lot about you." This he said in a different tone of voice, less businesslike, a tone I had not heard before in Philip. He waited for some kind of acknowledgment from me that he could continue in that vein. He must have seen in my expression the permission he needed, because he went on to say: "She tells me that you're a good friend. That she shares things with you." Philip was treading territory where he was clearly uncomfortable. He got up and went to the screen door presumably to check on Corky. He came back and sat down with some resolution to finish what he had started. "I myself am not very good at talking . . . about those things."

"What things?" I asked, although I knew well what things he was talking about.

"Things like the things you and Kate talk about. Dreams and things. Kate showed me this journal that she started where she writes down her dreams first thing in the morning. Then I guess she reads them to you." Philip was looking at his cup, tilting it as if the cup was a mile long and you could barely see whether any coffee filled its bottom. "I think that's good." But he really meant that he thought that it was bad. It was some kind of violation of a rule, but he was having trouble articulating the rule. "Kate really likes you." It was a novelty to see myself as a threat or a danger to anyone. I had never seen myself as such, but now Philip was reflecting to me a new image of myself. Part of me was slightly flattered inasmuch as I felt there must have been some forceful love for me on Kate's part for Philip to have perceived it. He was expecting me to respond. Out of sympathy for him, I did.

"I like Kate very much," I said. I said this in a straightforward and clear way. I didn't think anything was hidden there, but of course, there was. The way I liked Kate oscillated at different times from the tenderness of a father to the longing of an orphan, but the way I liked Kate was not in the simple way I conveyed to Philip. What he said next and the way he said it led me to think that Philip did not believe in the simplicity of my tone, either.

"Look," he said, putting his head down for a second and running his fingers through his carefully combed black hair, "I'm no poet . . ." Had Kate told him about my poem, perhaps read it to him last night when she got back from work? I began to feel like some kind of foil used by Kate to prick Philip back into sensitivity. Apparently it was working. Philip let the sentence dangle. It was not taking him toward the bottom line that he needed to get to in the next few minutes. The clock on the kitchen wall in the shape of an apple said almost eight o'clock and time for him to leave or else be a nervous wreck before his flight. "I guess what I'm trying to say is that Kate is not very sure of herself sometimes. Sometimes she just gets confused about things." Philip opened his eyes as if to ask me if I knew what he meant, if I could decipher the real message in his words. The messages that I took were various. For starters there was the "don't cause any trouble" message. I wasn't exactly sure how this message was uttered, whether in the form of a plea or a threat. When I didn't answer, he looked at the clock on the wall one more time. He was about to get up but decided to say something else. "I'm glad you two are . . . friends," he said. He stared at me again for a second as if to punctuate his hidden meaning. Then he stretched his lips in the form of a grin and patted me on the knee before getting up.

Philip pointed out a note from Kate on top of the counter by the toaster. Since he would not be returning until evening, he reminded me that I would not be there when he got back. He repeated his offer to hook me up with some government officials. I could help myself to anything, but I could not go riffling through Kate's drawers. Ha, ha. He yelled for Corky, who had disappeared down the block. I went outside and saw him place his black bag and a suitcase in the back seat. It was too warm for a raincoat inside the car so he took it off. Corky finally appeared but wiggled his way out of giving Philip a kiss. Philip asked him if he was embarrassed to kiss his old man in front of strangers.

DAY 25

By two o'clock it seemed we had done everything there was to do. We went to the neighborhood park, me pulling Corky in a wagon. We watched Sesame Street twice (once on regular TV and once on videotape). We spilled a thousand or so crayons on the den floor and drew Batman until I got the shape of his ears right. I did the drawing and Corky did the coloring. We built a raceway for Corky's Matchbox cars out of the Encyclopaedia Britannica and determined that fancier is not necessarily faster. We wrestled. We played hide-and-go-seek with a minor scare when the little devil disappeared for over twenty minutes; I finally found him nestled inside the dirty laundry hamper. We played football outside with an orange foam football that someone had taken a bite out of.

We lunched on hot dogs, macaroni and cheese (too crispy), and ketchup. We disgusted each other by eliciting monster burps from the bottom of our beings.

I reread Kate's note. It said optimistically that Corky had been known to take a nap after lunch.

"Would you like me to read you a book?" I asked.

"I don't want to take a nap," he responded, seeing through me.

"No, let's not take a nap. I hate naps. Let's just read a book," I said. Corky sized me up.

"Naaa," he said. Apparently, he had been deceived this way before by some other grownup. "Let's play hide-and-go-seek again."

"I tell you what. If we read a book together, afterwards, I'll teach you a bad word." I had learned at the firm-outing that this desire for a greater and more interesting vocabulary was one of Corky's passions.

"Teach me one first," he demanded.

"Let's find a book and then I'll tell you." We were still at the kitchen table. I tried to stand up to go over to his room where I had already seen a nice collection of books, but he pushed me down on the chair and then proceeded to sit horsy-style on my knees.

"O.K. But you have to promise you will never tell anyone that I told you this."

"I promise." Corky's eyes were gleaming with anticipated wickedness.

"Do you really promise?"

"I promise!" he squealed.

"O.K. Here it goes." I grabbed his head and whispered in his ear.

"Caca," he repeated, "I already know that word. It means poop."

"How did you know?" I asked.

"I learned it on TV. Now tell me a real bad word or else." He yanked my ear for emphasis.

"Ouch!" I said. I grabbed him and ran with him to his room before he had time to complain or squirm out of my hold. I plopped him on top of his bed. He began to jump up and down.

"Tell me a bad word," he insisted.

"Will you read a book with me after I tell you?"

"No." he said. Definitively.

I grabbed a book from a small bookshelf in his room. "Look, I bet you there are bad words in this book."

"No, there aren't. I read that book all the time. There's not a single bad word."

"I bet you there's at least one," I said. I opened the book and flipped through the pages. I was sitting on the bed. Corky came over and stood by my shoulder. "Mmmm. Not here. Not on this page. Look at this boy. I wonder what he's doing with all those toys."

"He went to the hospital to get his tonsils out and those are the toys in the hospital. See that . . . that's the doctor that operated on him."

"I see," I said.

"See, there's no bad words."

"We better read it. There might be a bad word in here." I went back to the first page and started reading, slowly. I used his pillow as a backrest and sat up in bed. Corky sat next to me.

Somewhere in the middle of our third book we finally found our first bad word.

"Pussy willow is not a bad word," he said, "It's a plant."

"Ahh, what you don't know because you're only five years old is that the real bad words are regular words that mean something else too." He pondered this for a few seconds.

"I'm *six* years old," he said. I waited a few seconds while he looked at the picture of a kitten chasing a butterfly in a field of pussy willows. I kept on reading hoping that he would not press me for further explanations. No such luck.

"What does it really mean?" he asked.

"What does what mean?" I asked absent-mindedly.

"You know, pussy willow." He began to suck his thumb, a gesture that I interpreted as the precursor of sleep. The truth was that I myself was getting kind of drowsy, which felt good, given where my mind had been the past twenty-four hours. I put the book down, slid my head onto the pillow and pretended to sleep.

"Wake up, wake up," he said shaking me.

"Shhhh," I replied. I could see through a slit in my eyes that his face was directly in front of mine. I sang in a whisper.

A la ruru niño
A la ruru ya
Duérmase, mi niño
Duérmaseme ya
Porque viene el cuco
Y te comerá

It was the lullaby that Renata had sung to me when I was Corky's age. It came out of the blue. I'm sure that I had not sung it or thought about it the last thirty-seven years of my life. Corky began to stick his finger exploratorily in my ear.

"Why do you have hairs in your ear?"

I kept on singing. Then all of a sudden he said, "My father knows how to speak French."

"Mmmmm," I said.

"Do you have a father?" he asked.

"No," I said.

"What happened to him?"

"He died when I was little."

"How little? Like me?"

"Bigger. Thirteen."

"I'm only six."

"I know."

My eyes were still closed. The soft pillow and the smell of Corky were beginning to suck me into semi-consciousness, except that suddenly images of Armanda and Nando began to twirl inside me like an unstoppable carousel.

"How did he die?" I threw my arm around him as if to calm his questioning.

"He died in a car accident."

Corky was quiet for the next few moments. He turned from facing me and laid his head on the pillow, looking at the ceiling. He held his arms up and opened and closed his fingers like puppets in the air.

"My grandpa died too," he went on. "He's in heaven." I did not answer. "Is your dad in heaven?"

"Where is heaven?" I asked, opening my eyes and feeling the comfort of anticipated sleep drift away.

"Up there." He pointed out the window at a patch of gray sky. "And in here." He poked a finger in my chest, startling me. "It's in here when you're alive," poking me again, "and up there when you die."

"Who told you that?" I asked.

"My mommy. Everyone has to die when they get old. My grandpa died because he had cancer."

"Yes," I said.

"Do you miss your dad?"

"I thought about this question, perhaps more than I should have because my silence was taken for an answer.

"I hope my dad never dies," he said. With this he turned his back to me. After a few seconds he declared, "I know what pussy really means."

"What?" I asked.

"It's when you're scared."

"Yeah?"

"Lonnie called me that word once when I wouldn't hang by my feet on the jungle gym. He called me a pussy. Is pussy the same as pussy willow?"

"Kind of," I said. Then as an afterthought and more to myself, "Everyone gets scared."

"I know," he said. I waited for more responses or more questions or even more explanations. But nothing came. After a while I heard his breathing deepen. He had fallen asleep.

DAY 26

I lay next to Corky for what seemed the longest time. I lay there until I could not breathe any more. When Corky touched my chest to show me where heaven was, I thought again, after many years, of Armanda's last letter. There it was before my eyes. The line where she poetically described how she would always carry a part of me inside of her, a little Ismael. The line from her letter appeared before me, naked of all the justifications and interpretations I had constructed over the years. The pain of never responding to this letter entered into me, at the very moment that Corky touched my chest, like burning, suffocating lava from hell. I got up quickly and headed to Kate's bedroom. I knew which side of the bed was hers because there was a small bookcase with some of the books I had given her. I stretched myself against her giant bed and hugged the smells of her pillow against me. It was a warm, comforting, arousing smell that reminded me of Armanda's hair, the way her hair smelled that last night before I left for Boston and law school and Trudy.

Armanda had put Nando to sleep in the bedroom, and she and I were lying on the floor in the living room of her small apartment at the Del Camino Motel, our backs reclining on the bottom of the black-and-white striped sofa. We were just holding hands, staring at the wall in front of us. The little black-and-white television that we had just finished watching a boxing match on was turned off. My plane to Boston left at 4:00 in the morning. We had about an hour left before I had to call a cab.

Armanda turned around to face me and then began to kiss my neck softly. Then she whispered to me in Spanish, "Let's dance the paso lento one last time before you go."

"Armanda," I said, "let's just hold each other. I don't want to make love tonight."

She had lain down and rested her head on my thigh while I stroked her long black hair. After a while I felt a coldness on my thigh.

127

"Why are you crying?"

She shook her head.

"Armanda, remember my promise that I would never lie to you? I always told you that I was going back. I never told you anything else."

She nodded slightly, her cheek still on my leg.

"Do you remember that night Norberto and I went to the Nine Tails and how you and I ended up together at the end of the evening? Never in my life did I expect to be so lucky. You were the most beautiful woman. De veras. When you came out to dance, everyone looked at you. Those who were not facing you moved their chairs and got ready to watch you. I still remember how once the music started to play, the noise of the conversations began to get softer and softer until everyone was quiet. Even the other women in the place were silent."

Armanda raised herself from the floor. Her eyes red from crying, her long eyelashes stuck together. She wiped her cheeks with the back of her hands.

"Did you like me?"

"Like you? I couldn't keep my eyes off you. At first it was your beauty. But then it was the dance. The song and you were like one. Everyone there wanted to be moving with you. I could see in their eyes that each one of the men was dancing with you in his mind."

"And you?"

"Also. In my mind, I was lying down on the stage, my pito pointing up at you, and then you lowered yourself slowly on top of me and began to pull me up with the grip of your panocho. Up and up I went until only my head and my feet were touching the ground, my back arched, and then you brought me gently down, your rayita holding me like a vacuum. Then you made me be still on my back, my hands on the floor, and with your arms up in the air you made tiny little up-and-down squat movements just on the tip of my verga and then you somehow managed to bend over to kiss my lips, holding yourself up with your palms and your knees, with me still connected to you, and you swirled your pelvis as if you were stirring a cup of coffee and you didn't want to clink the cup, only I was the spoon and you were the cup; and then you turned yourself around, lifting your arms and legs one after another like a long-legged spider, while I lifted my back not to lose our link, and when you finally rotated, I could see your culo in front of me, strong and shiny like a wet apricot."

Armanda smiled like a little girl and shook her hair backwards. "And then what happened?"

"And then after you finished dancing, you walked off the stage while everyone was clapping and whistling and I was looking at your eyes, trying to meet them with mine as you went by my table—I did and I winked and you winked back."

"I did not," she said, hitting me on the side of the head.

"¡Ay! Of course you did."

"You wish, cabrón."

"Then after I took Norberto home I drove straight back to the Nine Tails and sat in the area that you were waitressing while you weren't dancing. I asked you if you could sit down and have a beer with me and you said that on your break you could."

"So, do you remember what you said when we talked?"

"I remember that you told me that I looked like some guy in a Mexican soap opera."

Armanda giggled. "I tell that to everyone, you know."

"Bullshit! I'm the only one you ever told that to."

"And what else did you say?"

"I remember when the Nine Tails was about to close, I asked you if I could take you home and you said that you never let anyone take you home."

"That was true. I never did."

"But I told you to look at me and told you that your heart was telling you that you could trust me."

"Yes."

"So I came home with you. But you didn't trust me completely because you made me park a block from the Del Camino because you didn't want me to know where you lived."

"It was only that time."

"Yeah. Then you trusted me after that, except . . ."

"Except what?

"Except that you never wanted me to get too close to Nando."

"I told you why."

"You were afraid that Nando would be hurt when I left. You didn't want him to suffer as he had when his father left him."

Armanda hugged me and put her head on my chest. After a few minutes, I asked, "Do you think he'll miss me?"

"He misses you already when you don't come every day. He finally trusts you. And also you spoiled him buying him all those things."

I looked across the room and there next to the TV on a small coffee table was the picture of Armanda and Nando I had insisted they have taken. Armanda was dressed in a low-cut black dress, the one she always wore when we went dancing on Monday nights, her only day off from the Nine Tails. Nando was wearing a checked shirt I had bought especially for the picture, his thick black hair plastered with a green gel that Armanda bought in Juárez. Nando's face had the look of a scared little boy at the doctor's office wondering exactly how much hurt was coming.

"Do you have your picture?" Armanda asked when she saw where my eyes were focusing.

"I do, right in my wallet."

"Do you think you'll write?" she asked.

"I think I will," I answered.

"I'm not a very good writer."

"It doesn't matter."

"When I write it will be from my heart."

"Armanda, no more crying."

"I'm not crying."

"What are you doing, then?"

"I don't know, but I'm not crying."

"O.K. You're not crying."

I held her hard against my chest.

"Ismael?"

"Yes?"

"You don't have to say anything. I never asked you for anything. Just before you go, tell me what I was to you."

I searched for a response.

"You are the person my heart loves but can't have."

"You have me already."

"I mean, I can't stay with you."

"Because we're different?"

"Not so different."

"You have opportunities and things you want to do."

"I do have that, yes. I need to go back to law school. I want to finish what I've started. Believe me, it's something I've thought very hard about. Two weeks ago, I had decided not to go back. To stay here with you. Get a job teaching at the community college. Remember, I told you they were interested in me? You know how much I want to stay."

"Then stay."

"Armanda, I've never been as happy as with you, except that there's a part of me that says that it's not right for me to stay here."

"Not right? You think our love is not right?" This she said without anger.

"No, not our love. If I stayed here with you in El Paso, I would not . . . It's like Norberto's father said to me once: Norberto and I were helping his dad pick cotton when he asked me what I wanted to do, and I told him that I wanted to have a farm just like his and maybe have a chicken coop full of chickens and some lambs and pigs. Then he stood up and looked at me and said that it would be a sin for me to do that. I asked him why. He said that in his mind there was only one real sin in life and that was not to use all the talents that God gave each one of us. For him to have a farm was not a sin because he was using all God gave him, but for me it would be because God gave me more."

Armanda lifted her face, closed her eyes, and kissed my lips. Then she said softly, "I know you better than you know yourself, you know. I have always known that you would go."

"But you don't agree that I should."

"I don't want you to leave. I'm afraid for me and I'm afraid for Nando, who loves you like a father already. Our hearts are yours. But your heart is not ours. Your heart is not here."

"That may be, Armanda. Maybe I'm making a big mistake. Maybe I'll come back."

"I hope you do. But I will get used to whatever you decide."

"Do you mean that?"

"Yes. That is the lesson of the paso lento, ¿no? To learn to love truly."

"I never mastered all the steps of the paso lento, did I?"

"No one ever does completely. All we can do is try. But . . ."

"Tell me."

"Nothing, it's just that the paso lento only works when people give completely and forever to each other. Para siempre."

Armanda wrote three letters to me. I answered none. Armanda's letters contained drawings from Nando and recountings of the goings-on at the Nine Tails. My favorite letter had a poem about our spirits leaving our bodies and dancing together in a dance of love to a music that was made up of single notes from each star in the universe. It was my second year of law school and my life was being carried in a current toward Trudy, law firms, the East Coast, and all those places and people that seemed very different from Armanda and the Nine Tails and El Paso. When I received what was to be her last letter, I put the picture of Nando and Armanda inside the envelope and placed it in a wooden box where I laid, as if in a miniature coffin, my life's shames and regrets. In there I kept Renata's final letter, the one written by her niece telling me that Renata was about to die and asking me to go and see her. In there I kept the yellowed obituary of my natural father's death, which Lilia had given me when I deposited her in the St. Anthony's Convalescent Home in Harlingen, Texas. In the same box I also kept the blue margined and red sealed handwritten legal document formalizing my adoption by Theodore, side by side with Theodore's cracked Longines with the hands stuck at 6:32 P.M., the exact moment of his death.

I heard Kate open the kitchen door and yell, "Is anybody home?"

I got up from Kate's bed and went to the top of the stairs to answer her call. I did it in a loud whisper because I did not want to wake up Corky. It had been almost two hours since he went to sleep.

On the stairs, I put my finger to my mouth, then with my palms against my cheeks, I made the universal sign for sleeping and pointed toward Corky's room. She understood and motioned me down.

"How did it go?" she asked.

"We did great," I said.

She took me by the elbow and led me toward the kitchen. On the kitchen table were several paper bags filled with groceries.

"I hope you don't mind," she said, "but I had to go shopping."

"Any more bags?"

"A few."

Outside the late afternoon sunlight made me squint, and the air that was beginning to cool again made me realize that sometime during the day I had taken off my flannel shirt. I didn't have the slightest idea what had happened to it.

When I brought in the last of the bags, Kate had already changed into a white T-shirt and some very worn jeans.

"You like?" she asked, spreading her arms like a fashion model.

"Very much," I said.

I started mindlessly taking the groceries out of the bags, but Kate took my hands and sat me down as if I were some kind of grown-up version of Corky.

"You've done enough already," she said. "Sit down. I'm brewing some coffee."

She grabbed a white bag from inside the other bags and tilted it toward me. "Doughnut?" she asked.

"No, thanks."

"Suit yourself," she mumbled. She had grabbed a white powdered doughnut and stuck it in her mouth so that she could use her two hands to lift a grocery bag from the kitchen table to the kitchen counter.

"So, did you survive?" she asked, rubbing her hands on the side of her jeans.

"Corky or Philip?"

She looked at me. "They both have their moments, don't they?"

"Corky's O.K." I said. We both laughed.

"I take it you and Philip got a chance to talk."

"We did for a little while. I think Philip wanted to tell me something but couldn't quite get it out."

"Mmmm," she said. "Maybe I've been talking a little too much about you."

"What kinds of things have you been saying?"

"That I have the hots for you, that kind of thing." Her eyes landed softly on mine for a second and then she smiled.

"Don't kid me. I'm very vulnerable these days."

"Yes. Yes you are. What are you going to do?" She had taken all the perishables and had put them either in the refrigerator or the freezer. She placed the bags on the floor and sat down in front of me. For a moment, I felt incredibly fortunate to have her in front of me, looking at me and asking me questions. All mine, as it were.

"I don't know. Leave, I guess."

"Leave?"

I remembered that she had not been privy to my thoughts for the last twenty-four hours.

"Trudy and I are having problems," I managed to say.

"Is it serious?"

"It was last night. I'm not sure whether it's salvageable or not. Maybe it is. I just don't seem to have the energy or the will to find out."

"Oh."

"Go ahead," I said.

"Go ahead, what?"

"Go ahead and ask whatever it is you want to ask."

"It just seems kind of final."

"I guess it is."

"Why does it have to be?"

"Are we talking about Trudy?" I asked.

"The whole thing." She seemed a little irritated. "You have this air about you of finality. Losing a job is not the end of the world."

"No, it isn't," I said, quietly.

"I'm sorry," she said. "I'm not being very sympathetic, am I?"

"I don't want you to be sympathetic," I said, somewhat defensively.

She got up and poured two cups of coffee into the same white mugs that Philip had used that morning. She took the milk out and poured it into a little container that was shaped like a Holstein cow, pink udders and all. She put a bowl of sugar and two spoons on the table. It was only after I had finished putting in the sugar and the milk and stirring the coffee that she spoke.

"Would you like to stay for supper?"

"I'm not sure I can take any more of Philip," I said, after a pause.

"Philip won't be back until tomorrow sometime," she said.

I thought I had remembered Philip saying something different to me. But it was possible that my mind, rattled as it was, was playing tricks on me. The information that Philip would not be back that night sent a whole bunch of images reeling through my mind.

"What would happen if I stayed?" I asked.

"Whatever would happen, would happen," Kate said, looking at me directly.

For a while we sipped our coffee in silence, as if we were in some kind of standoff, each one waiting for the other to draw first.

"Kate," I finally said, "something is happening here that goes beyond losing a job and losing a marriage. I'm not sure at this moment that I can put all this into words. It has to do with you and it has to do with some things that happened in the past. It's all very confusing and I don't like the way it feels."

I thought I was done for the moment, but Kate's face told me that I was not done, that I should continue, that I was like a child rehearsing his lines before the school play, and that I was doing well.

"It's important to me that I don't fuck up this opportunity, because one of the things I'm realizing is that opportunities slip by and that this is very bad. I don't know why, but I believe that I must leave. To stay here, to look for another job, to try to patch things up with Trudy is really to continue in a way that wasn't right, somehow. What I really want to tell you and what I don't want to pass up is that for the longest time I've thought that I loved you . . ."

"Ismael . . ." She raised her hand as if to say that I did not have to say what I was saying or what I was about to say.

"Let me finish. I'm almost done. I promise you this won't get too corny or too uncomfortable."

"It's neither of those two things," she said, looking at me.

"But the thing is that at this moment I really don't know what love is. It sounds like some song that you hear on the radio, but it happens to be the truth. At this moment, I don't know what it is or whether—to be honest, really honest, which is what I want to be right now—whether it is something that I have ever really done. Loved someone, I mean."

I got up and walked to the screen door and looked outside thinking of what to say next. While I was looking outside I saw that my flannel shirt was draped over one of Kate's rose bushes where Corky had flung it.

When I sat back down again, Kate was still waiting for me to continue. I remember, seemingly for the longest time, looking at a strand of golden hair that dangled at her temple and caught the sunlight from the kitchen window. Inside me I could almost hear a voice saying, "Hello down there. Look what I've given you now. Why do you look a gift horse in the mouth? She's here and you're here and that's all that matters."

"You're hard on yourself," she said, breaking off my absorption. Then she went on. "I have always felt there are some things that are better left unsaid. Maybe because saying them gives them some kind of reality. Or maybe because I don't seem to have the courage that you have. Anyway, I'm not stupid, you know. I think I've always known that there was something special between us. I've been hoping that it was just a friendship. But, I guess if I had to be totally honest too, I would have to say that what I feel is not just friendship."

"It isn't?"

"I don't know why I'm saying this now. I really love Philip and my life very much. And I just don't think I could ever hurt Corky."

She got up, went to the sink, and emptied the remains of her coffee down the drain. Then she took out a glass and filled it with cold water from the faucet. She sat down and took a sip.

"You really make me feel the weirdest things," she said.

I must have made an instinctive motion to get up and go toward her for she told me with her hands to stop where I was.

"Don't come near me right now, please," she said. "This is all your fault. You seem so final about things."

"I'm sorry," I said.

She seemed not to have heard me. "Oh, Lord. For the longest time I really thought I was sick. I had this craving for you. At work I couldn't bear to touch you, not even to shake your hand. I just wanted you so bad. Oh, my Lord! It was awful. I couldn't make love to Philip. It was like some kind of sickness."

"You seem to have survived O.K. without my help," I said.

"Yeah, well, remember the time you told me that you had walked into your bathroom while Trudy was taking a steamy shower and that Trudy's back was to you and she didn't know you were there but that you could definitely see what she was doing through the glass windows of the shower? And remember how incomprehensible it seemed to you that Trudy who apparently had little desire for you in particular, still, apparently, was full of desire?"

"I do remember telling you that." I didn't go on to tell her that this was Trudy's secret—the only thing I ever regretted telling Kate.

"Well, I restrained myself then from telling you that I understood fully what Trudy was doing, because that was the only way I had of being close to you."

"Holy shit," I said. "This is so messed up. Something is terribly wrong with this picture."

"It's pretty funny when you think about it," Kate said.

I was suddenly struck with a thought. "I wonder if Trudy was being close to someone else too."

"Maybe it was her way of being close to you."

I groaned. There was a powerlessness about the whole thing that was disgusting.

"Listen, Kate. Don't you think we missed some kind of boat, that right now we're missing some kind of boat? I mean, what's

wrong with us? There are people around us who get divorces left
and right, who do this and do that, adjust a life situation here, add
something there until they get this happiness thing right. And here
we are enmeshed in a giant web of repressed wants. Don't you
think there's something wrong with us?"

"No, I don't think there's anything wrong with us," she said
calmly, as if she had thought about this for a long time. "I try to live
my life without hurting others and you do too. I don't always suc-
ceed. I mean, when I was driving home today, I knew that Philip
was going to be away and I knew I was going to invite you to stay
for dinner and I got terribly confused about what's right and what's
wrong, which is something that I never thought would happen."

"You think you're confused," I said smiling. "Maybe we think
about things too much."

"Well, maybe we do. Having principles is a curse."

We both tilted our heads upwards, for we heard a noise coming out of Corky's room.

"He's O.K. for a few more minutes. I trained him to stay in bed
or to stay in his room playing by himself for a while after he gets
up. It's one of my biggest accomplishments."

"Where do you draw the line?" I asked.

"What line?"

"I mean, where do you draw the line between sticking to principles and your own happiness?"

"I don't know. If you're very unhappy then you have to draw it,
I guess. If you're only semi-unhappy, then it varies. I don't know.
My marriage with Philip is not great-great. But it's not bad-bad,
either. And I think he genuinely loves me."

"I'm sure he does," I said. "I've been thinking about a lot of
things lately, as you probably have guessed. For many of these
things I don't have words. They're just these nameless moods that
circle in my chest like bats cornered in a cave. But there's one thing
that I think I'm now able to identify. It's that there is in me a place
for a deep, deep joy, which is not filled. Not filled. It wasn't filled
by work and it wasn't filled by Trudy. Maybe it's you, Kate, who
can fill it. I don't know. I thought it was you for the longest time.
Maybe it's unfillable by anything in this world. But God, I hope
not. And even if it is unfillable, I think the empty place needs to be
filled as best it can. I mean, we need to try to fill it. I have seen it

filled in degrees in others. People who like their work and who like—not just love, but like—the person they're spending their lives with. It was even full for me at some points in my life. I know it sounds very self-centered to say this, but maybe it's our obligation, the only thing that really matters, to try to fill our hearts as much as we can. Maybe that's the case."

There was a long pause when neither Kate nor I could say anything else. Then, in a tone that was different than before, more serious, more solemn, she asked: "Has someone filled that place for you before?"

"I don't know. I think now that maybe there was somebody who did, who occupied that place as much as it could be occupied, only I didn't have the courage to accept that person's love then. Today of all days, as I was playing with Corky and putting him to sleep, the memory of my cowardice came back to me with an awful force. I don't know. I feel so much regret. It's a hole of shame that has always been there, only I just now stepped into it."

Kate got up and smoothed her T-shirt. She seemed preoccupied, as if she were assembling the information she had received from me and needed to create a slot to store the new data in her mind.

"I'll be back in a second," she said. "I need to make sure Corky's O.K."

After a while she yelled at me to come upstairs. She was bending over the bathtub scrubbing a pliant Corky, who in the meantime was trying to touch his toes with his fingers. His usual blond hair was now dark-brown wet and padded down over his head like a helmet except for a tiny tuft springing up at the back.

She spoke without turning to look at me. "If you're dead set on going away then I think I want you to stay the night."

"What?"

"I want you to stay the night."

"What are you talking about?"

"I'm talking about the fact that you're living in some kind of loveless, guilt-laden, unfulfilled world even though the world is not that way at all and I don't want to be any part of this. I don't want you to leave here and go wherever it is that you're going with an image of me as one more loss. You want to go, then go. But I'm not going to contribute to whatever attitude is building up in you."

"I want him to stay, too," said Corky.

"Kate," I knelt down on the bathroom floor. She still had not turned to look at me.

"Close your eyes," she told Corky. She put one hand over his face and with the other she began to shampoo his hair. Her fingers were working strongly on his scalp.

"Oucharama!" said Corky.

"Sorry," said Kate.

"Kate," I repeated. "What else can I do? What *is* there for me here?"

"Nothing," she said. She seemed aggravated.

"You have a good life. You yourself just told me. Maybe it's not great-great. But it's not bad-bad."

She turned around and gave me a don't-be-a-smart-ass smile.

"Look, I'm not saying you should stay forever. It seems to me that you're dead set on going. You've probably been dead set on going for a long time and now you're finally realizing why you should go or where you should go. You have to do what's right for you. I mean, I would like you to stay. I would like to have you and Philip and Corky, all right? But I can't have that, can I?"

"Probably not. Not for long, anyway."

"I don't want to be an illusion. And I don't want you to be an illusion. I want to be real. Something happened that was good. I want you to be real. Not something unfulfilled. I hate that kind of soap opera stuff. And I hate dramatic good-byes. They make me think of cowardice and of running away from things. What? What's so funny?"

I was looking at Corky, who had stood up and begun to arch a stream of yellow pee across the bathtub like some kind of Roman fountain.

"Oh, shit, Corky." Kate slapped her palm against his white, wet, butt making a smacking sound that made it seem like the slap was harder than it really was.

"Ouucharama!" yelled Corky.

"Ouucharama, yourself!" Corky was set down in the water again. Kate got up and grabbed a multicolored beach towel, which she used to dry her arms.

"Do you want to stay or not?" She said this, her face directly in front of mine, her eyes looking into mine, steady and unblinking.

"I want him to stay, too," piped up Corky.

I remember grimacing and grabbing my head as if it were the container for some kind of liquid explosive that would go off if shaken too much.

"God damn it!" I yelled out. Kate squinted her eyes as if trying to figure out whether that was a yes or a no.

"God damn it!" Corky parroted, slamming the surface of the water with both hands.

I grabbed Kate by the shoulders. "I want to stay. You know that. You have got to believe that. And I'm so grateful for your asking. Things are spinning out of control so much faster than I can make sense of them that I have a feeling this is probably the last sane thing I'll do. But I have to go. If I were to sleep with you, I think I would dishonor something that came to me today and which I need to get me through."

Then I pulled Kate out of the bathroom, or she pushed me out, I don't know which, and there, by the doorway, slightly out of Corky's line of vision, I put my arms around her and then, after a while, we said good-bye.

DAY 27

t was around 10:00 P.M. when I got to the parsonage. After leaving Kate's house, I drove around aimlessly for an hour listening to a Spanish-language station. I drove and drove until I found myself in front of Reverend Boles's home. It was a white ranch on a cul de sac not too far from the church. Mrs. Boles was the gardener in the family. Even in the dark I could see the rhododendron bushes in front of the house trimmed even like a crew cut on a nine year old. The brick path to the front door was shiny, and there were no blades of grass sticking up between the bricks. Mrs. Boles opened the door. She wore a light pink terrycloth bathrobe, the front of which she was clasping tightly with her hand. She turned on the front light and peered at me, not recognizing me at first. When she turned on the light, it occurred to me for the first time that it was late to be calling on Reverend Boles, especially since I had no idea why I was there or what I wanted to say. Mrs. Boles must have had late visitors before, because once she recognized my face, she smiled and opened the door to let me in.

"Come on in, Ismael," she said. She sounded as if she had been expecting me all along.

"I know it's late, but I wonder if I can see Reverend Boles for a few minutes."

She nodded. She needed to get him from his study where he was pretending to read but was really watching a Red Sox game. It would only take a moment. I was to sit down in the living room and wait for him. She offered a cup of tea, but I declined.

A minute or two later, Reverend Boles appeared. He also was robed and ready for bed. His robe was plaid with blue flannel pajamas sticking out from underneath. I noticed that he was barefoot. He shook my hand, squeezing it and pulling me toward him at the same time. He too seemed to have been waiting for me. I wondered whether he and Mrs. Boles had received a call from Trudy, or perhaps there was a police bulletin warning everyone that a fence-jumping, shovel-wielding maniac was on the loose.

"Would you like something to eat or drink?" he asked.

I declined and asked if I could talk to him for a few minutes. In my mind I was still wondering what it was about, and it struck me that perhaps I had intruded for no purpose whatsoever on these good folks on what would otherwise have been a quiet evening.

Reverend Boles looked at me as if to gauge whether the situation called for semiprivate or fully private accommodations. He must have seen something in me that pointed toward the latter because he asked me to follow him to his study, which was a converted garage accessible only through the kitchen. I had been there before. He called it his hermitage; it was basically an old yellow sofa, a desk piled with papers, an old stereo, and bookshelves. Tonight there was a small black-and-white TV on top of a coffee table. It looked like it had been recently turned off, because in the middle of the screen there was a white dot that was still receding. He sat me down on the sofa and sat next to me, close enough for him to put his hand on my knee and to leave it there for longer than is acceptable by the norms of masculine protocol.

"Is something the matter?" he asked. Despite the fact that he had probably been in the same spot hundreds of times and had probably opened the same way, there was nothing formulaic in his voice. It sounded to the untrained ear as if he were really interested.

"I'm not sure. I don't know. I'm not sure I know where to begin. I was driving around tonight and I ended up here. Early this afternoon I was taking care of a friend's little boy, and I felt like I wanted to come see you. But now I'm not sure why or what it was that I wanted to talk to you about. I know this doesn't make sense. I don't know where to begin."

"Begin wherever you want to begin. Any point is a good point."

Reverend Boles was a chubby man with red cheeks who looked more like a well-fed plumber than a minister of God. He was the most unspiritual-looking person anyone could picture. He reminded me of what I thought Father Brown in the Chesterton stories probably looked like: totally material, totally flesh, totally earthly, and yet there was something about him that was baffling. This short and flabby mass of flesh came out in the pulpit with words that bathed the insides like ice water on a hot summer day.

The first time I saw him in the pulpit I had the impression that I was in one of those bad dreams where characters speak in a way different from the way they look—a man with a voice of a child or a woman with the voice of a man. There he was, cassock slightly tattered, white hair barely combed back, sifting through his note cards, looking as if he were trying to hold back gas, and then out it came—rolling cadences and images in sentences that actually made sense. The words were so simple, so inelegant, that all of a sudden the chubby man was no longer there; he disappeared; you forgot about him, and all that remained were those orderly thoughts that clarified and that acted like some kind of balm.

I remember the first time I came to his church. I had gone to pick up some doughnuts at the nearest place to get them, which happened to be in the next town over, and I was driving back to Oakridge when I saw all these people going into a flat brick church, the kind that looks more like a bowling alley. They seemed happy. These mothers with their shiny dresses and fathers with dark suits that you knew were only worn on church-related occasions, be it Sunday or a baptism, a wedding or a funeral. And they appeared happy, these people, as they hurried one another from the parking lot across from the church, telling each other—sometimes in Spanish—to be careful as they crossed the street. Anyway, I parked the car on impulse and walked in and sat at the very back. And then I saw Reverend Boles come in quite unmajestically from a side door and sit in the front while someone played an electric organ, and I said to myself, oh boy, this is a mistake. Nevertheless I stayed put, and suddenly I found myself in the midst of a sermon about the spiritual poverty of modern man. How poor we really are. How poor we really are in our expression, in the sentiments we stifle, in the way we make love, in the way we keep friends, in the way we pray. Consequently, I listened, and the next Sunday I was there again, and pretty soon I needed to be there every Sunday morning. When for some reason I didn't go, I was not the same. I was somehow more lost than before, more frazzled, more in a fog.

So there I sat in front of the Reverend Mr. Boles, not knowing what to say. I knew only that in my loosely developed scheme of things he was a stop I had to make before I left.

Without looking at him, I said, "The story isn't that complicated. I don't know why I'm having trouble saying it. I lost my job. Trudy wants a divorce. I'm losing things left and right. I just seem to be losing things, jobs, persons, home, a place. Am I making any sense?"

"Yes," he nodded.

But he was not doing anything to rescue me.

"I believe that I will be going away." I looked at him. "You'll need to find someone else to do the tapes."

Reverend Boles's eyes shone momentarily and a corner of his mouth twitched into a minuscule smile.

"What happened to your job?" he asked.

"Actually, you're partly responsible for that," I said jokingly. Reverend Boles tilted his head and furrowed his eyebrows quizzically. "Remember the sermon you gave at Virginia's funeral?"

Reverend Boles nodded. "The next day I was really irritated when my neighbor was, as usual, burning his deadwood on a beautiful day when I wanted to sit outside. So I jumped over the fence, put the fire out, and got into words with him. Then they found out at work, and I got fired."

"I see," he said, in a tone conveying a perfect understanding at the logic of it all, "and I started it all." He was trying not to laugh, which in turn made me laugh.

"It's pretty absurd," I said. I wanted at that moment to tell him about the seething emptiness in my chest and stomach that began with Corky's touch, but it seemed impossible to talk about that without making it all more trite and comical. The whole ball of wax could be summarized in a couple of paragraphs and would sound funny in the telling. I must have made some kind of movement that conveyed an intent to get up and leave, because he put his hand on my knee once again and moved closer to me, cornering me, as it were.

"Tell me again why you came here tonight. I can see you're in trouble. Although it's good, it's good that you can laugh."

There was a long silence while through my mind went images of Armanda and Nando, but I felt powerless to speak of them.

"Tell you why I came here tonight," I repeated to myself out loud.

"If you can," he said.

"I guess . . . what I want most to know is whether you believe."

"Pardon?"

"Do you believe? At Virginia's funeral you sounded, you sounded as if this was all, as if her life was all there is. Your words had no faith or hope."

For a while he looked at me as if trying to digest my words. He had a couple of ways he could go with what I said and he was trying to figure out for himself which was the best.

"All these things that have happened to you. Your job, your wife, all these things have taken you to a place of honesty. I can see that. It's the place of no more bullshit, if you excuse the expression. That's good. That's a good place. But it's also a hurtful place."

I remember feeling how good it was to have someone recognize that it all hurt, that all the unreality and machinations of my brain hurt like a disease. I thought of Trudy and the debates we used to have about my "depression" as she called it, with my saying that sadness came like a cloud and stayed as long as it pleased and her saying that the blues was something that you got rid of, acted upon.

"Listen, Ismael," Reverend Boles went on, "I don't have the answers. I'm just like you. Only not as smart." He smiled. "Some of the folks that come to my church have a simple faith. When they hurt, they pray. They believe that there is Someone who gathers up all the hurt and makes sure that it isn't wasted. They don't think about it much. It just comes natural to them. Virginia was like that."

"And you?" I asked.

"Well. Me? I'm not sure it matters much to mouthe the words that form my belief. I do my best every day. I try to comfort folks. I try to help people be better human beings in accordance with the Christian notion of what 'better' is, which is a good one in my opinion. I try not to hurt others. I try to enjoy life, such as it is. That's all."

"But if you don't believe in God, then all you do is a lie." I said this not accusingly, more like something I just discovered.

Neither hurt nor angered by my statement, he got up and walked over to the television set and ran his fingers across the top, his back to me. Then he turned around, returned, and sat down in almost the same spot where he had been sitting before.

"Listen, Ismael. I know you're hurting. I know you want me to give you something that you lost. Let me say this. You lost it a while ago. Long before Virginia's funeral. You may think that I don't have faith. But I do have faith. I have faith that some day you will hurt no more. I have faith that all this is nevertheless worthwhile. Right now you want me to give you something I can't give you, wouldn't give you, even if I could. That's one thing I know. When someone is in a no-bullshit place, pardon my French, you have to leave them there until it's time for them to climb right out. I believe that."

I nodded. Outside the small window of his converted garage I could see that it was totally dark. Getting in my car and driving on was not going to be easy. Perhaps I should stop at a motel nearby and wait until the morning. I wondered if Armanda still worked at the Nine Tails after all these years. How would I ever find her? And Lilia. I needed to stop by to see her, even if she didn't recognize me. For one thing, Kate was going to send me my last paycheck along with monies for unused vacation and sick time in care of Lilia's address. It wouldn't be an easy trip and I would have given anything not to start the trip that very night. All of a sudden I remembered that I had left the five-thousand-dollar check that Trudy had given me in the brown book of poems, the one that Trudy had read. My book of poems. My adulterous act. I remembered one of those poems there as I sat on the edge of Reverend Boles's couch looking at the patch of darkness outside:

Come,
rest your head on my shoulder
cry if you like.
Let me fill you with me.
I know you so well,
you don't have to say a word.
The beating of your heart
speaks your fear.
The rushing of your blood is your hope.
How can I show you that I am?
I have no thoughts other than your own.
I have no touch other than what you feel.

DAY 28

Trudy's car was in the driveway. The lights in the kitchen and in the upstairs bedroom were on. All other lights were off. My plan was to go in and get the five-thousand-dollar check inside the book of poems, but where had I left the book? The fact that Trudy was home filled me with ambivalence about whether to leave or not. Why not go in and say, " Hi, I'm back. By the way, we need to get some orange juice because we're running low. I'm back. Everything is back to normal. There was a little bleep on the marriage line. Nothing to worry about. It happens. I'm back. Back to eat breakfast with you on Saturday mornings, to rent movies together, to brush the silk skin of your Aladdin. I'm back to while away my days in companionship with you. That's not so bad. The courtesy and affection that we show each other. Is it so bad? I support you and you support me. Is that so bad?"

The door was locked. I was worried about what my first words would be when I saw her. I was undecided as I went from room to room expecting to see her at any moment reading a magazine on the living room couch with her legs curled underneath her, working on a brief in the den, lying on our bed watching television, or drying her wet face in the bathroom. How beautiful this house was, how comfortable in appearance, how homelike in demeanor. There were little touches of Trudy everywhere. Every room was coordinated in color and theme. There was thoughtfulness everywhere.

Trudy was not around. Was she hiding from me? I made my way down to the basement, the only place I hadn't been. It was cold and unused. There on the floor lay the leather book of poems with the edge of the check sticking out like a bookmark. There against the side of the sofa stood Abuelito's rifle resting peacefully. Trudy was not in the laundry room. I stood in the middle of the room not knowing which way to turn. I whispered Trudy's name and then I said it louder and louder. Then I yelled to her and to everyone that cared to hear that I was sorry. So sorry.

Outside, I saw that in my hands I was holding the book with the check and the rifle, even though I didn't remember grabbing them. It was quiet and cold outside. In the distance I heard Aladdin neigh and hoof, so I headed over there. Perhaps Trudy was there. It was unnaturally cold and my breath was exhaling in unsteady white puffs.

I could never truly tell if Aladdin liked me. I could never read his body signals. Even when he nodded at me with his forehead I wasn't sure whether that was a "glad to see you" or a "go away." He came over when I stretched out my hand and he blinked knowingly, but he seemed to be constantly wary of me. He was not at peace around me the way he was with Trudy. What did he sense about me, I wondered.

When Trudy was in law school there were at least three men who wanted to marry her. It was convenient that they all didn't live in the general vicinity. One was at Harvard finishing law school, another lived in upstate New York, a college professor of some sort, and the third practiced law in a D.C. megafirm. Trudy shuttled back and forth for a while, confused as to which one she should marry.

I know because that was one of our first conversations. We were gathered with a group of first-year law students and I ended up sitting next to her. Someone in the group was kidding Trudy about all the men in her life and she confessed that she did not know whom to marry. I remember telling her as soon as everyone else's attention was someplace else, "It's obvious you don't love any of them. If you're confused, then you do not truly love." It seemed simple and clear to me. Marrying someone was not like picking a college: O.K., this one has a good reputation but is in the middle of the city. This one has junior year abroad but is so far from any culture. . . . This one will graduate from Harvard and probably head for Wall Street. This other one already has a house in a pretty setting, but upstate New York is so damned boring. This one is kind, considerate, and generous, but I'm not terribly attracted to him. This one is sexy but still has growing up to do. Goodness, is that the way it was supposed to work? I didn't think so then, but maybe I was wrong.

One time Trudy and I were working in the barn. Trudy was mucking out the stall and I was carting loads away in a wheelbarrow when out of the blue I said to her, "Trudy, remember when we visited the marriage counselor?"

"Mmmm."

"We never answered her question about what had attracted us to each other. I'd like to know your answer now. Why did you pick me?"

She did not hesitate in her answer, which surprised me. "Because you were the only one who was smarter than I was. I was most of all attracted to your intelligence."

"Really? Smarter than all those other guys?"

"Yes. In a different kind of way, maybe."

"Like how different?"

"Different."

"Wow."

"You seem surprised. You don't believe me?"

"It's not that. I just . . . it's just that I've been thinking lately that any of those other guys would have made you happier. They would have been successful. They were already successful. They were ambitious and competitive and successful in a way that I'm not."

"I thought you would be even more successful," she said, continuing to rake and not looking up. "I thought you were more driven than any of them."

"Driven?"

"Sure. You may not want to admit it to yourself. But you were very driven and ambitious."

"What made you think that?"

"Honestly?"

"Yes. Honestly."

"I guess it was the way you went about winning me over. Just think about how you went about beating the competition. Don't tell me that wasn't competing. It was."

"Competing implies that I went about systematically doing something to get you to prefer me over the others for the simple sake of coming out on top. I don't think I did that. I wanted you, that's all."

"O.K., but you did things that won me over. You bided your time and were tolerant and patient while I was sorting through things. Then at the right time you made your move. Do you remember?"

"I remember that for a while there our courtship was very painful. You were quote-unquote in love with me but you were still seeing those other guys."

"But I stopped."

"Gradually."

"Maybe I still talked to them now and then but I didn't see them after you asked me not to, even though I thought at first that you had no right to ask."

"I don't remember asking."

"Maybe not directly, but you did. Remember the summer after our first year, you went to El Paso, sick of law school. You wrote to me toward the end of the summer. You said that you had been offered a job teaching English literature at a community college and you were going to stay with that woman that you knew. What was her name? She was the woman with the little boy."

"Armanda."

"Right. In the letter you said you had found or rediscovered a world that seemed to fit you better, where you were more—'at ease' were the words you used. So you wrote to say good-bye. Remember that letter?"

"I do."

"Well?"

"Well, what?"

"That was your ultimatum. That was your either me-alone-or-else."

"No, it was true. I did have a job offer and there was an Armanda."

"I know. That's why I knew you weren't bluffing. That's why I wrote right back after I thought long and hard and that's why I called and kept calling, talking to your mother, who preferred me to Armanda anyway, until she made you take the phone. I asked you to come back on your own terms. I told you over the phone that I was, for all intents and purposes, through with the other relationships. I asked you to give law school and us a chance. I told you what you already knew in your heart. That you were about to make a big mistake. You were about to saddle yourself with a kid and a woman who was not of your intellectual level and a job where you would have been bored out of your mind in a few months."

"And look at me now. I mean look at where I am. Do you still think I'm driven and ambitious?"

"I think you're driven and ambitious deep down. Maybe in a way different from me, but you are."

"How so?"

"I don't know. I want to be the best commercial litigator there is and be recognized as such. You want something else . . . you want to be immortal or something."

I stood there poised with a pitchfork of hay looking at Trudy as if I had never seen her before.

"What's the matter?" she asked.

"Nothing. Sometimes the things you say surprise me."

"Something happened to you. I don't know what. Somewhere along the line you sort of gave up. And now it's like you're ashamed of being bright. Like you're afraid of being successful."

"I'm not sure that's true."

"Sure it is. You're very ambitious. And restless. There's something in you that keeps you from being content, that's constantly pushing you to do more and be more. That's why you came back. That's why you chose me over Armanda. You left Armanda because you knew deep down that with her you would never grow."

Trudy began to put the bridle in Aladdin's mouth. I picked up the wheelbarrow and wheeled it to the back of the yard where we dumped the muck. I remember standing there over the hole we had dug thinking about what she had just said. It had the ring of truth but was not quite right, although it was hard—impossible almost—to articulate exactly how it missed the mark. When I got back to the stable, Aladdin's English saddle was already on and Trudy was bending the horse's back leg, filing his hoof.

"So . . . that's what attracted you to me. My ambition and my drive. My intelligence. That's why you picked me? And is that why we're disconnected now, because you think I lost those things?"

She looked up at me for a second and then went back to filing. She was using a big iron file with a wooden handle. The iron was the color of an old telephone pole and the handle was black with age and use. I had picked out the file for Trudy at an antique tool show years before we moved to Oakridge.

"There you go again. You did it with that psychologist and you're doing it again. You make me into this cold bitch image that you have of me. I respected your intelligence and your ambition. That was very important to me. I could never have married anyone whose intelligence I didn't respect and who didn't want to be successful at whatever."

"I'm not trying to make you into anything. It's just that there's something that doesn't sound right. It's all so calculating."

"Ismael, it's O.K. to calculate. We have a brain for a reason. If you don't calculate you make mistakes. Look, what did you do after I called you that time when I asked you to come back? How did you decide to come back to me rather than stay with Armanda? What made you choose me over her? You calculated, right?"

I was silent. Then, after a long while I said, "I must have."

"Right. What's the matter?"

"I'm just wondering."

"About what?"

"I don't know. About love, I guess."

"You don't think the two go together? Love without thinking is something else. Lust, maybe."

"I like lust."

"Yeah. Well, you would."

"I don't know. The word love is confusing to me. At least I know what lust is."

"What is it?"

"It's liking somebody powerfully."

"Liking their body."

"Yeah. But the kind of lust I'm talking about is more than that. It's liking the whole person, who they are, including their body. Wanting to be with them and do things with them including sleep with them. Yes. But not just that. Reading with them, talking to them, being quiet with them, touching them. It's more than just lust, it's more like . . . lovst. That's it. Lovst."

"That's love to me."

"But the difference is that this thing—lovst—is either there or it isn't. I can will love. I can force myself to care for someone and to do things that benefit them and to sacrifice my wishes for theirs, but I can't force myself to lovst that person."

"Well, I guess I disagree. Love to me is the decision made over and over again to stay with a person."

As I petted the undemonstrative Aladdin and recalled that poignant conversation with my wife, I asked myself what Trudy had meant when she said that love was a decision to stay with a person. At what cost was this supposed to be true? I walked out of the stalls and slowly headed back to my car. In the cold and dark patch of world that used to be my home, I realized that I should have pushed Trudy and I should have pushed myself about how we both saw love. I should have pushed further about when and where she thought I lost what she once thought I had; but I didn't, because I was afraid. I've always been afraid. Of things. Of truth. Of Trudy.

Now Trudy was nowhere to be found, and I was leaving. Or rather, I was being taken away by forces I could not control. I was opening the door to my car, putting Abuelito's rifle in the back seat along with the book of poems and check, all the while looking around me the way the recently dead must look at things.

I saw across my yard the front light of Bartholomew Meagher's house. What if Trudy was with him? I managed somehow to redirect the current taking me away from my house. I jumped the fence that I had criminally and tortiously jumped before, and I headed toward the great bay window from which I could now hear the sound of music mixed with laughter. I was on my knees crawling under the window. The laughter coming from inside sounded painfully like the half-screeches, half-giggles that Trudy emitted on particular occasions. I saw her in my mind on top of Bart the Fart riding to the finish line, tossing her hair sideways and tilting her head back in abandon. I slowly craned my neck to look inside.

She was there. Trudy was there. My heart was popping out of my chest. I looked again. She and Bart were sitting face to face on two Windsor chairs across a coffee table that was shaped like a wheelbarrow, a glass cover where the barrow used to be. Trudy had her back to the window, so I could not see her face. I could see her tan riding pants and her black knee-high riding boots. The tan riding pants had a patch of soft leather across her bum to protect her from the chafing horseback or saddle. Why was she wearing that particular tight-fitting outfit? Meagher was all smiles, sipping little sips of red wine and carefully putting his crystal goblet on a coaster the size and shape of a giant poker chip. Curling laughter came from both of them again. The thickness of the glass window and the music, which sounded like Al Jarreau, prevented me from hearing their conversation. I placed my ear against the side of the house, but all I heard was the coldness of the stone. This was crazy. I was ashamed as I saw myself on my knees, my head against a stone wall trying to listen to a conversation between my wife and another man. I was, after all, jealous or humiliated. I didn't know which or maybe both. There was also that anger which now had permanently settled, found a cozy corner in my stomach, and was emanating something that was bitter and constant. I could yield to that anger and do something right then and there. Instead, I sat against the wall. Who was I to be angry? Not more than two hours earlier I was at Kate's, and now I was on my way to Armanda. Who the fuck was I to be angry at Trudy? I crawled away from the window. I looked up at the sky and felt trapped despite its immensity, trapped, as if the sky were not a real sky but simply a canvas, like Van Gogh's *Starry Night*, and I was somewhere in there stuck in a tiny corner, disguised as a stroke of black paint.

DAY 29

I drove south in the general direction of Armanda. I planned only two stops, one in Mobile, Alabama, to see Spring Hill College and one in Harlingen, Texas, to see Lilia. I drove slowly, in no hurry to get anywhere. At my own speed. Stopping as I pleased. Taking detours as I saw fit. I didn't talk to many people along the way. And the people that I did talk to seemed to have been put there to give me a message that could only be deciphered later, much later.

There was the young woman in Charleston, where I detoured for a day so that I could see the sea. We must have talked for five hours, first on the beach and then back in town at a coffee shop filled with tour guides and off-duty cab drivers. She told me about going into hiding for two years when her world was falling apart.

She said she had placed herself in voluntary isolation in a little shack that her mother had near Myrtle Beach until she learned how not to hurt others or herself. She said that she knew she was healed when one morning she saw a moth the size of a basketball perched right outside her door. She said that seeing that moth was like seeing a creature from another world. It scared her and fascinated her almost shitless. The landscape of lunar grays, the hidden eyes on the moth's back, the two antennae, the folded wings that could spring open at any second, the dusty, feltlike fur of the moth's being. She knew she was cured from the need to hurt when she realized that she and that creature shared life on this planet.

There was the old man in the Wal-Mart just outside Pensacola where I stopped to buy some extra clothes. I was in line waiting to pay for a shirt, a package of three underwear, five tube socks for three ninety-nine, and a pair of gray work pants when I offered to let him cut in front of me since he was only buying a package of razor blades. He declined my offer and instead proceeded to make loud conversation right then and there. He insisted on buying me a cup of soup in the store's snack bar after we finished paying for our things, perhaps taking me for some kind of luck-less bum. He showed me a medal that had been given to him for valor beyond the call of duty during World War II. He said he had kept on fighting even after he was wounded and his fellow sol-diers retreated. He said he was just a nineteen-year-old kid that didn't know no better and, imagine, the government went and gave him a medal for just trying to stay alive. Then I gave him a ride back to his home, which was only a couple of blocks from the store and he showed me his whittling collection. Little miniature sculptures, some the size of my little finger, that he had made from dry branches and driftwood, all in the shape of different ani-mals and forms. Thousands of pieces. All over. On window ledges, on top of the TV, on bookcases, on kitchen cabinets. His wife had died a few months before, and she used to dust them with lemon oil, so now they didn't look quite as good. He asked me to pick one for my own. I took one in the shape of a mountain lion, and I kept it in my pocket until my arrest, when all the pos-sessions on my person were confiscated and not returned until after the trial.

There was most of all a rush of memories and images and a feeling of not knowing what had really happened and what I had imagined. They came at me, these memories and images, like the white lines of the highway, one after another, going past me fast and blurred.

Memory of one day getting a letter in my quiescent Boston suburb. It stood out from among the pile because it came in the thin envelopes marked with green and red Mexican stripes. My name and address were written on the front with a very careful and ornate handwriting, the kind that used to be taught in Mexican schools. I opened it and read the words dictated by Renata to her twelve-year-old niece. Renata said that she was very sick. That after years and years of taking care of her mother and her father, these two had finally died and now she was sick and in the hospital from where she was writing to me. She had a little medal and some other things that she had kept. These belonged to me and she wanted me to have them but she did not know how to send them to me. She was afraid to mail them. Then the letter ended, saying "tu nana que te quiere como una madre." Then there was another page written by the niece. She said that Renata was very ill. Los doctores no creen que vaya a vivir mucho. All she did was talk about how she wanted to see me before she died. Could I come to see her, please?

Could I come to see her before she died? Could I travel from Boston to Tampico to see the maid who took care of the boy? Could I come to see her before she died? No, I couldn't. It did not seem possible. It was only a short time before that we had gone through all that expense and time off to take care of Lilia. And Trudy was with me lovingly and ungrudgingly. Lilia was my mother, and it was proper that I take care of her in her hour of need. So I had taken two weeks off to be with Lilia. I found a very nice place for her in Harlingen, Texas. A warm place where María del Carmen, Lilia's remaining sister, could come to visit from Tampico. So off I went in a rented van with Lilia's TV set and easy chair and the chest of drawers that I had to dump behind the Piggly Wiggly grocery store in Harlingen because the nursing home would not let me bring it into her room. During part of the visit Lilia thought I was Perry Como and during another part she thought I was Antonio, the love of her life and my natural begetter.

And now another trip was called for. Another final letter calling for courage that just wasn't there. Another call from a person, a member of this world, who wanted me to be there at a deciding point in her life. Was I responsible for Renata? How was I to respond to her obvious love for me? Just how far do the ripples of love spread and what are its obligations? Are there degrees of duty depending on familial ties, on intensity of feeling? What gives? Could we not send money? Could we not get María del Carmen to visit her and pick up the little medal? Yes, of course we could. I agreed. It was too hard to go. I didn't even suggest that I should go. I wanted so very much to go. I did not.

María del Carmen called me to tell me that Renata had died the day after she had gone to visit her per my request. Renata appeared glad to give her the little medal, which she was sending to me, along with Renata's obituary. After María del Carmen called to tell me of Renata's death, I saw Renata's sweet face every time I closed my eyes. Every time I closed my eyes, no matter where I was, she would be there in front of me, smiling, calling me her son. Her image never went totally away, although at times it faded.

Now when I close my eyes I see her easily and naturally. She is there. Every time. Only now, I have developed the ability to add to her face the other ghosts of my early life: Lilia, Abuelito, Theodore, my own childhood face. Still, these other faces I must recall by mental command. Only Renata appears willy-nilly on her own. Even Lilia's painful grimace, the one she made a few seconds before dying, even that is faded. On the other hand, Renata is there. Except for the fact that I cannot control her presence, it is not scary at all to have her there. Quite the contrary.

Memory of Mimi carrying me into the warm waters of the Gulf of Mexico and at my urging showing me one of her big white breasts. I can still remember the pleasure and the fear of the revelation. With her back to the beach so that the rest of the family would not see her, Mimi kept going deeper, bobbing up and down with the waves. And there I was, hanging on to her neck, taking it all in, my giant pacifier.

Memories of Tampico, the place where I grew up, thank you, Fate, and the undisputed sin capital of the world. If you were to take a walk in the hot, sweaty sun of Tampico and sip cold lemonade at the noon-time meal, and if you were to sit by the beach in the evening with the cool breeze and the distant smell of rotten fish and salt and fumes from the refineries, you would know exactly what I am talking about.

Imagined memory of Lilia and Antonio on their own two feet, illegitimately begetting me, too impatient to lie down. I see them in the backyard of Abuelito's house, early in the evening when everyone has gone in to listen to the radio. I see Lilia and Antonio hiding behind the mango tree, Lilia kissing, groping, and swatting mosquitoes from her butt all at the same time.

Memory of my beloved whores. In Tampico, below the Plaza de Armas but before you get to the Mercado Municipal, I could walk and see the whores sitting by the windows fanning themselves with paper fans that have a picture of a Chinese woman drinking Coca-Cola. There they were. Las Putas. The whores. Behind barred windows, in shiny dresses, freshly bathed and talcumed and smelling of gardenias. As I think back on all the places I have been, and, except for the time I spent with you, Armanda, I don't think I ever felt as much at home as I did those afternoons walking past the sweet-smelling whores of Tampico.

Half-imagined, half-remembered memory of flesh and holiness indistinguishable. When Lilia was six months pregnant she went to Monterrey to live with the Sisters of the Sacred Heart. Everyone thought it would be better if she wasn't around when the baby was born. Not that Abuelito was particularly enraged. He took the news of the pregnancy calmly, as if he had already predicted the event in his mind. He asked Lilia who the father was but Lilia refused to tell him.

"If you don't want to tell me, that's your business," he said. "But don't dishonor the family."

Consuelo and María del Carmen, Lilia's two sisters, interpreted this to mean that she could not keep the baby. And so around the sixth month when the baby started to show, Lilia went to Monterrey to have the baby and everyone was told that she had gone to Mexico City to stay with Tía Carmelita and her crazy sister, Lele.

To hear Lilia tell it, the three months with the Sisters of the Sacred Heart was more than adequate retribution for her sin of passion.

"I was bored crazy," she said. "I crocheted tablecloths and I read. I read and read and read. I read all the novels of Galdós, and then some."

It didn't take the Sisters very long to find someone who would adopt the future baby. A very "upper crust" couple from Monterrey who were unable to beget in their own right. According to the Sisters, they were overjoyed at the prospect of being a mother and father.

Lilia visited the house where the baby was to live and saw the room where the baby would sleep.

"The wallpaper was light green with little red and green turtles," she said. "It would have been perfect for a boy or a girl."

Lilia took an immediate liking to the couple. She believed that the baby would be happy with them.

Once the baby was born and Lilia held him, she changed her mind about the adoption. She told the Sisters to apologize to the couple for raising their hopes in vain. The Sisters argued with her, reminding her of Abuelito, of the scandal she would cause if people in Tampico found out she had a baby on the sly. Lilia replied that she wasn't sure whether she would ever return to Tampico. All she knew was that the baby was hers and that was that.

Back in the convent, the baby was a hit. The Sisters couldn't get enough of him. They passed him around from Sacred Bosom to Sacred Bosom. They took greedy turns giving him his mamila and talcuming his little bum. He was adored like a little baby Jesus.

Lilia waited in the convent another six months, crocheting tablecloths until they were coming out her ears. One day the mailman brought a letter from Abuelito. He wanted Lilia and the baby to come back to Tampico, wagging tongues be damned.

Abuelito's house was a two-story wooden house made with the best American wood. It had been by far the best house in the neighborhood until Mr. Cedina, who owned the Coca-Cola plant in Tampico, built a brick house across the street. Unfortunately for Mr. Cedina, the brilliance of the brick palace was dimmed by the little shack next to his property that Abuelito had built for Tío Pancho, Abuelito's hermit brother. Abuelito refused to be either intimidated or rewarded out of his property.

At first, the baby and Lilia slept downstairs in the room next to Abuelito. The baby slept in a hammock tied to two perpendicular walls. When the baby cried, Renata, who slept in a cot next to the hammock, would pull a rope tied to the hammock and rock the baby until he stopped crying. When the boy got a little older, Lilia took the boy to her bedroom upstairs and put him in a crib next to her bed. When the boy cried, she would ring a bell next to her bed and Renata would come.

Renata was the boy's nana. She slept in a tiny room right off the entrance to the house. The boy liked going into Renata's room. It was like being inside Captain Nemo's submarine. There was a bed, a chair, a dresser and a radio. There was one small window that could not be reached even when standing on top of the bed on tiptoes. Renata and the boy listened to the afternoon soap operas on the radio. Lilia by this time had gone back to work at the B.F. Goodrich tire dealer. She was a secretary to Mr. Berfeler, the owner of the store and one of the richest men in Tampico.

Renata was not like Lilia. She was stricter and could see through the boy's tantrums. Renata got mad when the boy pretended to be sick so that he wouldn't have to go to school.

"He is not really sick," she would tell Abuelito and Lilia.

"Let him stay home if he wants," said Abuelito.

The boy would stick his tongue out at Renata.

On Mondays Lilia got paid, and when she came home she would bring the boy a present. Usually it was a comic book or something or other bought from the dark man who spread a blanket full of colorful toys on the sidewalk next to the B.F. Goodrich store. Some days

Lilia would not come home until very late. On those days the boy waited up with Renata until he could no longer keep his eyes open.

One night after he had fallen asleep waiting, the boy woke up to the sound of Lilia wailing. When he opened his eyes, the lights were on and Renata was trying to control the flailing arms of Lilia. Abuelito was in a long nightshirt uselessly ordering Lilia to calm down. When the boy started crying himself, Renata came over and caressed his head and told him that Lilia was all right, that the doctor was on his way.

Lilia calmed down after she was given an injection from a syringe that came out of a case that looked like a tiny silver coffin. When Lilia dozed off and the boy was being rocked by Renata, he overheard Renata telling Mrs. Cedina, who had come over to see what the excitement was about, that Antonio, the love of Lilia's life and the father of the boy, had died that afternoon after a short bout with cancer. The boy never saw him.

Memory of my "real" father. Theodore was my father. Believe me, I do not use the word lightly. For seven years or so he was my father. An old retired Dutchman who had come to Tampico for adventure. He ended up with Lilia and me.

I remember Theodore sitting in the living room of Abuelito's house explaining how he planned to marry Lilia, adopt me, and support the three of us with a social security check that seemed immense when translated into pesos but which turned out to be chicken shit in the States where Theodore eventually brought his new family.

Of all the places in the world, Theodore picked two acres of desert land on the outskirts of El Paso. We had the good fortune of being the first ones there. Not one house around for five miles. Theodore built the foundation, dug the cesspool himself, and had the house brought over by a giant trailer all the way from Odessa.

I spent my non-school days in desert warfare, battling sandstorms, collecting scorpions and horny toads, and watching big black beetles roll little balls of rabbit doo around in the sand. On school days I was driven twenty-two miles to the nearest public school where I, among other things, learned to speak English willy-nilly.

Lilia, in the meantime, was going batty. Lilia, the queen of conversation, had no one to talk to except Theodore, and then after a while, only me.

"The things I did for you," she would say to me later, after Theodore, the crazy Dutchman, had decided to end his life by crashing into a train overpass. "That was more than was expected from any mother. I married him for your sake. And I lived in that hellhole for your sake. I was never the same after that. That's when my nervous condition started, you know that. No, Ismael. You cannot complain about your mother and what she went through for you."

As time went by, Lilia spent more and more time visiting Abuelito in Tampico, leaving Theodore and me to deal with the smell of adult urine and migraines that incapacitated Theodore for days at a time. During the summers, I joined Lilia. My favorite part of those summers were his letters. They were about eight pages long, always addressed to me. He told me about almost landing a job, about making plans to install a sure-fire irrigation system that would finally sprout some grass; also, about my buddy Norberto twelve miles down the road, about the tulips that had bloomed in the desert, and the giant flagpole he had erected where he proudly flew our American flag.

One day I woke up to the sound of Theodore yelling. I looked outside my bedroom window and saw a trailer like the one that had brought the house from Odessa. They had come to take the house away. Theodore held them back with shouts and threats and promises to send a check covering the balance owed, but a month later they were back with the sheriff and the house was gone. We moved into a motel not too far from my school. Lilia had a nervous breakdown that landed her in the hospital. She was taken away by ambulance, sobbing uncontrollably. A few weeks later, Theodore convinced the owner of a brand-new sixty-foot mobile home that he was solvent enough to make the monthly payments, and we were off to the races again. Lilia took off for Tampico. She tried to take me with her, but I managed to convince her that it would be detrimental to my fledgling academic career if I left.

Soon Theodore got a very formal letter from Abuelito. If he was not able to provide for his daughter and his grandson as he had promised, then it would be best if daughter and grandson returned permanently to Tampico. Lilia would remain in Tampico and the boy was to be sent as soon as the school year was over. Theodore read me the letter.

"What would you like to do? he asked.

"I want to stay," I answered.

"Then, that's what we'll do," he said.

When summer came, I wrote to Lilia and told her that I did not want to go back. I told her, with a maturity beyond my ten years, that her place was with us. She had to give Theodore another chance. Lilia returned. She had only one condition. She wanted me transferred from the public school to the nearer Catholic parochial school. What that had to do with anything, I do not know. Perhaps it was her way of striking at the heart of the atheistic Theodore. Theodore, predictably, had a Dutch fit. Over his dead body would he let namby-pamby nuns fill the boy's head with mumbo jumbo. Why, those folks did not even believe in evolution. Father Sepúlveda, whom Lilia befriended, had told him so himself in one of his futile attempts at converting Theodore: We come directly from God. No monkey business.

Lilia was steadfast. Theodore was, too.

That night, Theodore was at the kitchen table puffing Lucky Strikes and drinking black coffee. Sheets of architectural plans were spread across the table and on the floor. It was Theodore's dream house. Little rooms and little doors that opened just so. Everything to perfect scale.

"It would probably be best for everyone if I went to Mt. Carmel," I said.

"What do you know?" he asked.

"I want to go," I said. "You may not believe in God, but I do."

Theodore looked at me long and steadily and then told me to go to sleep.

When Lilia came back, she took me to buy the gray pants and the white shirt that I would need for my first day of school.

And so it went. The mobile home too was taken away one day, but Theodore kept bouncing back with another place to live. Now and then he would land a job, or rather, someone would give him the "opportunity" to earn a commission by selling something or other. My favorite product was the liquid that would give car batteries eternal life, absolutely, or your money back. I enjoyed watching Theodore walk up to car owners who had left on their car lights by mistake and hear his pitch about how with the little bottle of elixir they need not ever worry about a dead battery again.

Father Sepúlveda introduced Lilia to some friends and in the years that preceded Theodore's death, she seemed more resigned to her fate, although she went to Tampico whenever she could. In fact, she was with Abuelito in Tampico the Sunday afternoon when Sheriff Williams, who also moonlighted as my Boy Scout leader, came by to tell me that Theodore had died instantaneously in a car accident.

Sundays were unusual days, anyway. I had decided, against Theodore's express directions, to continue as altar boy at Our Lady of Mt. Carmel. So Sundays were usually full of danger and intrigue as I went through a ritual of sneaking my altar boy cassock out the back way, placing it on my bicycle, and then telling Theodore that I was going out to ride bikes with friends. I had done this ever since Theodore caught me on the way to Father Sepúlveda's church, the black cassock flying in my face. Theodore stopped the car, grabbed my bike and threw it in the back of our Rambler station wagon. He and I rode in stony silence until we got home.

"What the hell are you doing?" he asked when we arrived and were getting out of the car.

"I want to do it," I said.

"It's such nonsense!" he said angrily, and I was afraid he was going to belt me across the face as he did when I did or said something that went beyond bad.

"It is not!" I said defiantly.

"Oh, bullshit," he said. "Why can't they leave you alone?" By "they," he meant Father Sepúlveda and Lilia.

"It's my choice," I said.

"Poppycock!" That was one of his favorite words (and one of my favorite ones to hear him say). "You are thirteen years old. Why don't they leave you be a normal boy?"

"I am normal," I said, somewhat hurt.

"That is such bullshit," he said. "Don't you think I know how much time you spend with that stuff? Don't you think I know about the foolish religious comic books that you hide under your bed? Don't you think I've seen you sleeping on the floor? Why do you do that? What have you done that you must punish yourself? Goddamn it! That's not right. You're supposed to be a boy. Play baseball. Look at girlie magazines. Pull your weenie. Be like other boys. Why do you sleep on the floor?"

"I want to do it," I said. I didn't feel like dwelling on this any further.

"Goddamn it to hell," he said.

So from then on I played hide-and-seek with my religious duties and the subject was never again broached, except perhaps indirectly a week or two before he died. Lilia had already left for Tampico and Theodore and I found ourselves fighting for the bathroom in the middle of the night, both of us racked with diarrhea cramps. Theodore's theory, which I accepted at the time, was that I was leaving a residue of detergent on the dishes and that this was the cause for our intestinal malfunctioning. I myself think now that it was more the constant barrage of creditors and the worry of how to pay them or how to evade them that kept us both loose inside.

He and I were fully awake around 3:00 A.M. sitting on the edge of his bed. He had just finished showing me the place in the closet where he kept all the life insurance policies and other important documents, including my adoption papers. He gave me very detailed instructions about how I was supposed to call a certain lawyer in town in case something happened to him. I was silent for a long time, wondering why he was telling me all this and what it would feel like to be without him. Then I asked him.

"Dad, how can you live without any hope of life . . . after you die? Don't you believe in something?"

"I believe in man," he said after some reflection. "I believe in the dignity of man. I don't need to believe in anything else."

That Sunday morning I walked in front of him with my cassock dangling over my shoulder, for some reason not feeling the need to hide from him anymore. He was sitting on the sofa, his gaze fixed on the decision he had, I now believe, already taken. I kissed him on the top of his bald head and said, "See you later, Daddy-o." He looked at me differently from any way that he had looked at me before and said good-bye.

Lilia arrived the day after the funeral. She had gone with some American friends to tour interior Mexico, so she could not be reached in time. Father Sepúlveda took me in until she got there. I slept in the recently deceased Father McCormack's room. The room was filled with statues of some of my favorite saints: St. Francis of Assisi with a bird perched on his finger and San Martín de Porres with a broom held against his chest, his look transfixed by a heavenly visitation.

One of the first things that Lilia said after she recovered from an annoyingly long crying fit was that she had heard from Father Sepúlveda that Theodore had killed himself. Mrs. Álvarez, the lady who lived in front of the overpass, had told Father Sepúlveda that when she heard the crash, she saw from her living room window a bloodied Theodore reverse the mangled Rambler about a hundred feet or so and then with full force ram the overpass again, half his body flying through the recently cracked windshield.

I found the insurance policies just where Theodore had told me they would be. There were seven policies. Some of them Theodore had kept for years, others he had bought as recently as the year before. All the premiums, every one of them, had been meticulously paid even though the monthly payments totaled almost half of what Theodore received in monthly income from his social security check and even though we had been living on Campbell's soup and crackers for the past three months. After lawyer's fees and after we paid Father Sepúlveda what we owed him, Lilia and I had about twenty thousand dollars left. That, and the social security benefits that Lilia and I would receive until I was eighteen (or twenty-two if I went to college) was more than enough for the two of us to live on. Lilia bought a white Falcon with red bucket seats, and as soon as her application was accepted, she moved both of us to subsidized housing.

DAY 30

It was evening when I got to Spring Hill College. I wasn't going to stay long. All I was interested in was taking the walk that I used to with Father Yakahima. The walk was about half a mile long, starting by the cemetery where the bodies of the Jesuits lie interred in simple anonymity and ending down the hill in a dark green pond, thick as gumbo soup.

I remember the first time: One evening around eleven, the phone rang. It was Father Yakahima asking if I wanted to walk down to the pond.

"There's a fucking hurricane passing through Mobile!"

"I know it," he said. "Meet me by cemetery. Ten minutes. I have flashlight."

His flashlight was a big red Eveready with a big handle and a big square battery. He was pointing it at the ground there by one of the graves. When he saw me he shined the light at the path he wanted us to take. We didn't say anything, mostly because we wouldn't have been able to hear our voices even if we had yelled. The wind and the rain were whipping so hard it hurt. We had to grab onto trees, to bushes, to each other or else we would have been buffeted away. Soon the only way to advance was on our hands and knees, feeling our way in front of us like blind and legless men. It was so loud and it was so certain that both of us were going to die at any instant that the only thing that we could do was shout, Oh Shit! Oh Shit! and laugh hysterically. When we finally made it to the pond, Yakahima began to take his clothes off and gestured at me to do the same. He found a rock to stick them under and without any ceremony whatsoever, he leapt into the black pond. I waited for him forever to pop his head up again, and when he did, he let out a tremendous yell loud enough to be heard even through the storm. I jumped in also and found the water in the pond warmer than the rain outside. My feet sank into a soft muck that after the first shock was actually caressing. I could feel green lily pods and cattails sur-

167

round and tickle me, and I could feel cold rain and wind pelt my head. Then my heart stopped and jolted into a cavity I never knew I had, as I felt in the black water a clamp on my ankles, and for a fraction of a second I pictured that two hands had emerged from the muck and gripped them. But I realized that it was only Yakahima when his head popped up in front of me and he was laughing, laughing, laughing.

The gray-haired Yakahima taught the two-semester history of philosophy course along with Father Pearse. We called them all kinds of names. The Jesuit tag team. The one-two punch. Ying and Yang. They were a living, walking synthesis to life's eternal dialectic between passion and reason. In the course, they each taught (and played) the philosophers they liked. Yakahima was Plato; Pearse, Aristotle. Yakahima was Augustine. Pearse was Aquinas. Kierkegaard and Hegel. Intuition and deduction. Yakahima and Pearse, the two great pigeonholes into which everything is wedged: Yakahima, full of life and mystery and self-expression. Pearse, orderly, methodical, tranquil. Yakahima was my friend; Pearse, my guide.

When you walked into Pearse's little room in the Jesuit's residence, he would give you his rocking chair and he himself would pull up his desk chair and proceed to listen to you as if you were the only thing worth listening to in the world. Then invariably you would say something that would cause him to go to one of dozens of shoe boxes that were filled with cards and which were stacked on top of his desk, on top of file cabinets, on bookcases, and on the floor. On each card he had a saying, something written by the countless philosophers and other great minds who had taken all too seriously this thing we call life. There was Duns Scotus (his favorite), Whitehead, and Plotinus, and even meaningful verses from his fellow Jesuit, Gerard Manley Hopkins. Pearse would find the right one sooner or later, the one that would clarify and shed light, and he would read it to you apropos of what you were saying, to show you that you were in good company.

It was Yakahima himself who thought I should ask Pearse to be my spiritual advisor, the person who would guide me in my budding prayer life. He thought it would be good for me to have a dose of Pearse's common sense. So it was Pearse and not Yakahima to whom I revealed, with some hesitation, my one incursion into madness.

"I want to tell you something that happened to me last week," I said to him one time, when our session was almost over. "I was doing the walking meditation that you suggested. It was in the early evening, by the frog pond. As I walked I was hit by a force that blasted me. It came from inside and from outside at the same time and it lifted both my feet off the ground and threw me face down on the grass."

Father Pearse drew his chair closer to me. He had a concerned look on his face.

"What did you feel?"

"I felt at once unworthy of any love and loved beyond any bounds imaginable. But the love was powerful and uncontrollable and I had no choice but to receive it. It was terrifying, but I felt no fear."

"Ahh."

"What was it?"

"Mmmm. What did you think when this was happening?"

"The whole thing only lasted twenty seconds or so. There was no room for thinking. Although I heard this voice in my head when I was pinned to the ground. It was my voice but I was not speaking. It was speaking of its own accord. I could only listen. It could have said anything it wanted. I had no control."

"And what did the voice say?"

"Please don't laugh. The voice called my name; it said, 'Ismael, Ismael, you are my beloved son with whom I am well pleased.'"

I paused to try to read in Father Pearse's face any sign that I was totally gone, that I was finally over the edge. But there was no smiling of any sort. His brows were knit in deep reflection.

"What was it? It was very scary."

"Nothing to be worried about."

"But I thought I was going crazy. A few seconds after it happened while I was still shaking the dust from my clothes, I wasn't sure that it had ever happened. Even now I'm not sure. I could have imagined the whole thing."

"Yes. These things have an air of unreality. In a sense, all of our interior life is like that."

"But what happened? And why do I feel embarrassed to talk about it?"

"Those events are like dreams. Their meaning can only be figured out by the dreamer himself. A dream interpreter can give various interpretations but it is only the dreamer that can say, yes, that interpretation is true. The truth to the dream is the meaning and the sense that the dream has for the person's life, you see. So it is with what happened to you. You have to discover the meaning. You have to patiently wait for its meaning to be revealed to you as your life unfolds. In a sense, you have to make the meaning, if you will. It will be your belief in the meaning and what you do with it that makes it true. Am I making any sense?"

"Sort of. But I'm in the dark and would like to understand."

Pearse smiled with kindly eyes.

"The best advice I can give you is to honor the experience but not be anxious about it. Keep it inside you as a comfort and as a remembrance. Its power will always be there and you can tap it as you will in ways that will be revealed to you. These types of things are gifts to be accepted gratefully. If they happen, they happen. The life of the spirit is usually much more ordinary. It is what you do every day, every second, even. It is what you do with the mentally handicapped people that you work and live with or with the migrant farm workers with whom you spend your summers or with your roommate or with me right now. St. Theresa of Ávila had a saying. I wonder where I put it. Let me see. Oh, let me just paraphrase it. I'll find the exact quote later. She said that when the wind blows we should put out our sail and when it doesn't, we should row. You see, we should concentrate on the rowing. That's what we can do. We should have the sail ready to set, and we should set it and let the wind fill it when the wind comes. But mostly our job is to row."

"In which direction?" I asked.

"Ahh. That's the rub. Row in the direction of the experience you just had. Row as God's beloved son. But even if you go astray, sooner or later there will come a new gust. When it comes, adjust your sail accordingly."

A few months before the end of my senior year, Father Yakahima and I were walking. It was late afternoon. The azaleas and camellias were in bloom. Pink, lavender, blue, white. Spanish moss hung from the giant oaks like a woman letting down her hair. Father Yakahima was walking fast for me, normal for him. I had trouble keeping up.

"So which way are you going to go?" he asked without slowing down.

"What do you mean?"

"What you going to do after you graduate?"

"Go to Columbia, I guess. Accept their scholarship. It's a good school and it's free."

"Yes. Very good school."

"I take it you don't approve. I'm not going to be a fucking Jesuit."

"I'd like to be a fucking Jesuit. Ha! Just kidding."

"I think I can do some good as a lawyer, and besides, I need to make a living. I have my mother whom I need to support."

"No doubt."

"You don't think I'm doing the right thing?"

"What I think not important. What you think?"

"I think that a law degree from a prestigious law school will give me the power to be effective. To do good. I think I can be a good lawyer."

"But what you like to do? Deep in here. What gives you joy?"

"There you go again."

"No, I'm serious. Of all the things you did in college, what do you like most?"

"The most? The very most?"

"Yes."

"Marybeth Fratillo."

"Shhh. Now. Why you want get an old man excited?"

"I liked writing those short stories that were published in *The Motley*."

"Good stories. Filthy, but good."

"It was fun."

"God wants you to have fun."

"Even when others are suffering?"

"Oh, boy. Where you get such ideas? Why you want to be a saint so bad?"

"Comic books."

"Comic books?"

"When I was growing up in Mexico they had these comic books called *Vidas Ilustres*. They were the lives of the Saints. I collected them all. They came out every Sunday. I bought them after Mass. During the week I tried to be like the saint I had read about."

"No wonder you're so messed up!"

"You don't think God wants us to be saints?"

"No. God wants us to be human beings. That's plenty hard."

"So what should I do?"

"That's for you to decide. I can tell you what I would do."

"What?"

"Find a way to listen to the voice in my heart and then do that. The rest will take care of itself."

I finally located Father Yakahima's gravestone. He had died fifteen years earlier. His stone was still white and was situated in the last row. Father Pearse's was there also. He had died a year after Father Yakahima. I believe that Father Pearse must have been lonely without Yakahima making him laugh irreverently. I lay face down on Father Yakahima's grave, my hands touching the soft green grass. I called to him once softly by name. Then I did the same on Father Pearse's grave.

The light from my flashlight was yellow, not white. It had been in the glove compartment of my car forever. The batteries were waning. It took me a while to find the path to the pond. Things had changed. New buildings had gone up. I found a path which seemed as if it were headed in the right direction, so I took it. Some place in the middle of the path my light went out. I shook the flashlight and got one final flicker before it petered out for good. I proceeded along in darkness by touching the branches on the side of the path and by feeling the dirt of the path with my feet. When my eyes adjusted, the half-moon gave off enough light for me to distinguish shapes. There was a clearing up ahead. It was the pond that gently opened up to me as another patch of black. The frogs and crickets were croaking and chirping up a symphony. I walked to the edge and took my clothes off. I stood naked, poised to jump, when suddenly I heard a noise different from the cacophony of frogs. I listened. They were human noises coming from the other side of the pond. I walked in that direction. The noises became slowly more distinguishable. A giggle. A sigh. A groan as if someone were in pain. Then I recognized the sounds of lovemaking. In front of me was a sleeping bag that was closed almost completely, but which was alive with lumps and shapes that heaved and moved like some kind of furry caterpillar crossing a road, inching its way to safety. I took a step closer and in doing so snapped a twig. The bag stopped moving.

"What's the matter?" said a male voice inside.

"I thought I heard something," said a female voice.

A hand stuck out and opened the bag. Then a head with blondish touseled hair popped up and looked at me standing a few feet away.

"Aaahh, shit!" yelled the blond head.

"Aaah, shit!" I yelled back.

"Who is it?" screeched a female voice.

"Who the fuck are you, you pervert?"

"I'm leaving. I didn't know you were here," I said.

"Let me outta here! I'm going to kick your ass!"

"What are you doing?" asked the female voice, alarmed.

Then in a flash he was out of the bag and was pushing me and swinging at me. I grabbed his arms and we grappled like naked Greek wrestlers trying to get a good arm hold. We came down on the ground with him on top and he pounded the sides of my head with his fists. With my open palm I jammed the tip of his nose upward and when he raised his hands to his face in pain, I turned him around and put my knees on his arms and my hands around his throat. His nose was bleeding and lather was coming out his mouth. I held him that way even though his partner was now pulling my hair and kicking me in the back. I squeezed him so hard his eyes were beginning to bulge out of his sockets.

"Stop or I'll kill him," I said.

When she let go of my hair and stopped hitting me, I turned around and looked at her. She was naked. We were all naked, I noticed for the first time. She looked so young. Kids, really. What was I doing?

"Let him go. Let him go." She was sobbing now, pushing at my shoulder, gently.

"I'll let you go. But you have to stay put. I came here to jump in the pond. I meant no harm. I'm going to let you go now. O.K.? You're going to stay put?"

He blinked "yes" with his eyes.

"O.K."

I released my grip and got slowly up. She kneeled down with him while he stayed on his back rubbing his throat.

"I'm sorry," I said. "I'm sorry this had to happen."

DAY 31

The St. Anthony's Convalescent Home in Harlingen is a one-story brick building with wings spreading in different directions like a good game of Scrabble. The parking lot faces the building across Rio Grande Avenue, which has traffic even at 6:00 in the morning.

Around 7:00 A.M. people began arriving at the St. Anthony's Convalescent Home. There were also some nurses in white uniforms coming out to the corner to wait for the first early morning bus. I got out of my car and entered. The place was strangely quiet. They had done everything they could to make it look decidedly unlike a convalescent home. As you entered there was a small lobby with oak bookcases and easy chairs. The bookcases were filled with the *Reader's Digest.* Everything looked exactly the same as it did nine years earlier when I first brought Lilia here. There was a small office where a big black nurse was getting ready to start the day. I introduced myself and asked if I could see Lilia.

"Oh," she said, "you're Mr. Díaz. We've been looking for you." The way she said it, she made it seem as if I'd won the lottery.

"You have?"

"Why sure. We tried everywhere. We called you at home but your wife said you weren't there no more. Then we called you at work and they said you didn't work there, neither. Then your wife called us back and said that you might be coming here directly. Then you also got a letter which I have someplace in here, let me see." She pulled a green file from an organizer on top of her desk. "Yes. Here it is. You want it?"

I took the letter and glanced at the return address. It was from Kate. Probably the check she said she would send. I put it in my back pocket.

"Why were you looking for me?"

She came over and sat me down in one of the chairs in front of her desk. She sat down in the other. She was looking very serious.

"I'm afraid I have to tell you that your mother is very ill. Very ill."

"How ill?" I asked.

"Very ill. Matter of fact, Doctor Sánchez thinks she's gonna leave us any day now. She got liver cancer. It just came to her like that." She snapped her fingers.

"Can I see her, please?"

"Surely. Surely you can. I'll take you right up. She's mostly been sleeping. Doctor Sánchez has her on some very strong pain killers. Morphine, you know. So she's been kind of out of it."

"Liver cancer," I said to myself.

"Don't you know it. Here we thought it was her heart or her mind that was going to go first and it turns out to be the liver. Who would have thought it?" We were walking down the quiet hallways then. A few guests, as they are called at St. Anthony's, were stirring. One or two were already out in the halls with their four-legged walkers in front of them. "But you know, there is just no rhyme or reason to what finally does us in. You think it's gonna be one thing and then something else hits you. I'm telling you, there's just no rhyme or reason."

"Has she been conscious at all?"

"Oh, you know her. She was always in her own world even before she got ill. She would just go about talking to this person and talking to that person. She wakes up now and then, but she doesn't recognize us most of the time. I don't know. She calls us something different every time. I was her Aunt Coca the other day. She was carrying on and on about how she wanted to go to this ball on this ship with all the cadets from the maritime academy something or other but her sister didn't want to take her because she, her sister I mean, didn't want your mother to steal away all the cadets. She's something, your mother. There's her room now. Why don't I leave you here for a second? I'll get you a cup of coffee and a pastry. You look like you could use one. I'll be right back."

Lilia was in a room with three other "guests." She was in the last stall, by the window, so that I had to walk by the other women. The beds could be separated by curtains that come around. Only Lilia's curtains were drawn. One of Lilia's roommates was standing by the side of her bed not doing anything, just holding on to the edges of the bed. She was wearing a turquoise robe and matching slippers. The other roommate apparently was still sleeping.

Lilia's face was thinner than I had ever seen it. It was really a skeleton with a cellophane-thin wrapping of wrinkled skin. Her white hair was sparse but neatly combed. She had a clear-tube line of oxygen over her head like a headphone connected to her nose. I went over next to her and touched her hand. I could feel her purple veins with my fingertips. After a while, I pulled up a chair and sat next to her, looking at her.

Around 9:00, Lilia began to stir. She shook the oxygen line from her nose. "No. No. No. No quiero," she said, as she moved her head from one side of her pillow to the other.

I talked to her as best I could, telling her, "Mamá, I am here. Es Ismael. Tu hijo." I managed to place the oxygen line back in her nose. Then I placed my hand on her forehead, but she whacked it away. I placed it again, and again she whacked it.

"Déjame," she said.

Doctor Sánchez came at 12:00. He shook my hand warmly and seemed genuinely glad that I was there. He told me a little bit about my mother. The disease had spread like wildfire, faster almost than he had ever seen. The cancer cells themselves might have been wreaking silent havoc for who knows how long. Doctor Sánchez felt that it was better this way. She would not suffer much. Even with all the morphine, however, there was probably some discomfort.

"Doctor," I hesitated to ask, but I did so anyway, "can you give up the morphine for just a little while? I would like to say good-bye to her, to let her know that I'm here."

"I see," he said. "Yes, I get that request sometimes. People think that will make the patient feel better. Actually it's to make the person making the request feel better."

"I realize that."

"I'll wait until three o'clock before I give her the injection, although I shall leave instructions with the RN to give it to her before if she starts getting very uncomfortable."

"Thank you."

He continued, "We have no way of measuring pain or of knowing how much a patient is in pain. Did you know that? With all our science we have no way of verifying whether a person is actually suffering. It's totally subjective. Pain is. What's a little pain for someone could be unbearable to someone else. Did you know that? We physicians depend totally on the expressions of pain that are given by the patient. Do you know what cancer feels like? No? Nor do I. I can't possibly imagine what it feels like to have your organs die while the rest of you is still alive. I can't possibly imagine. All I can tell you is that it must be horrible. Something beyond description. Ah, what do I know? What do we all know? Keep an eye on her. If she looks uncomfortable, call the nurse."

I dozed off and when I opened my eyes Lilia was staring at me. At first her glare was so fixed I was scared she was dead. But as I approached her, I noticed that she blinked.

"Antonio," she called out to me.

"No, no soy Antonio. I am Ismael, tu hijo."

"Antonio," she repeated.

I bent down to kiss her forehead but she moved her head away.

"¿Por qué me dejaste, Antonio?"

"Soy Ismael, tu hijo."

For a second she refocused on me. "¿Ismael? ¿El hijo de Antonio?"

"Sí, el hijo tuyo y el hijo de Antonio."

"No. El hijo de Antonio murió. Se lo llevaron."

"Soy yo. Aquí estoy."

"Vete, Antonio, vete. ¡Ay! ¡Ay! Me duele."

Her face was full of pain. Her fists were clenched. Her eyes were rolling. I wanted to get the nurse, but I waited instead.

"Mamá, ¿quién soy yo?"

"¡Ay! ¡Ay! ¡Ay! ¡Ay! ¡Cómo me duele!"

"Dime quién soy yo."

"¡Antonio! ¡Antonio!"

"No soy Antonio. Tell me who I am. Dime quién soy yo."

"¡Ay que me duele, mamá! ¡Ay! No puedo."

"Soy Ismael. Di que soy Ismael. Tell me who I am before you die."

"¡Ay! Ismael. Mijo. Sí. Eres Ismael. El hijo mío y de Antonio. ¡Ay que me duele! Pero no puedo más."

I went outside to get the nurse.

The rest of the afternoon, despite two more injections, she was restless and in some kind of delirium. She invoked her mother and her father and talked to them in painful monosyllables as if they were there, but she did not derive any comfort from their presence. Her whimpering was not loud. Her roommates did not seem to mind her agony at all. The one with the turquoise bathrobe watched television from a private set that had been placed on top a chest of drawers in front of her bed. The other one came and went to the bathroom constantly. At one point she peeked from behind the curtain and grinned at me as if to say that's as it should be. Mother and son. Together at the start and together at the end.

She finally died at eight o'clock that evening. I rang the alarm bell when I saw her stop breathing, but the floor nurse who responded was slow and deliberate and not inclined to treat this as any kind of emergency. The nurse seemed truly sad—the way she closed Lilia's eyes and folded her hands, and the way she combed her white hair one last time.

"God bless you, dear," she said.

I could stay if I wished. Doctor Sánchez needed to come and sign the death certificate. It could be an hour or two. "He usually comes as soon as he can, but sometimes he's detained." I chose to stay. When Doctor Sánchez came, he seemed surprised to see me there. He was dressed casually, in a white golf shirt with a tiny alligator, beige polyester slacks, and white tennis sneakers. Lilia's roommates were asleep. One of them had left the TV on which was now emitting a pale blank glow.

The doctor touched Lilia's throat. He lifted a heavy eyelid and shined a tiny flashlight on her frozen eye. He signed the paperwork that had already been filled out by the nurse.

"How did she do?" he asked me, barely looking up.

"She seemed very restless and uncomfortable."

"Yes. Even all that morphine doesn't do the trick completely. Good night."

A half hour or so later, two young men dressed in faded green jumpsuits came with a stretcher.

"We're going to have to take her," said one of them.

"O.K." I said.

I got up from my chair, stood next to her and said, "Adiós, mamá. Adiós."

DAY 32

Somewhere between Harlingen and El Paso, I opened up Kate's letter, which was still stuck in my back pocket. She was sending me my check for unused vacation and sick time and three months' severance pay. She had gone to Preston and argued that I should get what others had received in the past, at least. She said that Trudy had called her at work and had asked if she knew where I was. Trudy was very nice on the phone, but sounded kind of distant nevertheless. Trudy had received a phone call from my mother's nursing home about my mother's illness and she thought that Kate might know where I was. Kate said she told Trudy that I was probably headed toward Harlingen because I had asked her to mail my check there. Kate said that Trudy said thank you and hung up.

Kate said that even though nobody said anything openly, it was still a weird phone call. Kate wondered what I had told Trudy about her and me. For that matter, Kate said, she was still trying to figure out all the things we said that last night. She said that overall she thought we had made the right decision, even though now and then she wondered. Part of her felt that we had both missed something that ought to be taken and enjoyed when it comes. In any case, she wished me luck in finding whatever or whomever I was searching for. She said that she would like it very much if I wrote to her or called and that if I ever needed anything I should call her. She also wrote that Corky wanted to tell me that I was a pussy willow. She asked me what in the world that meant and what kind of things had I taught her little child.

After paying for Lilia's funeral (I could not bear, nor do I think that Lilia would have liked, the much cheaper process of cremation), I had about seventeen thousand dollars. It was enough, I figured, to live on for awhile if used judiciously. Sooner or later I would have to find a job, but I thought that for the time being I would dedicate myself to finding Armanda.

The Nine Tails, where Armanda worked as a dancer when I met her, had been torn down; in its stead was a Goodyear Tire store. The Del Camino Motel, where Armanda and Nando used to live, was still there. Don Martín and Doña Ramona, the two owners of the Del Camino, were also still there, barely. They were both in their nineties. I asked them when I was checking in whether they remembered Armanda and Nando, and they looked at me with a look that said "Boy, we can barely remember who we saw this morning." I asked them if they kept hotel records from way back then, and they did. They were all in boxes in the basement. I could look at them if I wanted, but they were all disorganized. Doña Ramona spoke to me directly and told me that ever since her husband had lost everything "upstairs," "acá arriba" she said, pointing to her head, ever since then, they had just thrown the boxes in the basement without any kind of order.

"Who's he looking for?" asked Don Martín, grimacing.

"He told you already. What, are you deaf too? A woman named Armanda. She used to live in 8B."

"Aaah. Ocho B. No, no me acuerdo. What does he want with her?"

"What do you care? Don't pay any attention to him. He's just a grumpy old man."

Apartment 8B where I wanted to stay was rented long-term to a man with one leg missing. But 9A, which was let to me, was almost identical. I spent the next week going through old checks and rent stubs. The Del Camino served both long-term renters and overnighters, so the multitude of boxes full of paper were totally unmarked. For lack of anything better to do, I began to put the boxes in chronological order. For my efforts I got ten dollars deducted from my weekly rent, per the insistence of Doña Ramona, so long as I promised not to tell her husband.

After a few days I found the box with receipts for the year when Armanda had lived there. I really did not know what I would find that could help me, perhaps some forwarding address that Armanda had left behind, or anything that could give me a clue. I had checked all the phone books. I had even gone to the school a few blocks away to see if they had any records of Nando. These records, too, were in storage, and the principal refused to send for them because the release of children's school records needed either the pupil or parent's signature.

In the box were copies of receipts that Don Martín had given Armanda after she paid in cash for her rent. There were receipts to Armanda that went for the year and a half that she had lived there. The receipts ended about a year and a half after I left, which was about the time that I got the last letter from Armanda. I took the receipts for that year to Doña Ramona to see if she could remember anything. I read to her the names of the tenants during that year and she shook her head "no" to almost everyone of them. One name she remembered clear as day, however, was Beatrice Lamont who had lived in 8C, a door away from Armanda and Nando. Doña Ramona remembered her because she was one of the few Anglos who rented a room long-term, and because Beatrice, who had moved out shortly after Armanda left, had still come by every Christmas for a long time afterwards with the most god-awful dry fruitcake anyone had ever tasted.

When I saw Mrs. Lamont, I immediately remembered her as the woman who had taken care of Nando when Armanda went to work.

"Uh huh. I remember Armanda and Nando as if it were yesterday. Matter of fact, I remember you too. Look at me. I have the body of a dead, rotten whale, one of them that ends up on the beach with those pitiful flaps, but my mind is strong, yessir, very strong. Somedays I wish the good Lord would remember me. Yessir."

"Do you remember me?"

"Sit yourself down there on that sofa. I haven't had a live visitor for a long time, except for the damned Meals-on-Wheels lady, and she's dumber than a thumbtack. I have instant coffee or tea, or I can get you some ice water?"

"Water, please."

"Hold on to yourself, I'll be right back."

From the kitchen I heard the banging of an ice tray on a table and then the sound of ice cubes sprawling on the floor. Then I heard her yell:

"Goddamn it! Damned hands don't move like they used to, that's for sure. Sorry, Lord, didn't mean to take your name in vain, but you know I don't mean it."

When she came back she was holding a tall, skinny, pink plastic glass that had a picture of a little girl holding daisies in her hand and lipstick smudges on the white rim.

"There you go. Now let me plop down right here. O.K., where were we? Yes. I remember you. You're the sorry son-of-a-bitch that left her. Excuse me to be so blunt but at my age, dear, I can say whatever I goddamn please, don't you think?"

"Yes."

"Well then, sit back and let me tell you the story of Armanda and Nando as far as I can tell 'cause I lost track of them after a while. Be a dear and fetch me those Salems from that little table yonder. Thank you. Do you smoke?"

"I do."

"Well, then this is gonna be fun. Go ahead and light up. There's an ashtray over on the kitchen table. There you go. O.K., where were we?"

"You were telling me what a sorry son-of-a-bitch I was."

"Ha! Yes I was, wasn't it I? Don't mind me, I'm just a pitiful old lady. Now, I recollect that you're the fellow I thought for sure was gonna marry her. The way you used to come over and play with Nando, and the way Armanda just lit up when she saw you and fussed about you when you weren't there. I thought for sure you were her one, and so did Armanda."

"She thought . . ."

"Of course she did. And you know it. She waited for you to write to her, and I myself kept telling her until I was blue in the face that she should hop on a Greyhound and get her fanny over there up north wherever you were. I kept telling her and telling her that it was her God-given duty to tell you and your God-given duty to know."

Here she started a coughing spell that lasted for half a minute or so. I went to the kitchen and got her a glass of water. She took it from my hand.

"Goddamn cigarettes," she said. When she stopped coughing she was red in the face and her eyes were watery. "I'm only sup- posed to smoke six a day. That's my own rule. Then someone comes to see me and I go hog crazy and smoke like a chimney. I don't know." She looked at me as if she had forgotten why I was there.

"You were saying that it was Armanda's duty to tell me . . ."

"Well, I told her that this waiting-around was plain crazy. I told her she had to tell you up front that she was carrying your child. It wasn't just a matter of love anymore, now it was duty and respon- sibility too, that's what I think, anyway. It was an obligation for her to tell you and you to know. So's to make sure you had a choice as to whether you wanted to do the right thing or not."

"My child? Are you sure?"

"Goddamn it! Am I sure? Shit! I don't know what the good Lord put in a man's heart, but I swear it's vile stuff. Am I sure? You know damned well that Armanda wasn't gonna fool around with anyone else. You know damned well it was your child."

She was fumbling for another Salem, but there was only one or two left in the package, and her swollen fingers had trouble taking them out. When she did, she put her cigarette in her mouth and pointed her face at me, asking for a light.

"Thank you," she said puffing out a stream of smoke. "God Almighty! I just don't understand what makes men do the kinds of heartless things they do. They're different creatures, that's for sure."

"What happened to Armanda?"

"Well now, there was a woman for you. She kept telling me that she wanted you to answer her letters because you wanted to and not because you had to. I told her to keep on writing to you even after you stopped. And I guess she did. But then she stopped and didn't yield to my advice."

"And the child?"

"For your information the child died later when he was about eight months old in a . . . tragic accident. Then shortly after that, Armanda left the Del Camino with Nando and a guy that drove a red truck. I don't know what happened to them after that except that about a year later I ran into her at the five-and-dime, and she was still very upset about the baby. She didn't want to talk about it at all, not at all. So I didn't ask her too much about it."

She looked at me as if waiting for me to tell her that it was O.K. to go on.

"You didn't know about the baby? You were doing whatever it was that you thought was so important and you didn't even care. It's too bad. Me and a whole bunch from the Del Camino went over to the hospital when she delivered. The baby was a sight of beauty, I guarantee you. When I first saw him he had a little blue cap to cover up the marks on the side of the head where those butchers in the hospital pulled him with them pincers they use. But then he got normal after a while. Armanda stopped dancing at the Nine Tails until she got back her figure, so she was working in some factory downtown. I took care of the baby and Nando while she worked. Boy, that Nando was something. He had such tantrums whenever

Armanda nursed or fussed over the baby. Then one day Armanda introduced me to the man with the truck. I guess he was the foreman or something of the factory where she worked. He seemed real nice and all, but I didn't see what Armanda saw in him. He was as exciting as a toilet seat. I thought at first that's what Armanda needed at that time, all in all, someone like that. But the son-of-a-bitch was not only boring but cruel. He just sat there and wanted to be catered to. Didn't want anything to do with the baby or Nando. I swear, I think it was him that first gave Armanda drugs to try. I don't think he used any himself, but he was a real cold son-of-a-bitch, in a quiet way, you know what I mean?"

I nodded.

"You sure you didn't know about the baby?"

"No . . . I mean there was some kind of obscure reference in a letter, but I was never sure. She never told me straight. I was never sure."

"Obscure reference my ass. I knew she finally wrote you about him. She named him after you. Damn Men! Holy Almighty! Don't anyone have any shame left? Well, now you know for absolute sure. I did something good today. Yessir, I did. Here, help me up."

I went over and gave her my hand and pulled her up. "I'll be right back," she said. Mrs. Lamont wobbled over in the direction of a bedroom in the back of the apartment. There was a cane next to her chair which she used for the first time. After a few minutes I heard a toilet flush and then the sound of plastic bottles falling and of pills rattling on the sink and on the floor and then another loud "goddamn it."

"Come over here!"

When I got there she was on a sagging bed next to an open drawer on her night table. She motioned me to sit next to her. I slid toward her when I did.

"See here."

It was the picture of Armanda and Nando, the same picture that was taken at my insistence with Armanda wearing her black dress with a white neck frill and Nando's hair shiny with the green gel that Armanda used to keep it from sticking up.

"Do you want it?" she asked.

"Are you sure?" I didn't tell her that I already had that picture back there in Oakridge, inside an envelope that was inside a box that was inside a drawer that otherwise stored sweaters and wool scarves.

"Oh, hell yeah. I'm gonna die any day now and all this is gonna end up as garbage. At least you'll appreciate it. Now help me up and let's go to the living room and have another smoke. What the hell, I don't feel like being good today."

"Do you have any pictures of the baby?"

"Your son, you mean."

"Yes, my son."

"Nope. Wish I did."

"Tell me, please. How did he die? You said a tragic accident."

She let herself fall on the bed again and I sat next to her. Then she lifted her head in my direction but her eyes were not on me. They were in the past. "He got run over in front of the Del Camino."

"But he was only a toddler."

She sat there in lost silence until it became clear that she was not going to talk about that anymore.

We walked back to the living room, her hand gripping my arm for support. When she had sat down again and I had lit her last Salem, she finished telling me all that she knew about Armanda and Nando. When Mrs. Lamont ran into Armanda at the five-and-dime, Armanda was thin and pale and wore a long-sleeved sweater even though it was the middle of summer. She had dumped the man with the pickup truck. She had started taking drugs after the death of the baby, but she had stopped and was working making mirrors for American cars at a maquiladora in Ciudad Juárez. Armanda asked Mrs. Lamont if there was any mail at the Del Camino, and Mrs. Lamont told her that there wasn't. Armanda said that maybe it was just as well.

"And that's about it. She promised to come visit me, but I never heard from her or Nando again."

Mrs. Lamont took a deep breath and started coughing again. After the coughing spell, she just looked at me. She had no idea where Armanda might be. She wished me luck in finding her, if that was what I wanted to do, and then insisted on getting up and walking me to the door. On the way out she asked if I would be a dear and get her a package of Salems and a giant bottle of Fanta from the Seven-Eleven down the street, which I did.

DAY 33

I finally found Armanda in a bar called El Caballito located in Zaragoza, a suburb of Ciudad Juárez. It was about a month after the manager of the maquiladora where they made mirrors for American cars recognized her in the picture that Mrs. Lamont had given me. He told me that he had seen her "making a living" in a Juárez bar.

She was sitting by herself, holding a drink and smoking a cigarette. Her head nodded suddenly every once in a while like someone trying not to fall asleep in church or at the opera. I sat down in front of her. She smiled easily and patted my hand, as if I had just returned from a quick errand.

"Hola, guapo," she said.

"Do you remember me, Armanda?"

"Ah, you speak English. I do too. I am expert in English."

"Ismael. I am Ismael. Do you remember me?"

"Oh, but of course I remember you," she grabbed my shoulder and pulled me toward her, "you are my guardian angel."

"Armanda . . ."

"Shhh . . . How do you know my name if I haven't told you it?"

"Look at me well."

Armanda opened her eyes wide with exaggeration, pretending to focus on my face.

"You are very guapo. You remind me of someone from las telenovelas, I don't know who." She raised her hand to the bartender and waived two fingers at him. He came over with two beers and waited for me to pay him.

"Uuuy. You are very rich," she said as I opened my wallet. She wiggled her fingers and pretended to reach for the money, but I wrapped her hand in mine and held it.

"Armanda, we knew each other." I lifted her head by her chin to look at me.

A man from a table across the bar came over to where we were, stumbling as he walked.

"¿Te está molestando este gringo, Armanda?"

"He's no bother," she said to him, "and he's not a gringo, are you, guapo? He's from the telenovelas."

I looked at the man, and he and I locked glares for a few seconds. The rest of the people in the bar were quiet and staring at us.

"Oh, come on!" yelled Armanda with a wild gesture of her arm. "Pedro, pon la música que tengo ganas de bailar." Armanda was standing and stretching her arm toward me, asking me to dance to a mariachi song that had just started playing on the multicolored jukebox. I took her hand and allowed her to pull me out of my chair. On my way up I brushed against the man who was still standing there. He was a young man . . . tight blue jeans, boots, and a cowboy shirt halfway opened. He put his hand on my chest, stopping me and causing Armanda to jerk back.

"¿Me la estás regando, cabrón?"

"Mira, no sé cuál es tu problema. Yo sólo quiero estar con ella. ¿Se puede, no?"

"Any time, ése. Just let me know," he said, shoving me back with his hand.

Armanda came back and pushed him. "What do you want with me, pinche Mario? Ya déjame en paz. I have nothing to do with you. Fuck off!" Then in a softer tone, to me, "Come on! Stop the bullshit! Let's dance."

"Nando me dijo que te cuidara. ¿O ya te olvidaste?" This he said to Armanda. He was standing legs parted, arms at his side.

Armanda started toward him, her hand raised to slap, but I put my body in her path, detaining her. "¡Dile a Nando que me deje en paz!"

I pushed her away from the man named Mario and slowly toward the wooden platform. When we got there, it seemed as if she had totally forgotten the incident. She placed her hand on the back of my head and tried to look into my eyes, but her own eyes were wobbly and unable to stay in one place. I put my arms around her waist and brought her close to me. Her body was still tight and strong but also softer than before. She was light and comfortable in my embrace. I buried my face in her short hair that smelled of coconuts and jabón de manzanilla.

"Hey, what's the matter?" she said pulling me away from her. I rubbed my eyes with my wrist. "Hey, come on. This is happy time. Come here." She pushed my head against her lips and with her tongue licked my cheeks and my eyes. Then she held me again tightly, moving only her hips very slowly until the song was over. When we went back to the table, Armanda ordered two more drinks.

"Armanda, let's go some place. Let's go some place else. I'll take you."

"Oh, no," she said. "I have to stay here unless you get a permiso, which is very expensive."

"How much?" I asked.

"I don't know," she said. She yelled at the bartender. "Pedro, ven pacá!" The bartender came over. I noticed for the first time that he was wearing a white shirt, a black bow tie, and a permanently ingrained grin.

"Este señor wants to take me out with a permiso."

"How much?" I asked.

"Son sesenta dólares por toda la noche." Pedro replied, expanding his grin even more.

"Está bien." I opened my wallet and gave him three twenty-dollar bills. Pedro bowed and took the money.

"I need some too," said Armanda, her head bobbing and smiling. I opened my wallet for her to take what she wanted. She took two twenties.

"Thank you!" She rolled the money in the palm of her hand, stood up, and waved the money at the other women in the bar.

"I go get my things." She walked out through a set of green curtains that opened up to a side building. When she did that, the man who had come to our table started after her. I made a motion to stand up to intercept him, but Pedro the bartender motioned with his head that I should not follow. Pedro sat in the chair in front of me. He started talking to me.

"Is much better if you let things be with her. That man is sent by her son to watch her and to make sure she gives him all the money she makes. He gives her drugs. Right now he is giving her drugs. Is better if she gets injected here. La nurse gives her the shot. She can't do it herself. So someone gives her the shot. When her son gives her drugs, it's very dangerous. Once he gave her too much and she was in the hospital almost dead."

"The nurse?"

"Oh sure. La nurse checks los clientes for diseases before they go to the back with any of the girls. She gives clientes rubbers also. This is very safe place."

"And her son, ¿se llama Nando?"

"Sí. Do you know him? He's a very evil man. He's a narcotraficante. Everyone knows him. When you take her home, make sure he not there. If he's on drugs he is very dangerous. He's killed people before for nothing."

When Armanda came out, she actually looked awake. She had put on lipstick and eye shadow and rouge, and there was a sprightliness to her step so that she seemed to skip and hop like a little girl as she walked.

"Come, come," she said to me, "Let's go."

As we walked out of El Caballito she waved to all the women and laughingly called them names, and they in turn yelled back at her. As I got Armanda into my car, I saw standing in the doorway of El Caballito the man who had come to our table and gone with Armanda to the back.

In the car, Armanda was full of energy. She found a radio station that she liked and turned the volume up. Then she stuck her head out the window and began to sing and laugh.

"Why did you cut your long black hair?" I asked.

"Ah, you remember my long black hair?"

"Yes. It was beautiful."

"And so? I am not beautiful now?" She ran her fingers through her hair and tousled it.

"More beautiful," I said.

"You are a bullshitter!" she said, and grabbed me tightly between my legs.

"¡Ay! ¡Vamos a chocar!" I screamed as I straightened the car back into my lane.

"¿Vamos a qué? ¿Vamos a cochar? We are going to fuck? Is that what you said?"

"No, chocar, chocar, not cochar."

"Oh, how sad. I prefer cochar. Go that way. I want to show you where I live."

I turned in the direction where she wanted me to. It was an unpaved street with potholes large enough to devour a whole wheel in one bite. Adobe houses lined the street on both sides, some of them plastered and painted in yellows and greens and even reds and others showing only the bare mud adobes with sticks of straw sticking out here and there. In front of some of the houses, people sat in wood and straw chairs or on turned-over buckets and wired milk crates, drinking beer and tequila and postponing as long as possible the heat of the desert night.

"Drive slowly. Turn off lights now. You see that house with green door? My house. Debajo del flower pot is the key. You must take me back there tonight. I tell you now because I will be too loca later. But if you see a black car in front then you must drive me down the street to la nurse's house. Prende las luces. I'll show you where. Turn left here. Ves. Esa casita número 39. There lives the nurse. I can stay with her anytime."

"It's Nando, isn't it?

"Do you know Nando?"

"I do know him, from when he was little."

Armanda was silent.

"You remember me now, don't you?"

Armanda turned the radio on again. "I don't want to remember anything, anything. I just want to live now." She stuck her tongue inside my ear until I cringed my shoulders with pleasure, and then she laughed and started singing the song that was playing.

"Armanda, who was that man? That man in El Caballito that came over to our table?"

"Don't worry about him. He's not that tough."

"What kind of drugs are you taking?" I reached over and started to pull the long sleeve of her dress.

"Come on, now," she said, yanking her arm away. "You have to just take me as I am. No questions. We just celebrate. O.K.? Let's go dancing. Tengo ganas de bailar."

"Armanda, I think we should find a motel. I don't think you will be able to dance in a little while." Her eyes were beginning to close for longer periods of time, and her words were slurred.

She had her eyes closed for about five minutes and I thought she was asleep, when without opening her eyes, she said, "O.K., no dancing tonight, except maybe our paso lento. The one I teach you." I tried to pursue this further but she did not hear me. Her eyes were closed by now and her head rested heavily on my shoulder, so that I was unable to obtain the recognition of our past together that I so much needed from her.

I found a motel, and with the help of a young boy that worked there, I placed her on the bed. I took her shoes off and then her dress and covered her with the green bedcover. Then I watched her. I ordered a six-pack of Tecates and a fresh pack of Delicados, and I watched her from the chair in front of the bed. She was unconscious all throughout my watch, but she was also very much alive—alive, but in a different place. Her body twitched, and her eyes rolled and darted every which way behind her eyelids. She whispered things that I could not understand, and she laughed and she smiled. I got the impression from watching the movements of her body and the sounds she made that the place where she had gone was a friendly, comforting place filled with warmth and safety.

Around three in the afternoon of the next day, she opened her eyes wide and looked at me as if she had never seen me before. I was still sitting in the same chair where I had sat all night. She pointed at an empty bottle of beer as she grimaced with her tongue that her mouth was parched. I picked up the phone and ordered another six-pack and another pack of cigarettes. Armanda sat up in bed and pulled her black bra strap over her shoulder. She caught me looking at the fullness of her breasts.

"Did we make love?" she asked, pulling up the cover and glancing down at her waist and legs.

"No," I said, making a disappointment pout with my eyes and mouth.

Armanda laughed. "Give me a cigarette." I gave her the last Delicado and lit it for her. She tapped the bed, asking me to sit next to her. "What is your name, anyway?"

"I'm Ismael. Don't you remember?"

"I'm very hungry. ¿Qué hora es?"

"It's around 3:00 P.M." There was a knock at the door. Joselito, the young boy who had helped me with Armanda and who had supplied me with beer and cigarettes throughout the night and half the day, was there again, holding a tray of Tecates, a glass full of limes, and two packs of Delicados.

"Buenas tardes, señora," he said to Armanda without appearing to notice her seminude body.

"¿Tienen algo que comer?" Armanda asked him.

"Sí señora, si quiere le traigo el menú."

"¿No tienen menudo?"

"Sí, señora. Muy buen menudo con pan francés."

"Bring us two plates, please," I said to him as I paid him. "No te preocupes, guarda el cambio."

"You are very generous," said Armanda when I came to sit next to her. "Are you rich?"

"I have a little money."

"Good."

"Why?"

"Because then, mi vida, we can be together." She got up and went to the bathroom. When she came back she opened another beer and sat next to me on the bed. There was a glow of bliss around her as if she were still in the place where she had spent the night.

"Mira, mi amor," she said, "como sabes, I have a habit. I need to make money so that I not suffer. If you like to stay with me, you can. Pero tengo un hábito and I have a son who is more sicker than I am. He is angry all the time. I want to tell you."

"Armanda, I need to talk about the past. I need to talk to you about our . . ."

"No."

"No, what?"

"No past. I don't want the past ahora. In a couple of hours I have to go to work. First you take me home so I can change. You can meet me at work later."

"El Caballito?"

"Yes, tonto. Where else?"

"I don't want you to work there."

"Oh, listen to you. Pareces mi esposo." Armanda took a gulp of the beer and reached over to unbutton my shirt. There was a knock at the door. I went to open it and got the menudo from Joselito.

"Here, I am going to pay you for the menudo and for another night."

"¿Qué haces? I have to go to work," said Armanda, smiling from the bed.

"Muchas gracias," said Joselito.

"Don't you ever rest?" I asked him as he was leaving.

"Oh, sure, I had a big siesta already."

The menudo was red with chili and thick with tripe and big grains of hominy. Armanda and I sat against the bed and put the big, hot bowls on top of pillows in our laps, the four pieces of pan francés between us, the limes and beers and salt shaker on the night table next to the bed. We ate in silence, and after we ate I convinced Armanda that we could spend another night together. I would drive by her house and if Nando's black Impala was not there, I would go in, pick up some clothes for her and then go to the Caballito and leave sixty dollars with Pedro. If Nando's car was there, then I would come pick up Armanda and drop her at home. We would then meet later at the Caballito. I resented the fact that Armanda had to report to Nando, but I thought that for the moment it was best to go with the flow of circumstances, just as, for the moment, the flow dictated that I stay away from the past.

As it turned out, Nando was not there, which meant, according to Armanda, that he had disappeared on a drug binge of his own and would be out for several days. Pedro, the bartender, was not there either. He came in around six o'clock and it was only 5:00 P.M. when I got to El Caballito. The daytime bartender did not look as though he could be trusted, so I asked him if the nurse was there.

"¿La nurse? Sí, está atrás haciendo las camas. Go in, go in. She's back there."

La nurse was an old lady dressed in white with a Red Cross pin on her lapel. She had on a full dress with cream-colored buttons running all the way down the front. Her hair was gray and pinned up in a bun. She had a sour, squinting countenance which I suppose was a natural side effect from the duties of her job.

She was bent over putting clean sheets on a bed. I gave her the sixty dollars and told her to give it to Pedro the bartender. I also told her that Armanda was still with me.

She took the money and dropped it in a very large side pocket of her white dress. I gave her five dollars for her trouble. She took that money too and put it in her pocket without looking at me or thanking me.

"You making trouble for her," she said in English as I was leaving.

"Nando?" I asked.

"Sí."

"If you see Nando or that man that watches over Armanda, tell either one that I would like to talk to Nando."

"No es posible," she said.

"¿Por qué?"

"Think of her," she said. "She not a free woman. She is slave by her son and by that maldita droga. She very sick."

"I know. Tell Nando that I want to talk money with him. I will give him much money if he lets me be with her. He'll understand."

La nurse looked at me, her eyebrows furrowed, as if I too was on drugs.

"What do you want with her? There are plenty women younger, más bonitas, que no son drogadictas."

"I know her from many years ago. Please tell Nando what I asked you."

"I tell him. I hope he not kill me too."

"Thank you." I started to walk away.

"She ask you for drugs tonight. Don't give her. What I give her yesterday is enough for the night. You bring her to me tomorrow morning at my house. I give her another injection then. It better if I do it. I give her small doses so she not too crazy."

"O.K."

"I need money to buy drug for tomorrow. I have to buy from the man you had a fight with. Give me twenty only."

"Last night it was forty."

"Forty. Shh. You just like Armanda. I tell her she needs to know how to negociar. That Mario asks for forty and she gives him forty. Her son asks for all the money and she gives him all the money. I tell her hide some for you. She not listen. Give me twenty. I get the same mierda for twenty. Also, don't pay again sixty for a permiso. You can get it for forty. Pedro keeps for him the other twenty you gave him yesterday."

"But I just gave you sixty."

"I keep the other twenty for me. Now you learn."

DAY 34

Almost every night, except when Armanda did not show up, I was at El Caballito. In addition to what I paid for our beers, I gave Pedro a twenty-dollar tip every night so he was O.K., from a business perspective, with my monopolizing Armanda. Every other day I bought injectable cocaine from Mario. On weekends I bought a small bag of "mula" or very diluted heroin. That more or less kept Armanda from going wild with the pain of craving. After a while Mario and I became begrudging business friends, although I knew for a fact that he would kill me in an instant for whatever money I kept in my wallet. He showed up less and less at El Caballito, and when he did, he sat with Armanda and me and told us about the drug wars that he was involved in.

The women who worked there and the other regulars took me in also as part of their crazy world. I was especially liked for my daily purchase of tacos al carbón for everybody from the restaurant down the street. I usually got the tacos around 3:00 A.M. when business was slow and everyone was waiting for 5:00 A.M. to come around so they could go home. The other women called me "el güero" because my skin was light for a Mexican and because everyone that knew any English at all insisted in talking to me in that language. The women also called me "el novio de Armanda" because I was constantly at her side at El Caballito or taking her out on a permiso to do "date" things like going to movies or shopping at the mercado or spending afternoons at Mexican rodeos. The women of El Caballito teased Armanda that she should not be so egoísta, that she should share me with the rest of them, to which Armanda responded mostly by telling them to go to la chingada. Except that one time out of the blue, she told them they could have my body if they wanted and if I wished, so long as my heart remained hers. That was the only time that Armanda, in so many words, admitted that she cared for me.

199

Except for that time when she mentioned "our paso lento" and except for the conversation we had a week before she died, Armanda never talked about the past. She never accepted my invitations or responded to my prodding to remember. I also ceased to prod. The mere hint of the past brought such pain to Armanda that I joined with her, resignedly, in her necessary amnesia.

I like to think that in those early days in El Paso, Armanda did remember "us" in some vague way, the way an unexpected scent reminds us suddenly of something indefinable in our past. I like to think when Armanda insisted on taking me to the back rooms of El Caballito or when we were out on a permiso or when we found ourselves alone in her house and she proceeded to laughingly undress me, despite my nervousness that Nando would walk in, that during those times she was led by a remembrance of me that lingered somewhere in her flesh and that urged her on. I would like to think that those moments, filled as they were with the compassion of two lonely and lost human beings, when we more than anything took harbor and anchored ourselves for as long as we could in each other's grasp, there was something in Armanda's body that remembered our past communion with a memory that senses retain but which minds lose. It seemed as if during those moments, there was a quenching of the nervous cravings that otherwise consumed us. I know that for me, those moments were like taking a nap after the noontime meal in Abuelito's house when I was a small boy—letting myself gently drift into a sleep filled with the coolness of a Gulf breeze and with the distant cries of street vendors, imbued with the peace of knowing that everyone I loved in the whole world—Abuelito, Lilia, Renata—was in the house with me, also resting.

There were many moments like that. But most of the time, Armanda was like someone to whom you have just said good-bye and has slowly started to walk away; or like someone slowly dying before your very eyes, a setting sun who now and then briefly flared with a burst of girlish laughter, sticking a devilish tongue in my ear, grabbing my crotch or accusing me loudly in a crowded place of bullshitting her about something.

But if Armanda did not let me talk about our past, she had no objection to talking about my past in the East or about our future. My conversations with her deep into the night at El Caballito started with her asking me to recount the details of my previous life, what kind of house I had, how many rooms, what Trudy was like, if Kate was pretty, what kinds of things I did as a lawyer, where I went for fun, and ended always with elaborate and very specific descriptions of my plans for our new life together. Armanda listened to all of it, mostly in silence, her face shining with a delight that is seen in children's faces when they are watching a riveting but very scary movie. My plan was to make an "arrangement" with Nando and then live together at the Del Camino where I was promised rent-free lodging in return for managing the place for Don Martín and Doña Ramona. Then I would put her in a hospital where it would be hard for her at first, but she would recover slowly with my support and care. Finally, I would get a job at El Paso Community College where I had already submitted my application. She could work too or learn a new trade, something like hair styling, which she mentioned she had worked at for a while but had given up. I think she indulged me in my enthusiastic machinations so many times that one day it hit her, the way a stone sinks to the bottom of a clear lake, that I was serious, very serious.

Armanda and I were the only ones dancing at El Caballito even though the place was full and noisy. It was around 11:00 P.M., and I had been elaborating to Armanda a few new details of my plan when she had suddenly stood up and headed to the dance floor. I followed her even though it seemed as if she would dance alone if I had not come along.

It was a Tito Puentes mambo, one of Armanda's favorites that was playing, and the pace was fast and happy. We were dancing apart, holding hands only to facilitate the mutual twirling and twisting that we enjoyed doing. Then, in the middle of the song, she took my arms and we began to dance body-to-body almost without moving but still responsive to the blasting trumpets and rhythmic drumming of the song.

"¿Por qué?" she asked more to herself than to me.

"Why what?" I responded.

"Why do you want to take me to El Paso?"

"Because I want to be with you."

"Do you really want to live with me forever?"

"Always. Para siempre."

"Why?"

"Porque te quiero."

"Ah. How do you know you love me for sure?"

"I don't know. I need you to live and you need me to live."

"You need me?"

"Yes."

"And I need you." Armanda said this lowering her eyes in a way that looked to me like shame.

"It's O.K. It's O.K. to need me for my money. Isn't it?"

"Maybe," said Armanda.

"Armanda, I don't know the words to say it. We need each other. Our bodies and our minds and our hearts need each other. I don't have the words to explain it."

"I need to know without bullshit why you want to be with me."

"I love you, Armanda."

Armanda looked in my eyes and pleaded softly. "Ismael, no bullshit right now. Tell me really what is here en tu corazón."

We stopped dancing. I felt as if her eyes had sucked me into that big tunnel where I had been falling in darkness and terror way back then since Corky's fateful touch. Then, after a while I spoke, hearing the sound and the meaning of the stuttering words for the first time as they came out.

"I want to be with you because I am so full of guilt and vergüenza. I need you so much to forgive me for abandoning you and my son and Nando back then. You're my only cure for that pain. Without you I have no meaning. My shame is wasted. I need to make up for that. I don't know how to do it other than by caring for you. Te encontré. Estoy aquí porque te encontré. I was allowed somehow to find you."

Armanda, with a blank and serious expression on her face, nodded slightly as if to confirm that that had been her thinking also. She turned and headed for our table, holding my hand in silence. I had never before seen the look of sadness in her face that she had then. After a while she got up and headed toward the back rooms of El Caballito. I stopped her and said, "Armanda, no drugs. Not tonight."

"No drugs," Armanda said reassuringly.

When she came back she went directly to talk to Pedro at the bar. She brought back a bottle of Mexican brandy and two small glasses with ice. "I want to drink this tonight," she said.

After she poured the brandy, we clicked the glasses and with the brandy still in her mouth she kissed me long and tenderly on my lips as if for the first time.

"When she finished kissing me, she said: "What makes you think that Nando will let you take me to El Paso?"

"He doesn't rule you. Are you prepared to leave him?"

"He's my son."

"He is your grown-up son. Don't you think that it would be good for him to separate from you?"

Armanda bit the top of her finger. "I don't know if I can. I need him too. I need to take care of him, como tú necesitas cuidarme a mí."

"But it's different. Nando needs to take care of himself. For his own good."

"Sí, lo sé. But he needs more time. He is ill. You do not know."

"There is nothing you can do to stop that. How can you right now prevent him from dying from an overdose or getting killed by a gang?"

"No puedo," said Armanda shaking her head brusquely. "It's not just that. He will die if I abandon him."

"Armanda, let me talk to him. In your heart you know that we will be doing the right thing. You can't belong to Nando. It's not good for him. He must learn to separate from you. I'm not proposing that we move far away. We'll go to El Paso and make a living there. Nando can come see us. We can visit him. The money I make will be in part for him so he doesn't have to steal to get what he needs. I don't care if he takes advantage of me as long as he allows us to be together."

"Ismael, la verdad es que I rather have drugs than you. I know in my heart that is the truth. I don't think I can give up them for anyone. I bullshit you if you think I want to change. Too late for change." Armanda looked at me with a defiance in her eyes that I had seen many times before. It came when drugs were not available or denied to her or sometimes when in the middle of a drug state, her stupor was interrupted or her will opposed.

"Listen to me for a second. I know that already. I know a little bit what that hunger is like, not like you do, but a little. That hunger is not you. It is something else. It comes from someplace else."

"I don't want to change."

"Then don't change. I will still be with you."

Armanda looked at me steadily without blinking for the longest time. Then she took a wrinkled pink tissue from her purse and blew her nose. "I want ask you something," she said.

"Ask me."

"If I ask you to leave and never see me again, you do it?"

I could feel my glass heart rattle loudly with steel marbles, my lungs fill with the dustiest cotton, the top of my palate cover with flour. I could not figure any purpose to the question other than that it was a real question that she was asking with no rhetorical overtones whatsoever. I remembered thinking in a flash that perhaps she wanted me to experience the equivalent of what I was asking her to do. After what seemed like a lifetime, I answered, full of trepidation for what her response might be.

"If you asked me, Armanda, if you asked me seriously, I would do it."

"You do it because you agree with me that it is the best and not because you have no choice?"

"I would do it because you ask me."

Armanda squinted her eyes and fixed them on me as if waiting for the inner detector in her soul to signal whether I could be believed.

"Bueno," she finally said with a firm nod of her head.

"Bueno what?" I asked.

She took the glass of brandy to her mouth and drank all that was in it in a gulp. Then she sighed loudly and told me, "Nando is home tonight. He plays poker with friends at the house. Talk to him if you wish."

I jumped up immediately from my chair so that I would not have time to focus on the fear of meeting Nando. The move was so quick and decisive that Armanda looked shocked. "I'll be back," I said.

DAY 34 (LATE EVENING)

Outside Armanda's house three cars were parked, not including Nando's black Impala. There was loud rock music coming from the house; the words of the song were in Spanish. I knocked and knocked on the open door but no one came. The front door opened into the kitchen. The party was happening in the living room, which was off to the side. I went in. There were four men playing cards on a tin table that seemingly had been moved from the kitchen. There were bottles of rum and tequila and Mountain Dew strewn all over the floor. The room was in a haze with the thick smoke of marijuana.

Mario, the man that Nando sent to watch over Armanda, was sitting down next to a stocky young man with raven black oily hair whom I took to be Nando. Mario whispered something in his ear. Nando looked up for a second and then continued to draw two cards from the pack. "Ya le cayó caca al mole," Nando said. The two men with their backs to me turned around and laughed.

"Quiero hablar contigo," I said.

"Hey, ése. You want to talk to me, ése." Nando said rocking back in his chair. "Pero . . . the question is, why do I want to talk to you?"

"I want to talk business with you."

"Ahh," he said, slapping his cards on the table and sliding the pile of dollar bills in the middle toward himself, "es business. El gringuito quiere hablar de business." He stood up and came toward me. He was shorter than Armanda. The top of his head barely reached my chin. With Armanda, I could dance cheek to cheek with only a slight bend of the head. I remembered his rounded face and his eyebrows that uninterruptedly lined his forehead from temple to temple. He stood about five feet away from me, his hands in his back pockets pushing his pelvis forward. "Talk business to me, baby," he cooed.

"I want to buy five hundred grams of coke, the kind you sniff, not the kind you inject, and I want to buy one hundred grams of mula."

"Oh, five hundred grams of coke and one hundred grams of mula. That's very big order." Nando turned his head over his shoulders to look at his friends behind him, who laughed at his sarcastic tone. "What else do you want?"

"I want to give you three thousand dollars."

"Three thousand dollars. Why, you think I'm cute?" Laughter again.

"I give you three thousand dollars and you stay away from your mother for two months. She comes to live with me in El Paso. After that you can visit her if she wants."

Nando glared at me for a few seconds as if I had just insulted his honor in a way that could only be cured by my sudden death. The other people around the table turned their chairs around to look at me. Nando picked up a bottle of tequila from the floor and then slowly went to the tape player and smashed the bottle so that the music stopped with a twangy bang, and plastic and glass flew all over the room. The men around the table stood up. Mario was shaking glass that had landed on his lap. Then Nando turned around and talked to me with a smirk. I noticed that his hand was bleeding and that he still had the jagged neck of the bottle in his hand.

"Ten thousand dollars up front and a thousand for the drugs. I see her whenever I fucking want."

"No deal," I said. "She's a whore and a drug addict. I want her but not that much." I turned around to walk away.

"Don't ever turn your back on me," yelled Nando. I turned to face him. "Eight thousand más one thousand for the drugs más five hundred each week you want me to stay away."

"Look. I don't play games. You think I'm afraid of you? You can kill me right now, I don't give a shit. I knew you when you were little." I took out my wallet and showed him the picture I was carrying, my hand trembling despite my efforts. "This is a picture of you and your mother that I had taken. I knew you and your mother. I'm not going to hurt you or her. She was the mother of my son, your stepbrother that died. I'll give you five thousand dollars and a thousand for the drugs and one hundred every week. When I get a job I will continue to give you whatever money I can. Everything I have is your mother's and yours. That's all I can do. I'm not playing games anymore.

"Give me the money."

"I don't have the money now. I can give it to you tomorrow."

"Give me the money in your wallet. Now."

I opened my wallet and gave him the two hundred dollars or so that was in there.

"You are one big pendejo," he said, grabbing the wad of dollars. "You think she stays with you. She is using you for convenience. No need to, how you say, hustle, for mula or craca. It's easy for her. When the money is gone, she will be here with me. Hey, it's easy for me too. You think she prefers you? You are in fantasy, ése."

"Maybe so."

"Maybe so. Maybe so. You don't have much money, do you? What, maybe you had fifteen thousand total. Minus the two thousand or so that you have spent since you been with my mother. Ha? I'm right. Hey, ése. We finish your money quickly. It will go in two months, maybe one. Hey, why look at gift horse up the ass, is that how you say? Then when you have no money, all like before. If you get job so then we take money you have if enough."

"I'll be here tomorrow morning with the money and to get Armanda's things."

"O.K. O.K., man. Come here with the money. And you take my mother. Is not first time I rent her for money. I know you don't disappear. I don't worry. She will never leave me. You know that too, don't you?"

"I'll be here tomorrow. Then you must stay away for two months."

"Sure, sure, whatever you say, ése. I find you if I need you before, don't worry. I know where you live already, the Del Camino. Hey man, I may be loco but not estúpido."

Then he drew closer to me, pulling me toward his face with a finger hooked on the top button of my shirt. He stood on tiptoes and whispered in my ear. "I want you to take this with you. I know you are the father of my stepbrother. I know you are the man who fucked my mother in her mind and fucked me also. You fucked up two lives, man. I want to tell you that. I want to tell you something else. Come here. I killed your son, ése. Want to know how? I tied him to that fucking triciclo that you gave me and I rolled him down the little hill of the Del Camino. You know how the exit is like a little hill that goes down into Alameda Avenue? I tied him with this gray tape that you bought to fix the noise of the air conditioner and I rolled him down into the street and saw the little fucker go splash by a truck. Crunch. Crack. Crack. Splat. Take that with you, puto."

DAY 35

got to Armanda's house the following afternoon. She had requested time in the morning to be alone with Nando. Armanda was sitting beside the kitchen table with two suitcases by her side. In the living room where the card playing had taken place the night before, Nando was sprawled on the sofa, shirtless and in boxing shorts, watching some kind of Mexican movie. On the kitchen table lay two packages wrapped in aluminum foil and tied with a cord. They were both inside a plastic bag which was full of sliced serrano and jalapeño peppers. The smell of the cut chiles filled the air and stung the eyes. I sniffed deeply.

"For dogs that may be on the bridge to El Paso. That way they don't sniff drugs," said Armanda.

"Ahh," I responded.

Nando got up and came to the kitchen, a cigarette dangling from his lip. He stared at me. I took a white envelope where I had put the money out of my back pocket. I offered the envelope to him. He nodded at the kitchen table, and I placed the envelope there. Armanda got up and picked up her bags. There were no attempts on either side to say any kind of good-bye. Armanda's eyes were deep red. Perhaps they had been fighting.

"I'll hide this in the car," I said, taking the packages from the table.

"Yo te ayudo," said Armanda. She grabbed her two bags. "Nos vemos, Nando." Armanda said this while I held the screen door open for her. Nando nodded.

I put the drugs in the trunk underneath the spare tire where I had hidden and forgotten Abuelito's rifle. Then I opened the door for Armanda. She looked back at the house and Nando standing in the doorway and paused, filling me with an instant fear that she was not going to go through with it. She waved at Nando and got in. Just before I ducked my head to get in the car, I heard Nando say to me in a dry monotone:

"Don't forget what I want you to know. Crack. Crack. Splat."

"I don't forget," I said. "I won't forget."

In the car Armanda asked me to drive to a nearby drive-in bar. It was like a drive-in movie; you ordered food and liquor by yelling into a radiolike apparatus which hooked on to the car window and blared music when you weren't pushing a button to communicate with some voice a million miles away. After a while, Armanda asked me if we could stop by El Caballito to say goodbye, and I knew, to get a dose from the nurse. In my preparations for our "escape," I had not omitted the fact that for a while Armanda would still need drugs and that I would have to be the one to inject them into her. Armanda had a phobia of doing it herself, although she would, of course if there were no one else available. The problem was her very thin, very wobbly and very used veins that were like the nerves of a cooked chicken and which only an expert could find. La nurse and Armanda had let me watch the procedure a few times at my request, and I had even successfully accomplished the feat twice, but it was something that made Armanda worry. I thought she might be thinking about it as she sipped her beer in silence.

"I can always bring the nurse to see you," I said. "I just think it's a good idea to stay away from El Caballito and from Nando for a while."

"I don't care," she said.

"I won't leave you alone."

"I'm not worried about it," she said. There was a tone of quiet resignation to her words. She was not happy, but neither was she cold or distant. "What did Nando mean?"

"When?"

"When we left. What did he mean when he say, 'don't forget what I told you?'"

"Oh, I think he meant not to forget to come back and give him money every week."

"You lie," she said, piercing through me and seeing exactly what I was thinking and feeling. "You hate Nando, don't you?"

"Yes, I do."

"Not just because he's bad for me."

"No. I never felt this way before about anyone. I hate him as a person."

"You are like him in some ways." She said this in a way that was meant to inform me of something which she knew I already knew.

"Help me," I said. Neither one of us was looking at the other. It was as if we truly were watching a movie on some imaginary outdoor screen.

"I make no promises," Armanda turned to look at me.

"Promises of what?" I asked, not following the train of the conversation.

"Promises that I will be able to make it. To cure my habit."

"I ask only that you try. I don't want you to die. You're dying now."

Armanda turned around quickly with what looked like anger.

"It's O.K.," she said. "I like truth. It hurts but it feels good."

"I don't mean to be hurtful."

"I don't think detox hospital will work, but I try. You have to tie me with a rope one day and take me no matter how much I hate you. I will hate you. I will hate you with all my heart. You know that?"

"Yes."

"But not soon. I need time."

"I'll surprise you one morning," I said grinning like the devil, to which Armanda responded by splashing my face with beer.

It all happened fast and more or less as planned. A couple of weeks later, I grabbed Armanda while she was in one of her dream states and put her in the back seat of my car with the help of two of the old men who lived in the Del Camino and of Doña Ramona, who guided us with cautions to not hit her head, to watch her dress, to put a seat belt on her. I whisked her off to a medical center outside of Las Cruces, New Mexico, about an hour and a half away. She was to stay for two months, and I would not be able to see her for two weeks. The young doctor who received Armanda and whose features resembled a Latin version of Kate, informed me of the procedures while Armanda continued sleeping on a stretcher beside us.

"Every detox center has its own therapeutic style," she explained, her thumb on Armanda's pulse. "The difference lies in how tough each place is with the patient. There are those who don't believe in making it too uncomfortable for the patient. Then there are the cold turkey ones, which are not much more than a padded cell. Of course, the type of treatment a patient gets also depends on what's covered by insurance or, as in your case, how much the patient's family can pay. This treatment you have chosen is top of the line. Two months of therapy is expensive but it has the best recovery stats of all treatments. We don't guarantee any results. We can't. It all depends on how much the patient wants to heal herself. When all is said and done, it still comes down to willpower, I'm afraid. We will probably be recommending some form of outpatient care after she leaves. Some form of twelve-step support group is good also, but in my experience, not by itself and not at the beginning. It's helpful down the line. Some combination of continued drug therapy with group therapy run by a qualified psychologist is probably the best. Here's a pamphlet that describes our outpatient treatments and facilities. Here at Buena Vista Center we follow the middle approach. Not too tough but not too soft, either. We start patients on drugs that produce similar effects to what her body is used to—let's see—cocaine and heroin, hmmm; and we slowly start to give her less and less of these nonaddictive stimulants while the real poison works its way out of the body. This is done in conjunction with individual counseling and group therapy plus good food, exercise, crafts, and other fun things to keep her mind occupied. The hard part starts in about a month when she will be off everything except maybe some mild antidepressants or sedatives or maybe even some "uppers," all depending on her state. This is when we're going to need you. She'll be facing the prospect of no more drugs and that will be hard even though her physical addiction will have been eliminated. Something like a mental addiction will be there, and that's where we win or lose. Now, I need to go get her in her room and get her ready. It's better if you're not here when she wakes up. I will be her medical doctor. I will be in charge of her body. Doctor Quineiros is her assigned psychologist. There will be nurses and aides that will also be with her as she goes through this. Now you need to go to the second floor and ask the nurse to give you the psychological questionnaire. Please fill out this questionnaire about her mental history and tell us anything that may be of help to Doctor Quineiros in his individual counseling of her. We'll see you in two weeks."

I bent down and kissed Armanda on her lips and for some reason made the sign of the cross on her forehead the way Renata used to make it on me before I went to sleep. Then I went up to the second floor and wrote everything I could possibly think about Armanda. I wrote about how I had left her and Nando years ago, about my son that was killed, about how and where I had found her, about how much drugs she took, then I pleaded to the invisible Doctor Quineiros to make her whole, to make all of us whole, to do all he could for all our sakes.

DAY 36

I survived my first visit with Armanda. She was sitting in a triple room, not unlike the one where Lilia had died, only the other two beds were unoccupied. Armanda was sitting up in her bed watching TV. The nurse at the front desk had warned me that Armanda was going through a time rougher than all expected. She was very irritable, so much so that she and another patient had beat the dickens out of each other the day before over an imagined insult. Now she was doing "timeout" in her room.

"I gant out," were the first words she said to me. The skin around her left eye was purple and green and looked like the shiny eye of a fly. Her lower lip was swollen and hanging like a ripe plum.

"¿Cómo estás?" I asked.

"Ake me om ere at ow!" she ordered me, not quite pronouncing all the words.

"Soon. Soon. I will take you from here."

"I wan alk o Nando!" Armanda said grimacing from the pain in her mouth.

"Soon. Soon we will talk to Nando," I said, drawing a chair next to her bed.

"I ask Nandoo ill ou."

"You will ask Nando to kill me?"

"Hes."

I stood up and looked at her to see if she really meant it. By the way she pushed my face away with her hand, I knew that it was not a pure wish, but an ambiguous desire. I opened the bag I had brought with me. A carton of Viceroys mentolados, her favorite cigarettes made in Mexico, or maybe just sold in Mexico at a much lower price. Five giant Baby Ruth bars. Lip balm, appropriately enough. A new lighter. A new mirror and rouge and comb set. Agua de naranja. Jabón de manzanilla con coco. Chicles Adams. A new pair of sunglasses which she put on immediately and which, fortunately, were big enough to not rest on her new shiner. Three pairs of silk underwear. A pair of purple slippers, a sun dress, assorted magazines in Spanish, and the one that made her eyes light up for a second: a portable tape player with her favorite tapes, Javier Solís, Tito Puente, Cuco Sánchez, Vicente Fernández, La Negra, José-José, Armando Manzanero, Lo Mejor de Agustín Lara y sus Mejores Intérpretes.

For the rest of that visit, she was sullen and silent. I took it as a hopeful sign, however, that when I was leaving her room, she said "hey" and I turned around in time to see her firmly and with passion point her middle finger up in the air.

The rest of the visits were better by degrees, if you can call someone who is subdued and without much animation "better." But I was told by the Latin Kate and by Doctor Quineiros that it was normal, that it was necessary to have Armanda on some kind of heavy antidepressant. This prescription recommended by Doctor Quineiros and prescribed by Doctor Sandovar (Latin Kate's name) was because Armanda had shown violence toward herself during the first month of withdrawal and even now spoke of dying as a better alternative to living without drugs.

"She is extremely dependent on her son, even more so than on the drugs," Doctor Quineiros said to me. She is conflicted and deeply wounded as a mother. It's as complicated as I've ever seen."

"Does she talk about the death of her second son, my son?"

"She acknowledged the death of baby Ismael. It was a big struggle for her to get to that point. But she called his death an accident, and I did not think it was the right time to probe further. Are you sure Nando killed him as you say?"

"Yes, I checked into it with the El Paso police. The baby's hands and feet were tied with duct tape to the tricycle. Nando was six years old at the time. He was taken into psychiatric care but no charges were brought by the D.A. The case even made new law in Texas. It's discussed in law books. The police also showed me Nando's record. Whew! In and out of reformatory school from age ten onward, sniffing glue, stealing, assault, then when he was sixteen an aggravated assault and rape conviction for which he did two years in an adult prison."

"Well, all that is in her, causing a pain that's catching up to her."

"And me? Does she talk about me?"

"No. I mean she talks about you in the present, but she doesn't talk about you in the past."

"I see."

"It's understandable. You're part of a trauma that she doesn't want to remember. Except that now you're back and this is, like, riling up her subconscious. Your departure, her pregnancy, Nando's jealousy toward the new baby, and the hurt of seeing his mother hurt by your abandonment, the baby's death, and now that you tell me, the love and guilt and hate that she must feel toward Nando, her flesh and blood and the killer of her flesh and blood. No wonder. All of this is in her head at some deep level getting stirred up. And now there are no drugs to keep things calm. But she says good things about you. She says you can help her tear away from Nando, who needs to be separated from her mother love so that he has a chance. She hopes that Nando can come here too sometime in the future, with your help. And she hopes that you will stop hating Nando and understand why he is the way he is."

"Oh."

"Can you do that? Can you stop hating Nando and reach out to him as Armanda wants?"

"I honestly don't know."

"Just remember that what she's doing in part is for you. She's trying. You may not see the effort, but effort is measured differently in different people. Given her circumstances, what she's doing is heroic for her."

"What more can I do?"

"If you can afford it, leave her here another two weeks. We need to find the right medication for her so that she's not zombied out all the time, and the extra time will give the individual and group therapies in tandem a chance to progress. Then I think you need to bring her back for weekly individual sessions with me. Can you afford it?"

"Yes, I think so. I'm running low but I still have some money left. Every week I give Nando money so he doesn't come looking for her, but I have a job starting in the fall at the community college teaching pre-law and a paralegal course on real estate, and in the meantime I'm a substitute teacher at the Catholic high school. I also manage the Del Camino, and I translate romance novels into

Spanish. I even got Armanda a job working at a hair salon. She'll be a receptionist while she learns to cut and style hair."

"That's very good. That's very good. If you can just work things out with Nando so that he's a safe part of her life, that would be most helpful."

Armanda came home with me two weeks later than expected. She seemed calm and looked younger but somehow more timid, more afraid of life. Fortunately, I was never away from her for very long. I did most of my work at home except for my time teaching at the high school, which was mostly in and out for me. My job at the community college was all set, and I was busy preparing my lessons and looking forward to the courses, except that I feared leaving Armanda alone in the fall. She still seemed very fragile. She did not go to work at the hair salon where I had finagled her a job. Instead, she worked at the Del Camino, helping me manage and also clean it with the help of Annette, the young daughter of one of the women from El Caballito. Annette made the trip from Juárez to the Del Camino every day by taking four different buses. It was fun to see the two of them tackle room by room, taking out a bundle of sheets and stuffing them in the canvas carts and taking out rolls of toilet paper and soap and putting them in each room. It seemed like back-breaking work, but Armanda liked it. As the days went by, I saw Armanda smile more and more and even joke with the retired old fogies who lived permanently at the Del Camino and who lusted unabashedly for her.

In the afternoons before Annette took the bus back to Juárez, she and Armanda cleaned the pool. Armanda, barely clad in a leopard bikini bought at the Woolworth's down the street, blasted her favorite dancing songs from her tape player, and she was at her very best, gyrating and suggesting such things with the pool skimmer and the vacuum hose that I was afraid some members of the geriatric but merry audience who daily lined the pool would drop stone dead at any moment, their hearts short-circuited by a deadly surge of joyous energy.

Every Friday morning I took Armanda to the Buena Vista Center for an hourly visit with Doctor Quineiros and every Wednesday night I dropped her off at the Church of San Martín de Porres, where in the basement Drug Addicts Anonymous met to tell their stories. Armanda did not let me come the night when she

told her story, but I would have given anything to be there. Sometimes partners or spouses were invited, and during those times I
noticed that Armanda did not participate much in the discussions.
She sat there with her legs folded in her chair, smoking and drinking coffee. She listened to the comments because I would catch her
smiling or giggling when something funny was said, or I could see
her eyes well up with tears when some sad story involving children
was told. When the moderator, in an effort to include everyone,
asked her a question, Armanda would sit straight in her chair and
respond directly to the question in a truthful and heartfelt way, but
with as few words as necessary.

During those visits I understood that she was there because I
wanted her to be there and she did not believe that the sessions
would do any good or in any way prevent a return to the inevitable.
I knew she was thinking about how long she could last. I could see
her having a harder and harder time making it through the day and
through the night. She'd wake up early in the morning and make
herself a glass of Kool-Aid and tequila which she refilled every
hour or so and sipped throughout the day and most of the night.
She never got fully drunk because the tequila was drunk slowly and
in small doses, but I knew she was anesthetizing herself from feelings that were beginning to stir once again. I knew that she thought
of Nando more than she let me know. She had not seen him since
that day I put her in my car and drove away. Nando had not come
looking for her, probably because every week I would drive to her
old house and give Nando, or leave under the flower pot beside the
door, an envelope with two hundred dollars. When he was home I'd
go in and tell him about Armanda even if he acted as if he was not
interested at all. I told him about Armanda, her success at the center, and how she was working at the Del Camino, trying to stay on
a good path. I told him about my jobs and my future teaching job,
which would bring a good enough salary. I don't know whether
bringing Nando money and letting him know that there would be
money available in the future was my way of reaching out to him
the way Armanda wanted me to or just another way of paying off
Nando so that he would not reclaim Armanda.

One night about a week before her death, I woke up with
Armanda sobbing next to me in bed. She was biting her lips, trying
to stifle the noises that sounded like the cries of a wounded animal.

"Armanda, ¿por qué lloras?" I asked her.

She tried for a few minutes to stop, her two hands covering her face. Her chest was heaving and her eyes were wide with the look of someone who had suddenly remembered something horrible.

"Why did you never come back?"

"When?"

"Many years ago. Why did you never answer my letter? Even when I told you about your son?"

"Ay, Armanda. I ask that every day. I don't know. I was afraid. I wanted another life, the kind I thought I should have. I wanted more than I thought you could offer me. I did not know then what I know now."

"Qué lástima," she said, the sobs quieting down. "Life went by us."

"Life is still here. We have time."

"Time for what?" she asked softly.

"Time to change things. Time to live."

"Sometimes it isn't possible to unturn our mistakes. We must live to make up for them in the way that life says."

"I know. But we have to try. We have to keep on living to make up for them."

"Sí. Pero, I died already. I let myself die long ago. There is no strength to come back any more."

"Armanda, remember how you once told me that you learned the paso lento in part from your mother who was a curandera?"

"Yes."

"You need to heal yourself now. The way you learned from your mother. We need to heal one another. We've been doing that, you know."

"And I am healing you?"

"Yes."

"¿De qué?

"From my past."

She put her arm around my chest and drew close to me.

"Ismael, I want to tell you something. I have forgiven the past. You shouldn't stay anymore. You don't have to stay."

"Lo sé."

"¿Por qué, Ismael? No desperdicies tu vida. Vete."

"Armanda, solo tú me comprendes. ¿Recuerdas el paso lento? Do you remember how, with practice, the dance takes you along farther and farther hasta que un día you finally learn to dance the paso lento?"

"Sí."

"That's why I want to stay."

She smiled and reached under the sheet to touch me. "Mira," she said, "el viejito quiere bailar."

On the day of her death the following week, I came home from teaching and found the door to our apartment slightly open. As I opened the door I was struck by the stench of burning heroin. The door to our bedroom was closed. I could hear the sound of a man wailing. The door was locked. I pounded on the door.

"Está muerta," I heard from inside. It was the voice of Nando.

"Abre la puerta," I yelled.

"Give me la mula," shouted Nando from inside. His words were slurred, almost incomprehensible.

"¿Cuál mula?"

"In back of your car!"

I went to my car and opened the trunk. Underneath the spare tire there was still one of the two aluminum packages that Armanda had made. The smell of the cut serrano and jalapeño chiles was gone. There was Abuelito's rifle which I now bolted together. Inside the chamber, there was the sole bullet that I had placed a long time ago in the basement of my house, just before I got Kate's call.

I walked back into the apartment and kicked the door to the bedroom open. In one hand I had the rifle and in the other the package of heroin. The curtains were drawn and the bedroom was dark. When my pupils adjusted, I saw Armanda motionless in the bed with one of her arms limp over the side. Her blouse was torn open, showing her black bra. Nando was kneeling on the floor undressed except for blue underwear and tight brown socks that stretched to his calves. He was facing the window curtains, his hands outstretched to the dark heavens, his head lolling loosely around his neck. I dropped the heroin package on the floor and went over to touch Armanda's hands and face. I put my face on her naked chest. There was no heartbeat. I closed her eyes and lifted her so that her head rested on a pillow and covered her body with the bedspread. Nando, still on his knees, was trying to open the package of heroin, trying to cut with his teeth the string that Armanda had wound tightly around the aluminum foil. He looked up briefly at me and smiled in such a way that I saw before my eyes the image of the little boy Nando I once knew. I picked up Abuelito's rifle, which was leaning against the bed. Calmly, I walked behind Nando and put the end of the rifle in the small indentation between his neck and his head. Nando's shoulders cringed as if he were being tickled just before I pulled the trigger. A jet of black vomit shot out of his mouth, and then he doubled over, twitched, and did not move again. I went over to Armanda and lay next to her until Annette found us in the morning. I asked Annette to call the police.

DAY 37

In my cell there is a window. It is covered with some unbreakable but scratched up, tinted Plexiglas through which I can see out but no one can see in. A poor specimen of a window to be sure, but still a window. And out of this window I have seen the stars, the moon, the sky with its infinite shades of blue and black, clouds the shape of dreams and most of all, I have seen the skinny willow down in the courtyard below. On the drooping limbs of this tree I have seen robins and cardinals, finches and sparrows, and yesterday morning as the sun rose, I saw the tree shine from within as if on fire. I write about the window now because it strikes me that the cell need not have a window at all. It could have been all closed in. I see no necessity for it, but some kindly prison architect must have thought it would be good to have. I am grateful to whoever added this amenity to the design.

DAY 38

*G*rosvenor, who I gather is in tight with the commissioner, came by this morning, and, after beating around the bush with small talk, told me that a date had been set. The new governor wants to push things along, do something soon after taking office, to show people that he means business. I, appeal-less as I am, make fine fodder. When? Soon. Sooner if possible. Before I change my mind about appealing. The thing is, the commissioner has some discretion here, according to Grosvenor. Not by much. But an extra few days is not out of the question. Arrangements have to be made. For one thing, our little place apparently does not handle executions. We are here, it turns out, because the execution site is overcrowded. The event requires a trip and perhaps a short stay in Huntsville.

Grosvenor giggled when I asked him if the short stay was for acclimatization purposes, like an athlete getting to a high altitude place a week or two before an event. But here is what the commissioner, through Grosvenor, wants to know. How am I doing? How am I doing with what I am doing? How much time do I need to wrap things up? Grosvenor gestured at my typewriter with his eyebrows when he said this so I figured he was talking about this writing.

"I'm done," I said.

"You've been working very hard. The commissioner is very much aware," he said. "It looks like a book."

"Grosvenor, you know very well what it is. You've read parts of it."

"I apologize. My motives were good, however. I'm worried about the state of your soul. It's my job. Part of my ministry."

"Yeah, well. I'm worried too."

"Anyway, I've told the commissioner about what you're doing. Mr. Gómez has also reported to him. He thinks it would be good if you finish as much as you can. But he needs a ballpark date so that he can arrange things accordingly. Delay a little. Throw some red tape. Whatever."

225

"I'm not ready yet." I was not thinking of the writing. I was thinking more of my jaguar work.

"I know you're not," said Grosvenor. "None of us are." Then he paused and changed his tone of voice. I had an inkling of what was coming. "Ismael . . . what about Jesus Christ?"

"What about him?"

"Have you let Jesus Christ be the lord and ruler of your life?"

"Grosvenor, listen. I appreciate your concern. Really, I do. A couple of weeks ago I probably wouldn't have. And I'm sorry about the scene in your Bible class. That was silly. But now I need to be left alone."

"He will come to you if you let him."

"Stop. Please."

"O.K., but answer one question."

"What?"

"If you don't want to talk about Christ, why do I see you poring over the Bible?"

I could have told Grosvenor to go busybody someone else. I could have even picked him Botswana-like and thrown him out without too much problem. But I answered his question as best I could. Not because I thought he had a right to an answer but because I wanted to. I felt at that moment as if nothing that Grosvenor could do or say would bother me.

"I like reading about Christ. He was a jaguar too."

"A what?"

"It's just something I've been thinking."

"My. Oh my, Ismael. There are others who are smarter about these things than I am, for certain. You are one of them for sure. All I can say is that you read the Holy Book as if you're searching for something. And what you're searching for is there. It's there, all right."

"Lately, I guess you're right. I have been searching for something in there. You're right. But it's not what you think. It's something different. I've been searching for clues as to why Christ simply went to his death. Why didn't he defend himself or run away? He could have lived to fight another day. He may have done the world more good."

"He died to save us. You and me. To deliver us from our sins."

"I'm sorry. I just can't understand the ransom theory. It just doesn't make sense to me."

"Why else? It was the sacrifice required by God the Father. To save man. Why else? Why do you think he died?"

"What would have happened if Christ had not died? What sins exactly was he delivering us from? And didn't we keep on committing them after he died? What sort of God can only be appeased through the suffering and death of his son? If that's the reason, then I want nothing to do with it."

"It's a mystery, Ismael, we don't know everything. I can tell you that for me his redemption was like when you see your little baby sick and you pray to the Lord with all your heart to take away the pain from that little baby and give it to you. And God can do that. He takes the pain away from some and gives it to others, but for some reason He just can't get rid of all the pain there is in this world, not altogether."

"I just don't understand why he died so voluntarily. All I can think of is that maybe he was trying to tell us something about how a beloved son of God lives and, for him, living like a beloved son of God involved a kind of daily voluntary dying."

"He did that, yes, he did that. He wanted to teach us how to die to the flesh and how we, like him, shall resurrect first in the spirit and then in the flesh. I believe that something changed when he died. Something in the very chemicals and the very matter-of-factness of the universe changed when he died. His death was like a big injection of hope where there was none before. The evil that is in us, the ugliness were forgiven and we ourselves became the inheritors of his kingdom because of his death."

"That part I don't see so well."

"Oh, Lord, Ismael. You don't have much time left, son. You shouldn't be doubting so the word of God. Lord! So, why do you think he went to his death?"

"To teach us, as I said. And maybe because he was guilty as charged. He said he was the Son of God. That was blasphemy, a crime by the rules of his world. He came to the world to live in the world and in doing so accepted its rules. Now he had to yield to them. Somehow he saw the will of God in obeying those rules. Besides, it was not in his makeup to run away from what life presented, whenever and however life presented it."

"But he was the Son of God. He wasn't blaspheming."

"By the rules of his world he was."

"Do you think he was the Son of God? All you have to do is accept him as your savior and you'll be saved. Trust yourself unto him, Ismael. It's that simple, Ismael. I am not acquainted with all your fancy thinking, which is beyond me. But I know that to be saved you just have to give yourself to Jesus the way a little child gives himself to him, no questions asked. That's all. Then everlasting life will be yours. Do you believe that Jesus Christ is your Lord and Savior and the Son of God? Do you believe that he will be awaiting you when you take that final step, Ismael?"

"I believe in his courage. I believe in his ever-present, steadfast sense of purpose. I believe in the way he squared up to adversity and in the compassion he felt for his fellow human beings. And I believe that there are times when I myself am inexplicably filled with a courage, a purpose, and a compassion like his own. More than that I cannot say."

"At the moment, anyway. But we have time for you yet to say what I believe you yearn to say."

"If you say so."

"Let me do this. Let me go back to the commissioner and try to get you as much time as possible. But I need to be honest with you. You need to start wrapping things up. And I don't mean just your book, either. You need to start thinking about . . ."

I was staring at, of all things, a speckled ladybug that had somehow miraculously managed to find her way into my cell. There she was, right on the concrete wall, peaceful as can be.

"Ismael?"

"Yes?"

"There's a favor I want to ask you. I would like you to listen to my confession. I would like to confess to you as a representative of our Lord and to ask your forgiveness for what I've done. I need your forgiveness as much as you need to forgive me."

"Grosvenor, honestly. I am in no mood or condition to forgive anyone right now. I don't want to hear your confession. I am not anyone's representative. Look, Grosvenor. Please go now. No to the confession. Not now, not ever."

DAY 39

Grosvenor's Confession   (abbreviated version)

I want to confess my sins to you, my brother in Christ, and witness to you about how I was saved through the power of God.

I was, for as long as I remember, a God-fearing man. At the time of my fall, I was an elder in the Presbyterian Church in Las Lomas, Amarillo, Texas. I rose to be an elder by virtue of my hard work and dedication to the church and because I was blessed from early days with the gifts of preaching and administration.

By profession I sold insurance and I was very good at it. Many of my clients came from the church or were referred to me by members of the church, and in that way there were many worldly blessings that I received directly from my spiritual life.

The two went hand in hand and I can
understand how the Good Bible says that those
who walk in the ways of the Lord shall prosper
all their days . . . not just in the hereafter,
but right here and now. For the Lord clearly
says that he comes to bring us life and to bring
it to us abundantly.

I guess that all that prosperity must have
gone to my head. I began to think of myself as
special in the eyes of the Lord. That is why I
think the good Lord allowed me to fall into
temptation.

The Lord gave me a lovely wife and two
beautiful daughters. A better-looking family
could not be found anywhere in the Texas
Panhandle or elsewhere. My wife was beautiful.
My two daughters were the sweetest creatures
a father could ever wish for. They were lively
and frisky like young girls tend to be, but they
also grew up in the shade of God and the
church. They taught Sunday School, each one of

them since they were little. They took care of little ones in the school nursery, and they were in the choir and in the Youth League too when they grew up.

When my eldest, Eliza, was but sixteen years of age, she accepted the care of mentally handicapped children as her God-ordained ministry, and she would bring over to the house a young mentally handicapped woman whose name was Esther. Now Eliza, God bless her, used to tell me that taking care of these innocent souls was more a gift than a burden. She said to me "Daddy, someone like Esther has more to offer me than I can offer her."

"How so?" I asked.

"Because, Daddy, Esther's close to God just the way she is. The rest of us have to try hard to get close to Him."

Can you imagine a sixteen-year-old coming up with something like that? Well, I was so proud of Eliza for the way she was witnessing our

Lord every day in the things she did that I never gave it a second thought to have Eliza bring Esther over all the time. Sometimes she would come and stay for the weekend or a vacation week since apparently her own family didn't want anything to do with her.

The home where she lived encouraged what they called "normalization" which you probably are acquainted with, seeing as how you told me when you were in college you used to live in a halfway house for the mentally handicapped, a fact for which I praise the Lord, for I know that deep inside you there is the special love of God, the very same that led you way back then to seek out these angels of the Lord.

One day Esther was helping me with the dishes because I asked everyone eating at my home, whether kin or guest, to help out with the chores. If they ate at my house, they worked, and that's all there was to it. Esther and I were doing the dishes, and Esther was about the same age as my daughter, mind you, when all of a sudden I started looking at Esther as a woman. I always knew she was a woman, don't get me wrong, but you know what I mean. All of a sudden I was seeing her as a woman for the first time. Lord Almighty, I finished up those dishes fast. After that I stayed away from Esther, so much so that even Eliza noticed.

"Daddy, what's wrong? How come you don't cater to Esther anymore, the way you used to?"

I'm telling you, Eliza was and is a gifted child of God. Nothing could escape her perception. Well, I knew I couldn't keep anything from her, so I told her.

"Eliza, now, you're old enough, so I'll tell you this. I don't know if Esther knows it or not, but she is a woman just like any other woman. She may not be pretty. But she sure is a grown-up woman."

"Oh, Daddy. You're such a fuddy duddy."

"Now, what exactly does that mean?"

"Why, don't you know that you probably just paid Esther the biggest compliment she's ever received?"

"How do you figure?" I asked.

"Well, you see her as a woman, that's how. Everyone else sees her just as a handicapped child. You should spend more time with her. Getting her to see your respect for her as a grown-up woman would be the best thing that ever happened to her!"

"Is that so?"

"Sure. Now here. Take this load of laundry to the basement and help Esther do the loads. She's down there right now folding."

To this day I do not know whether the Devil used Eliza to get to me. The Enemy will use whatever means he can, and I don't doubt that he used Eliza's words to encourage me that it was O.K. to be with Esther and to feel for her the way I felt.

I did go down to the basement and I did help Esther with the folding. Little by little I let go of the reins of my passion, just in bits so that no one noticed, not even me, to be honest with you. My wife was unsuspecting on the whole, and Eliza managed to leave Esther and me more and more alone, trusting me and thinking no doubt that all I had within me were the intentions of Christian compassion. I hardly had to think of any excuses. It was the laundry one day. It was gardening the other. It was going to the church to do the altar. It was this or it was that until Esther was really familiar with me and had gotten used to joking with me and what not.

My insides were everyday more overcome by Esther. The way she had of just looking at me with those adoring eyes whenever I did something nice for her. The way she listened to and did everything I said. I don't know if I had ever felt anything like that. It got to be that all I could think of was having her completely to myself, and these thoughts got to be so ever present in my mind that I began to get accustomed to them and think of them as normal. I was getting old. I had a paunch and was going bald. My lovely wife was always there to fulfill her marriage vows and she mostly came to me whenever I asked her, but she never sought me out or made me feel attractive, the way Esther did. Besides, I thought to myself that all this was good for Esther. And to tell you the truth, I had never seen her happier. She used to bug and bug Eliza to ask her over, and then after a while she took to calling me directly and asking me if I could come pick her up from the home where she lived, even if it was only to get an ice cream cone at the Dairy Queen.

I'm going to skip a lot of details only to let you know that little by little I started touching Esther in such a way which she felt, and I

236

made myself believe, was just what friends did when they were having fun. I honestly don't think she thought about what was happening. She just responded spontaneous-like to the affection I was giving her and she never gave it a never-mind about whether it was right or wrong.

Well, before you know it, I began to notice that Esther did not mind where I touched, as if all places in her body were the same. Then after that, it just happened. I started doing with Esther all kinds of lecherous and lascivious acts wherever and whenever. Esther just went along totally obedient to whatever I asked her to do, giggling and calling me "Oh, Ronnie," when I was doing it. That's what she called me for some reason. She just smiled and looked into space or she would comb the few strands of my bald head with her fingers, while I had my way with her. Afterwards, I would treat her with a little present. A comb and mirror set, a red purse, a new dress, perfume, little things like that to let her know I cared.

Then it happened that some time went by and I didn't hear from Esther, nor did she come over to the house, but I didn't want to inquire for fear of being too obvious. Finally, I asked Eliza whatever happened to Esther, and Eliza with a look that burned my conscience and my soul, told me that Esther was grounded for a month because she was caught with Billy, one of the boys that went to school with her, doing it in the back seat of the school bus, while the rest of the passengers cheered on.

"Doing it?" I asked shocked and heartbroken all at once.

"Daddy! They were making love."

"Right there in the bus?"

"Right there in the back of the bus. Billy told her that he wanted to marry her, and she just grabbed him and made love to him right there. She doesn't know any better. It's not her fault. No one ever talked to her about those things."

When Esther finally came to see us, I was burning up with anger and jealousy. All she could talk about was Billy this and Billy that. Billy and her were going to have ten kids and Billy and her were going to Disney World and Billy and her were going to live in a trailer that the state was going to give them and Billy was going to get a job at Luby's and on and on. Instead of letting her go and being happy for her, all I could do is simmer with rage.

So one day, Ismael, I killed her. Just like that. I asked her if she and Billy would like to go bowling with me. When we were bowling, I asked Billy if he could bowl a set on his own while I took Esther to my car to show her a surprise I had bought for both of them. And there in the car, which I had parked behind the bowling alley, I began to kiss and grope at

Esther, and she let me at first, but then when I tried to go further she pushed me away and started telling me she wanted to go back to see Billy. This got me so full of hatred that I grasped her neck and choked her until there was no life left in her.

And now you see, my brother Ismael, what you have done is nothing compared to what I have done. Yet, I have found forgiveness for myself and others in the Lord. Please forgive me for both our sakes. For you yourself will not find peace until you can forgive the likes of me and accept me as a brother in Christ, someone who is like you in many ways, kin in the ways of the flesh. Please forgive me so you may forgive yourself. For in forgiveness lies the path to our salvation. Yours and mine.

Amen.

DAY 40

Kate pulled me away from the doorway, but just far enough so that we were not within Corky's field of vision. We could hear Corky splashing in the tub and he knew that we had not gone far. Our tender hug turned naturally into a gentle kiss, only the kiss became abruptly hard and restless on Kate's part. As we kissed, Kate's hand searched below for my response and found it. She knelt down and I tried to lift her up or kneel down with her, but she held me up while I cupped her golden hair in my two hands and in my being I felt light and airy, like the second before the roller coaster plunges down. Then, with one abrupt movement of her head, she took me in so completely that I was instantly reminded of Armanda and when I looked down, it was Armanda herself who looked up and smiled and let me know in her own way that I was created for her and she for me.

I open my eyes and for five seconds or so I actually do not know my location. I am lying down in some place in some universe that I cannot recognize and I see no object either natural or manmade to show me where I am or guide me, except that from between my legs extends a fulcrum, a tangible and hard symbol of my lostness and my longing. It is crying out into the heavens painfully, although it is being gently caressed at its base and point of origin by some lips attached to some person whom I do not recognize. I am breathing quickly and sweating. I try to sit up, but whoever is down there pushes me softly down again.

"What are you doing?" I ask when I finally orient myself and realize that I am still alive. I ask the question inquisitively, without alarm.

Velop, who I never before thought of as having handsome features, looks at me.

"Close your eyes, sweetheart. Just go along. You were having some kind of loud nightmare, so I came in, and found you like this. Hard as a rock. Look at you. My, my, it must be all the weightlifting you've been doing."

"Velop, stop."

"Sweetie, this is my way of thanking you. This is the only way I know how. It means a lot to me to give you this little gift before . . ."

"Before what?"

"Oh, darling. Don't make me say it. This is for helping me. You've been a sweetheart to me. You wrote that letter to Merv, which the bastard never answered, but that wasn't your fault. And you wrote that letter to your friend Mr. Niven and now there are two Harvard graduates working on my habeas corpus. They wrote to me. Actually, the associates are volunteers from your wife's firm. She got them. Pro boner, as they say. They think I have a real chance. They found the weak link in my case as I always suspect-ed. I never should have been charged with a capital offense. Oh, my honey, they think they can get my sentence commuted. So, enough talk. Let me get back to business."

Velop must have seen me glance across the hall.

"Oh, don't worry about Botswana. He's asleep. And even if he wasn't, he would understand. He knows when he has to share."

There's a giant grin on Velop's face. "He's not as bad as you make him out to be, you know."

I manage to sit up and pull a sheet over me.

"Why?" asks Velop plaintively.

"It's not my way."

"Oh, sweetie. I know it isn't. Don't you think I know that? You can close your eyes and think about your love, the lucky lady."

"No."

Velop gets up, shrugging his shoulders. He goes over to the desk. The light is still on. He picks up a book on insects that Mr. Gómez managed to find for me and looks at me with an "Insects? Really!" look. Then he grabs a handful of unopened letters that were covered by the book.

"You know, sweetie. You really should answer some of these. What I would give to get this kind of mail. Look at this, a letter from the National Legal Defense Fund."

I am now standing up and putting on my pants.

"You shouldn't have told him."

"Told him what, my darling? Told who?"

"Niven. About my situation. When I wrote to him I didn't tell him."

"Oh, sweetie. They knew you were here. I just told Mr. Niven that you were refusing to help yourself. I didn't tell them any details. I don't know any details. You're so reserved. Mr. Niven told your wife, I suppose. Oh, baby, don't begrudge me."

"It doesn't matter."

There is a pause during which Velop is thinking how to best say something.

"There's something I need to tell you," he says softly.

"I know."

"I know Grosvenor told you about the new governor and all. This is different."

"What is it?"

"Honey, rumor has it that the commissioner is not doing too well getting you more time. The turkeys in Austin are really putting up a fight. They want it done right away. I think they're afraid that you'll appeal."

"Oh."

"Why don't you appeal, my love? There's still time. All you have to do is make one phone call. To this here Legal Defense Fund or to Mr. Niven. In his letter to me he asks me to talk to you. You've not answered anybody. He says that a Mr. Preston in his firm knows the governor himself from some kind of Republican committee or other. He's already put in a good word for you. But they need you to help yourself. Just give me the word. I'll call him for you."

"I don't know."

"You don't know. What don't you know? You can tell me."

"Velop, I did it. I did what they said I did and more, much more."

"Oh, honey. Look at you. Come here, baby. Come here. Let it out. Let it all out. There you go. It feels good to say it out loud, doesn't it? Yes it does. There, there. Tell Uncle Velop what you did. It'll do you good."

"I'm O.K."

Velop waits for more but there is nothing more forthcoming.

"Of course you did it," he says after a while. "We all did. I did it too. I told you so way back then. That's not the point. Oh, honey, you're too hard on yourself. Don't torture yourself so. Life does that for you. That's life's job. You have to help yourself. Oh, my. What does Cortina say?"

"About what?"

"About appealing, about you trying to save yourself. You and he spend a lot of time together. Is he giving you that mano a mano macho shit about staring at death in the eyes and all?"

"No. I mean yes. But not like that." I laugh.

"Oh, it's good to see you laugh, sweetie pie."

"How much time do you think I have?"

"I don't know. I'll ask Mr. Gómez if he can find out. He can riffle through the commissioner's papers and phone messages. I reckon that here, a week tops. Then they ship you over to Huntsville and then it's a day or two. Oh, look at me! I'm getting goose pimples just thinking about it. Look at me, you're making me cry. Do you have any hankies? Here, let me get a piece of toilet paper. Wow!"

I head over to the desk and stack the letters neatly. Then I pat the pages of this book. Velop comes over and looks at the many white pages that are filled.

"You've worked so hard with all the lawyering and now this writing too," he says.

"I hope I can finish it," I say.

"I'll go now. I can see that you want to be alone. Please think about what I told you. All it takes is one phone call. Bye, bye, my love. Kiss, kiss."

DAY 41

This morning, right after Grosvenor informed me that I was leaving for Huntsville in five days, Mr. Gómez walked in and told me I had a visitor.

"She says she's your wife," he said. "She's very pretty. I saw her myself."

"My wife?"

"Yessir. The commissioner approved one of the private conference rooms right off the visitation hall."

I sat there in front of the typewriter mulling over Mr. Gómez's words without noticing that a small crowd had gathered at my cell door. There was Cortina and Grosvenor and Velop, all looking at me wondering what I was going to do. I didn't have to ask what Cortina was thinking; I knew by the way he looked at me that he was watching to see whether I would act like a jaguar. Trudy was what life brought me today, and my task was to meet what was given, whether good or bad.

"Today of all days," I said.

"Today is as good as any," said Cortina.

"Don't you want to see her? She came such a long way," said Velop.

"It's not that I don't want to," I said, "It's just that I had gotten used to . . ."

"It's O.K., man," said Cortina, "you'll make it. You won't come undone. Not at this point."

I got up and followed Mr. Gómez slowly out of the hall and past the many doors that took us to the front of the building. Finally, Mr. Gómez brought me to a door that was half glass, through which I could see Trudy. She had a briefcase next to her and her hands were folded on the table. It made me smile to see her there, her hair shorter than I had ever seen it before, her face wrinkled a bit more around the edges of her eyes. She got up when I came in, hesitated a second, and then came toward me and hugged me hard for a long time. Her body against mine and the force and meaning behind her hug reminded me of the first night of our marriage.

We sat down in front of each other. "You came a long way," I said awkwardly.

"Oh, it's not too far. I've been trying to see you for a while, but I wasn't sure."

"I know, I received your letters. Thank you."

She smiled, and her lips quivered as if she were trying to hold back tears.

"Oh God, I told myself I wasn't going to let myself do this," she said as she hunted for a tissue in her purse.

"It's O.K. A lot has happened."

"A lot," she replied.

She wiped her eyes and then blew her nose. While she was rubbing it, she said, "Would you believe that until Niven found out, I hadn't heard a single word about you? I knew that your mother had died, but from there I knew nothing. So many months and months. I knew where you had gone, though."

"You did? How?"

"One day, about a month after you had left, I called Kate and asked her if she had any idea."

"Kate," I repeated her name to myself, but my face must have lit up with her sudden memory because Trudy smiled with recognition.

"She's a very good person and a very beautiful woman. Actually, I called her up just before I came here. I told her that I wasn't sure whether you were going to let me see you because you hadn't answered any of my letters, but in case I did see you, I asked her if she had any messages, and she gave me a letter to give to you. I have it here."

She started to open her briefcase but then stopped, apparently deciding that she would give it to me later. She was speaking naturally and with ease as if the two of us were sitting in an outdoor cafe in Harvard Square waiting for our movie to start.

"Anyway, about a month after you left I called her up and asked her if she knew where you might have gone after your mother's death. She was very nice to me and said that she had seen you just before you left and that you mentioned something about looking for someone in your past. Someone you thought you had wronged. Anyway, I thought it was probably Armanda."

"You remembered her," I said.

"You and I had talked about her before, but . . ."

"Tell me?"

"After I talked to Kate, I went down to the basement and looked through your things. I'm sorry. I just didn't know if and when you would come back."

"It's all right. There's no room for secrets anymore."

She looked at me as if suddenly remembering where she was and why she was there. Then she continued.

"I found a letter by Armanda, which I also brought for you." She looked at her briefcase but again decided not to open it just yet. "Anyway, I thought you might have gone back to El Paso to look for her."

"Trudy . . ."

"What?"

"I'm glad you came."

"Are you sure?"

"I wasn't sure at first when Mr. Gómez told me you were here, but now I am. It's just that it has taken me a while to come to terms with my memories and with my life, and I was afraid to have all that past come rushing back at me again."

"I needed to see you, Ismael. I feel somehow responsible— well, maybe not not responsible, but a part of all that happened."

"Yes, you are a part, but no, you're not responsible."

"No, let me finish. I thought long and hard before I came here about whether I was coming because of guilt. And there's probably a little guilt. I mean, I did kick you out of the house. But really I'm here because no matter what, you still need to fight this. You don't answer Kevin's letters. You don't respond to folks who want to help. Why?"

I looked at her and shrugged my shoulders. "I'm not sure why. I have some thoughts I guess, but mostly it's just that what I'm doing feels right."

"Kevin had a group of the best appellate lawyers look at all of your papers, the transcripts from trial court, everything. I have, too. We truly believe that you do not merit the death sentence, even by Texas standards."

"I know, I read his letter. Thank him for me."

"But . . ."

"Let me see. Let me see if I can explain it. I guess I feel that there comes a time when you have to accept what fate has given you and learn to be friends with it somehow. I guess I could try to fight this on and on, but at some point it just becomes more important to start getting ready to die. I don't think I could do that if I were hoping and fighting to get a reprieve."

"But there's still a chance. And most of all, your crime—if you want to call it that—does not deserve death."

"But who's to say? A group of people interpreted the law to say it did, and then a judge agreed with them. Trudy, I just thought about the day that you and I went to Faneuil Hall with about a thousand other immigrants and their families, and there I stood with my hand raised, promising to follow and obey the Constitution and the laws of the United States. And remember how long and hard I thought about whether I should take the step from resident to citizen? Boy, was I proud that day. I thought that for all its problems this country is as good as it gets on this earth, mainly because of its laws and the protection to true freedom that they afford. I often think about that day."

"Oh, God, Ismael. Oh, God. You've given up, haven't you?"

"I know what I say sounds defeatist to you. Like I somehow want to die or like I don't care about life anymore. But really, that's not the case, not now anyway."

"What?" Trudy had put her head down and was looking at the table, her hands knotted.

"It's like I'm not running away anymore, and I'm not looking for another place to be. It's like in letting things be, I'm who I'm supposed to be, finally. You know, in a way, I feel very lucky. I have an opportunity to know that I am dying and to die without pain. How many people can say that? Really, I'm no different from someone who has been told that he's terminally ill. I have it much better in that my body and mind, most of all my mind, is in good shape. But the choice that someone who is terminally ill and I have is the same, how we live until we die."

"I won't win this battle, will I?"

"No, not today, anyway. But, I tell you, if suddenly I was told that I would not die, I would be O.K. with that."

"I don't understand you, Ismael. I don't. I guess I never did."

"I do have a favor to ask you."

"Tell me."

"If it happens that I do go to Huntsville, I'd like you to be there."

"There? Where?"

"There, in the building, when it happens, wherever they let you be. I would like to know that you're there."

Trudy reached out to hold my hand. Her look was strong. Her hand was trembling but firm.

"Why?" she asked.

"I think that having you there would give me comfort."

"I don't know, Ismael. It's . . ."

"It's a lot to ask, isn't it? And whatever you decide I'll understand, but I need to ask it. And I have another favor to ask you." She lifted her eyes toward me. "I've been writing every day. And my writing is beginning to look like a little book."

"What's it about?"

"Oh, how things came to be, how I ended up here."

"I hope you didn't paint me too badly."

"If I had time, I would go back to those parts where I wrote about you, and I would make sure that I didn't. But, I want to give the book to you. To do with as you see fit. Most of all, I want you to know me and to forgive me if you can."

"Forgive you for what? For falling in love with someone else or for being in love all along with someone else? I don't know what you want me to forgive you for!"

"For whatever I did that hurt you."

Trudy shook her head as if to say that I had no inkling of how much it all hurt.

"Tell me."

"Nothing. There's no fault here, really. I thought about it for a long time. When things go wrong in a marriage it's because of two people. It wasn't just you. I know that now. Still . . ."

"I hurt you."

"Maybe it was self-pride. I felt rejected. First about Kate and then Armanda. I don't know where I fit in the picture. Did you always love Armanda, even while we were married? All that time with me, were you really with her? And what was Kate to you? And why couldn't you have written those poems to me? I don't deny it. I hated you for a long time."

"And then?"

"You left. You just left with no word about whether you were dead or alive. I don't know. I kept on living; that's what I did. I got up in the morning and went to work. I spent time with old friends. I made new friends. I did what I needed to do. I struggled until I believed again that your rejection of me didn't mean that I was unlovable. That's what I did."

Trudy . . ."

"Shit! I didn't want this to happen. This is not the time."

"It is the time. It's exactly the right time. I wish I could respond to your anger."

"It's not . . . it's not really anger anymore. It's not anger."

"Whatever it is, I appreciate it. Now more than ever. If we're not honest now, then when?"

"O.K., just tell me this. Honestly tell me this: If you could have only one person in Huntsville and Armanda were still alive, who would it be? Me or her? Or Kate, even? I don't know. Tell me from your heart."

"Trudy, I no longer deal with hypotheticals. The fact is that life gave me Armanda, and it gave me you, and I made choices at different times for you and for her. Now life has brought you here, and you are alive, and I would like you to be there if you could. It's important to me to recognize that need and to ask you, that's all. I'll understand if you're not there."

"You want me to be there, but Armanda will be in your heart."

"That is also true. Armanda is in me. Even if I got out of here and you and I were back together, she would still be with me. She's someone who has always been with me. I wish I had recognized her presence way back then when we had problems so that I could have tried to figure out a way to live with both of you."

"Maybe that's not possible. Maybe what we all have to do is choose, and you never had the courage to choose."

"Maybe."

Trudy looked at me not knowing what to do next. She bent down and began to take things out of her briefcase.

"I brought you Kate's letter. I thought you might also like to have Armanda's letter, and . . . here's the little medal that I found in Renata's letter. Let's see, what else? I have some documents I want to leave with you. I have a petition for clemency for the governor, but the commissioner has to approve it first. I have a letter from you to a Texas attorney, a friend of Kevin's, authorizing him to file appeal papers on your behalf. I have law briefs that I want to leave with you. At least take a look at the arguments that we use as to why what you did doesn't fit into the type of crime required for the death penalty under Texas law. Kevin and his team worked so hard, and they also happen to be right. Just read them. Please."

"I will."

"Do they let you make phone calls?"

"Yes."

"Here's my number. Let me know what's happening. Let me know if you decide to file an appeal. All it takes is one phone call to file the papers. O.K.?"

"O.K."

"I'd better go now. I don't know what to tell you. I feel so helpless and so disappointed in all of this, in how this turned out. It's all such a waste. I don't know whether I will be at Huntsville or not. I don't believe that what you are doing is right, and frankly, it's a lot to ask. I just don't know. I'd better go."

DAY 42

Kate's Letter

Dear Ismael:

Trudy called at home yesterday and told me that she was flying down to see you. Tonight I have asked Philip if he and Corky can go miniature golfing so that I have some time to write to you. So here I am. As usual, I have stared at the piece of paper for an hour now while making myself two vodka collinses. Now, thanks to a certain airy and warm feeling in my brain, I just started writing with absolutely no idea of what I want to tell you. I just decided to write as if this letter were no different from any other letter to a friend.

Lots of things have happened since you left. It seems as if lots of time has gone by too. There I go, stating the obvious. Well, let me try once more. In terms of things happening, I want to tell you that I have a little girl now, whose name is Frances, but we call her Fran. She is nearly two years old and is a joyous little being. The other thing that happened is that a few months after you left, I left the firm and am no longer a practicing lawyer. Would you believe that, after all it took me to become a lawyer, I could shed the profession like a winter coat on a spring morning? I did it, though. One day soon after you left, I saw clear as daylight that I was not happy, and I decided that the job was not for me. Of course, I couldn't leave right then and there. I bided my time until Philip and I could swing it financially, and then I left. I have been keeping busy being a mommy to Corky and to Fran—and get this—I am now an assistant youth director at a church in Dorchester. I'm in charge of the after-school program at the church, taking care of kids after school. Most days Corky and

Fran come with me, and they have a ball. I am also spending my evenings at Harvard Extension taking courses in psychology. I am going to be a youth counselor one of these days. So how's that for things happening? Can you believe it? Sometimes I can't believe it myself.

Philip is doing well. He has been very kind, putting up with all my career twists and supporting me (emotionally and financially). I don't think it was too easy for him at first, especially the part about my not being a lawyer. Poor Philip, I think his image of me and of our life together came tumbling down. But he's hung in there while I rebuilt or rediscovered myself (the same thing?) and I think he likes the new product. By the way, I think he secretly blames you for the loss of my big income. Just kidding. Although he's right in a way, you know. This is the part of the letter where I start to get serious, only because I have to.

I do have you to thank for many, many things. We touched each other, didn't we? I mean, our lives collided there for a few moments in time and then proceeded on, slightly altered and in a different direction because of the collision. I believe these types of collisions happen many, many times, even in the course of one day. Someone touches us and we are different, somehow, even if we just expand to accommodate the touch.

But there are collisions and there are collisions. Ours was a good one, wasn't it? I don't know how I served your life, but I am beginning to understand how you served mine. The pain and the beauty of your love helped me to discover my soul. I guess she was always there, but it's as if I saw her only after I saw her in your eyes. Like when we are face to face with someone and we see ourselves reflected in their pupils. It's true. I never knew I was so beautiful until I saw the way you looked at me. I never knew I was so worthy to be loved until I felt your love.

Wow! Now I'm really on a roll. I almost sound like you in that melodramatic (but very touching) poem that you left for me on your last day of work. Oh, Ismael. Of all the things I learned from you, this is one of them. That it's O.K. to be corny when I want to be with whoever I want to be. At home and at the church where I work I often say "I love you" to those around me. On a whim, even. And I tell the poor in spirit wherever I meet them how rich and beautiful they look to me. And the other thing I learned is that there is a kind of friendship that I never imagined possible. It happens in this lifetime between two people, and it is so out of this world that the persons involved can only compare it to romantic love, and to be sure, the pull of the souls also pulls the bodies; how can it be otherwise? Even so, it is not romantic love, it is just love with a big, big L.

I know you know by now what I'm talking about. That's why now you miss me as much as I miss you even though you're happy to have Trudy at your side, and I'm happy that in a few minutes Philip and Corky will return, and Corky will pull out of his pocket a bright green golf ball and will giggle while I give him the customary scolding for "golf ball lifting," and Philip will pull out of his shirt pocket a little eraserless pencil the size of my thumb, and he will put it with a hundred other little eraserless pencils in the kitchen drawer along with the garbage bag twists and the dried-out tubes of Crazy Glue.

So I say goodbye for now, Ismael. I know you will do what is right for you and that you will follow your heart the way you always did. You don't need me there to know that I am with you, just as we never needed words to know our love was there.

Kate

DAY 43

Armanda's letter.

Querido Ismael, mi amor:

Perdóname mi English. I think I like to write in Spanish better but I know that you want that I practice English. So, I keep trying. Still I am in school learning like you want me. In school I sit and repeat repeat always many words and memorize. But now I look for almost each word in the dictionary. Terrible. I not can not translate in my head very fast. Nando is much better than me. He learns from TV and little friends. Nando misses you very much. He asks for you always. He thinks of you when he plays with the toys you gave him. The soldiers, the triciclo, the ranch with all the pigs and cows and horses. The ranch makes me think of you too and the chicken farm you want. Remember?

Yesterday he saw me cry and he asked me if my heart was broken. I told him no but he was sad too all day. I cry because I call your mother to get the phone number of you but she said that I not call any more. She said that you were to marry with someone in New York in a little while. Then she hang up. Ismael, you never told me about another woman but I know all the time there is someone. I not ask you because I do not want you to lie to me. Also I knew that your body and your heart do not lie to me. Your body and your heart tell me you are for me and I am for you. I know. You know also deep in you that I am the person destiny for you. I miss you. In the morning I get up from bed I feel alone alone and I carry aloness all day with me like a hole without end in my chest. My body needs you. It hurts with pain verdadero. My body hungry for your body always in place where we dance the paso lento always. I know you have your life. I never want you to leave

the life you choose. You never promised me
nothing. I respect you for that. Only I want to
tell you my need for you this time and ask you
write please if you want. I want to tell you I
carry inside a part of you for always. A little
Ismael. So you will be forever with me en
cuerpo y alma.

Armanda.

DAY 44

ortina said that in his opinion I had made good progress in becoming a jaguar. He asked me if I thought that to be the case as well. I told him that for some reason fear had left me. He said that was good and that I shouldn't worry if it came back. I told him that I wasn't worried. He said that he knew I wasn't. He said that if fear came back it would be different, and I agreed with him. Then I told him that along with fear, hope had also left me and that I didn't know if this was good or not. He said that being a jaguar had no rules. That it was up to me, whether I could live better with hope than without it. As for him, he said that he did not care for hope. It was something that he killed daily if it was there. I told him that I wasn't sure whether that would work for me and that maybe killing hope like that was a form of cowardice.

I told him that I wondered for myself whether there was not a kind of hope that was good and necessary and that maybe I would find this kind of hope and make it part of my way of seeing things, but maybe I would not. Cortina said that was fine, that being a jaguar was different for each person and that each person made his own courage as he saw fit.

Cortina asked me further if I had decided to appeal. I told him I wanted to finish this book today so I would have some time to think about that. He asked how I would decide whether to appeal or not. I told him that mostly I would listen deep down the way I had learned to listen and that I would look at life and death con los ojos del jaguar. He said that was as it should be and that he was proud of me. This last thing he said was not easy for him. I could tell by the way he briefly looked at me and then away from me. Then before he left, he asked whether I would continue writing in my book if I decided to appeal and if the appeal was granted. I said that even if I appealed, this book was as complete as I could make it. He said he understood and then asked me if there were not someone out there whom I thought worth staying alive for. I told

him that there were people I could live for if that was the right thing
to do. Cortina said he understood. Then he shook my hand and left.

Later, Botswana came by to tell me that Jimmy, for whom the
Olympics were named, was better than me by a longshot. The way
Botswana tells it, Jimmy will always be the champ. He possessed
great powers of concentration, although unlike me, he relied on a
prop to awaken his imagination. It seems his girlfriend managed to
sneak to him through secret sources a handkerchief imbued with
the juices of her passion, secreted specifically with Jimmy in mind,
one supposes. This handkerchief, which was replaced with a freshly scented one every two weeks or so, Jimmy held against his nose
while he lost himself in forceful reverie. Jimmy was taken to
Huntsville about a year before I arrived. He remains respected by
all, and his influence remains pervasive, seen by the fact that
Wooly cannot live without his own white handkerchief containing
the fragrances of his Josephine.

Botswana said he could keep Grosvenor away the last hours
before the bus to Huntsville, if I wanted. I asked him what he wanted in return for that, and he said he wanted my ass, and then smiled
a smile that went from ear to ear. I thanked him for the offer but
told him that Grosvenor was no bother to speak of. Besides, La
Pelona already had my ass. He asked if La Pelona was the same
white pin-up girl that was used for the Jimmy Olympics. I told him
that the pin-up girl was La Mona, not La Pelona. La Pelona was
Spanish for the grim reaper, the same one that is coming to get
each one of us.

"You got that right," he said.

The commissioner has agreed to a small party of sorts. Three
Lone Stars apiece have been granted as well as my favorite dish,
maybe, if Mr. Gómez can swing it. I asked Mr. Gómez if something
Mexican could be cooked up. He said that it could, but he would
not recommend anything too spicy, knowing as he did who did the
cooking. He said besides that I didn't want to get my diarrhea back
again now that I appeared to be cured. He asked what would be the
one thing that I would most like to eat, and I told him I would like
some tamales de puerco y de pollo if such a thing were possible.
He said he would have to try to get them from the outside, but that
it just might be that my wish could be granted. He asked me also if
some of the inmates for whom I had done some lawyering could

attend. They had been asking Mr. Gómez for a chance to come by
and pay their respects. I told him I saw no reason why not.

Velop is very melodramatic about my departure. So I have
asked him for both our sakes to stay away from me. He has largely
honored my request. Although every once in a while, like just a second ago, he comes by and touches me, albeit in appropriate places.

Grosvenor has largely stayed away, perhaps sensing that
Botswana is on to him again. He keeps trying to get me to utter
magic words which he believes will be the difference between some
kind of heaven and some kind of hell. I am tempted to utter them
just to make him happy and also earn some final peace . . . from
him, at least. What would it hurt? I cannot, however, utter them just
for Grosvenor's sake. Besides, without fear there seems to be no
need for words. It is entirely possible that the words will burst forth
naturally and gracefully from my heart, without Grosvenor's or
anyone's prompting, and I will not stop them if they do.

Finally, there is Wooly, whom I have entrusted with a most
important task. I asked Wooly if he will take outside the ladybug
that has cohabited with me these past few days. How she got in
here is beyond me. She must have made her way riding on Wooly's
clothes, on his way back from a painting job. And even more amazing is the fact that this little being has decided to stay, offering
herself to my devoted contemplation, and is totally at ease with me.
She likes it mostly around the sink, which I plugged up so that she
would not be drained away. Or she stays on the willow branch that
Wooly snuck in for me. But sometimes I put her on the desk where
she motors back and forth, climbing over papers and letters and
even moving carefree through my hands and fingers as I type.

In the only book on insects that Mr. Gómez could find, I discovered that ladybugs are voracious eaters, sometimes devouring
hundreds of aphids in a single day. Since I don't believe there are
aphids around here, except perhaps some that escape my eye, I
don't know what she lives on. The crumbs of bread that I leave out
for her remain intact, as far as I can tell.

Wooly has agreed to take the tiny critter out in an envelope.
Wooly already thinks I'm crazy anyway. He has been instructed to
let her out on one of the lower branches of the willow in the courtyard below. He will do it this afternoon while I look on from here.
He promises to wave when she is free.

DAY 45

How beautiful is your silence.

DAY 46

Dear Commissioner:

Enclosed please find a signed petition for clemency. I add what follows as a response to the section in the petition that asks for a personal statement as to why clemency should be granted.

I committed the crime for which I was convicted and I am responsible for other crimes of the spirit which are, if you can imagine, much worse. The application of the death sentence is legally justified.

I am sorry for the life I took. I will spend the rest of mine in atonement for that and for all else that needs atonement. I have found my own way to contribute to life in gratitude for life. If allowed to live,

I will continue with your assigned tasks of lawyering and weight lifting and with my own discovered task of telling stories. Stories of those around me that seek to be told and heard and thus redeemed.

Commissioner, whatever your decision, you have allowed me to prepare for death, and I am grateful.

I must stop now, for Trudy, who has been urging me to complete the petition, is waiting downstairs to take it personally to the governor, if you approve it. She is worried that she will not have the time to do all that needs to be done. I think we have all the time we need.